**The world was going c1
for the ride ...**

Sounds of imagined footsteps followed her down the hall. Her hands shook slightly as she inserted the key in the lock. Panic welled up in her throat. She looked left, then right. She was alone. She jiggled the key, willing the door to open.

Finally, the lock gave. With a sob, Madeleine slipped inside.

She slammed the door behind her, leaned against it and stared into the dark apartment. Each labored breath calmed her pounding heart. The realization that she was home safe settled into her body and her mind, allowing her muscles to relax. She shook her head and smiled at her vivid imagination. Pushing away from the door, she stepped toward the kitchen.

Something stopped her. Like a wall of black air, surrounding her.

She couldn't see it, but she could feel it. She stepped back. It was behind her. Around her. Frozen, unable to move, barely able to breathe, she opened her mouth.

A hand reached out from the dark and grabbed her throat, cutting off her scream.

"Maddie, you've been telling secrets."

This book is dedicated with love to my mother, Eunice Green, and in loving memory to my father, John Green. You taught me I could do anything and patiently listened while I told my stories. You raised a dreamer and now the dream has come true.

Special thanks to Wendy Douglas, for keeping me on track and always asking "why?"; to Gayle Heywood, for listening to the beginnings of my stories for 21 years and always wanting to read the end; and Sylvia Biondich, for unwavering support in whatever I do.

Silver Dagger

***

T. L. Sinclare

SILVER DAGGER
Published by ImaJinn Books, a division of ImaJinn

Copyright ©2002 by Tracy Green
Printed and bound in the United States of America. All rights reserved. No part of this book may be reproduced in any form or by any means (electronic, mechanical, photocopying, recording, or otherwise) without prior written permission of both the copyright holder and the above publisher of this book, except by a reviewer, who may quote brief passages in a review. For information, address: ImaJinn Books, a division of ImaJinn, P.O. Box 162, Hickory Corners, MI 49060-0162; or call toll free 1-877-625-3592.

ISBN: 1-893896-86-2

10 9 8 7 6 5 4 3 2 1

PUBLISHER'S NOTE:
This book is a work of fiction. Names, characters, places and incidents are products of the author's imagination or are used fictitiously. Any resemblance to actual events or locales or persons, living or dead, is entirely coincidental.

Books are available at quantity discounts when used to promote products or services. For information please write to: Marketing Division, ImaJinn Books, P.O. Box 162, Hickory Corners, MI 49060-0162, or call toll free 1-877-625-3592.

Cover design by Patricia Lazarus

Prologue

The boy clenched the blade in his fingers, then relaxed his grip. He took a short breath, and, in one smooth motion, pitched his arm back and forward again in an overhand throw. The dagger glittered as it spun through the air and landed, point first, in the wood plank propped against the wall.

"Very nice, lad. You've got the best knife hand I've seen in years."

The boy glowed under his father's praise.

"Now, remember, when you're faced with a vampire, always aim for the heart and always use pure silver."

His father repeated the same lesson each day, but tonight the child had a question.

"Why silver, Papa?"

His father held up one finger. "A silver dagger is the only thing that will kill a vampire. Aim for the heart, then leave it there. That's the only way to know they're truly dead."

The boy picked up the next knife in the box. "Are there a lot of vampires, Papa?"

"Too many." The man chuckled. "But fewer today than there were last night."

The child smiled in return. His father was a great vampire hunter, and one day, he'd grow enough to join him on the hunt.

"Now, remember, always keep your knives with you. Silver is your only protection. Vampires are evil creatures. Don't give them a chance to get close."

The boy nodded. He flipped the silver dagger over in his hand and flung it at the target. It penetrated the wood plank, an inch away from the first knife.

"Very good, Stephen. Very good."

One

Madeleine Bryant squinted through the rain at the nervous young man blocking the door.

He looks too young to be an axe-murderer.

Don't go there, she warned herself. *You don't* know *these people are axe-murderers.*

It had started as a joke. Danielle had been reluctant to introduce her new friends to Madeleine.

"They're kind of quiet people," she'd said.

"Are you sure they aren't axe-murderers?" Madeleine had asked.

"Yes, cousin, I've fallen in with a group of axe-murderers. That's how we entertain ourselves on Friday nights."

Madeleine had laughed. She wasn't worried. Danielle was a sensible young woman with a good head on her shoulders. She wasn't going to get involved in anything stupid—like drugs, or heavy duty sex, or white slavery rings, or—

Madeleine gave herself a mental shake and focused on her mission—find Danielle and get the hell home.

She'd hoped to be home before the storm hit, but she'd missed that by about five minutes. Five minutes of standing in the rain waiting for this young man to open the door.

"C-can I help you?" he asked. His body was wedged between the door and the frame, killing any hope of seeing inside the house.

Madeleine brushed the wet hair off her face and tried to look harmless, nonthreatening. She'd given up on looking professional when the clouds opened up. Rain pummeled the ground, exploding on the brick steps and splattering Madeleine's nylon-covered legs.

"I'm looking for Dylan," she announced with

confidence, though she had no idea who Dylan was. He was a name in Danielle's address book. The flurry of red hearts around his name had to mean something. "Is he around?"

The young man bit the edge of his lip. Worry, panic, maybe fear, flashed at her through his deep brown eyes. He leaned forward, his voice dropping with his height.

"Are you a *friend* of Dylan's?"

Madeleine didn't know what being a "friend" meant, but it might get her inside.

"Yes," she smiled.

He didn't seem happy about her answer—more resigned than welcoming—but he stepped back and opened the door. "Come on in. Dylan's out but he'll be back soon."

Madeleine hesitated, suddenly realizing what she was doing. *This is probably a bad idea.*

A stranger's house, a rainy night, and a weird man at the door. All the makings of a bad horror flick.

She inhaled deeply and tried to laugh at her own thoughts. Unfortunately, in all the horror movies she'd watched as a child, only the scantily clad heroine survived to the end—and she wasn't dressed for the part.

Water dripped off her hair and fell inside her collar. A shudder ran through her body as a single drop drew a trail down the center of her back. The cool night air plastered the wet material of her silk blouse against her skin.

Horror flick or not, she was going inside. She offered the young man a tight smile and took the final step into the house.

The door snapped shut behind her. Madeleine flinched, and the tiny hairs along her arms stood straight up. It's the cold, she assured herself, knowing it wasn't.

It was obviously too much to hope that lights would be blazing and a comforting fire would be roaring in the fireplace to welcome her inside. There was only one way to describe the entryway in which she stood—dark.

Covered lamps and a few well-placed candle sconces lit the hallway with a pale, weak light. It took a few minutes for her eyes to adjust, but that gave her time to finish dripping on the expensive Persian carpet that covered the floor. She glanced down at the ring of water surrounding her legs, and her shoulders sagged. *Great. Let's crown my wholly unproductive day by dripping on a stranger's expensive rug.*

She refused to even look at the state of her shirt. It was the last silk blouse in her closet, and it was probably ruined after five minutes in the rain. Her struggling law practice didn't allow for luxuries. Silk would be replaced by polyester.

A lock of hair fell against her cheek. Madeleine pushed it away. She'd cut her hair short so that it would be easy to maintain. It also meant her hair would be sticking up in all sorts of interesting shapes as it dried. She brushed aside the worry. She wasn't here to impress these people. She was here to find Danielle.

"Why don't you come on in?" Madeleine jumped. She'd forgotten the young man was still there. "Dylan just ran out to—" He paused. "You know, *get something to eat.*" It sounded like a code phrase he expected her to understand.

She didn't, but she nodded anyway. "He should do that."

The young man's lips curled in a mild disgust. "I guess."

She followed him down the dark hallway, which opened into a huge living room. A long, curved staircase wound up the back wall. The low lighting continued, though the streetlights shining through the windows added a bit more illumination.

"Have a seat. He'll be back in a few minutes."

Madeleine nodded and rubbed her hands together to warm them. Cold and nerves sent tremors over her skin.

Her blouse and skirt clung to her body, providing that oh-so-pleasant clammy feeling. Home was sounding better and better all the time. The small apartment with paint-peeled walls wasn't much of a home, but it was hers. She'd get home, turn on the lights, and crank up the heat.

Madeleine strolled across the room under the watchful eye of her escort. None of the elegant brocade furniture filling the room looked sturdy enough to handle a dripping wet polyester skirt. Finally, she rested her hip against the back of a chaise lounge.

"I'm also looking for Danielle. Is she around?" She asked the question casually, but she watched him closely, looking for any reaction to Danielle's name.

The young man shoved his hands into his pockets and stared at the carpet. Seconds later he raised his eyes and looked at her. There was no flicker of recognition. "I don't think so. Is she a *friend*?"

Madeleine shrugged. "Who can tell these days?"

Her companion just nodded and went back to staring at the rug. Madeleine relaxed a little as she looked about the room. Bookshelves lined the walls, with volumes stacked every way possible in the available space. She'd always been able to tell a lot from a person's bookshelf. This house boasted of everything from Jane Austen to hard-core science fiction. It was a collection that made her fingers itch.

A neat stack of magazines sat on the end of the coffee table. Her eyes landed on the top copy—a comic book called *Vampire Warrior*. Blood dripped from the vampire's fangs as a barely dressed woman reclined in his arms. Matching blood dribbled down her neck. Crimson words slashed across the cover—*The Draw of Blood. Has Galor Killed His Only Chance for Redemption?*

She stared at the blood red words and felt her chest tighten. Something about the cover was strange. It looked real. Frighteningly real. The vampire's eyes vibrated on the cover, drawing in unsuspecting victims.

Movement in the corner of the room pulled Madeleine's attention from the strange book. She turned and looked up. A waiflike woman walked slowly down the stairs, her fingertips resting lightly on the dark wood banister. Dull blond hair hung limp around a face that was dominated by the dark circles under her eyes and the tired set of her mouth. She carried exhaustion like a burden.

She looks like Danielle. The thought shook Madeleine as she watched the other woman. Danielle had sworn it was lack of sleep causing the pale skin and dark circles. She'd followed that statement with a dreamy smile and a knowing giggle. Madeleine wondered again if it wasn't drugs. She hadn't pressed Danielle for information about this new boyfriend. It hadn't seemed important at the time—young love was always intense.

Then Danielle hadn't come home. Now, Madeleine wished she'd asked the question.

She took a deep breath and told herself not to worry. *Danielle's a sensible girl.* Madeleine stared at the pale woman. *A sensible girl with strange friends.*

The woman glanced into the living room. The surprise on her face was clear even through the dim light. She hurried down the steps and rushed to the young man's side.

"Nick, who is she? What's she doing here?"

"She's a friend of Dylan's."

They made no attempt to drop their voices, so Madeleine made no pretense of not listening.

"Did you invite her in?"

"Well, sure. I couldn't leave her—"

Madeleine could see the moment of realization and the spike of fear that followed.

"Oh my God."

"He's coming down," the woman warned.

Tension bounced between the couple. They both straightened where they stood, like students in the principal's office. Madeleine felt the muscles in her own neck tighten in sympathy.

"Nicholas."

Madeleine jumped as a deep, masculine voice invaded the room. That one word sent shivers down her spine that had nothing to do with the cold. She looked up. And gasped. A man stood halfway down the staircase.

She had only a moment to register the fact that she hadn't seen him enter. The thought disappeared seconds after she conceived it, replaced by his image. Dressed completely in black, he filled the room with his presence.

He was tall, well over six feet, she thought, though it was hard to tell with him standing on the stairs. His black boots probably added an inch to his height. He seemed intent on ignoring her, so she took the opportunity to check him out. She let her gaze wander up his legs, strong powerful thighs wrapped in black denim. The black turtleneck molded to his chest and arms.

His black hair, brushed off his forehead, framed his strong face. His cheekbones were etched lines creating tempting shadows and hiding secrets. She couldn't see his eyes—he was looking at Nicholas—but even from across the room she felt their strength.

He was stunning. Handsome, yes, but beyond the mere physical beauty was strength. *Power.*

He doesn't look like an axe-murderer, she thought, trying to jar his image loose with a bad joke. It didn't work.

He *didn't* look like an axe-murderer—he looked far more dangerous.

Nicholas raced to the bottom of the stairs.

"I'm so sorry. I forgot. She said she was a friend of Dylan's and—"

The newcomer raised his hand. The groveling stopped. "It's not an issue."

Nicholas spun around to look at Madeleine. "You mean

she's a—" His shoulders dropped. Panic and guilt crossed his face.

"Yes, she is." He moved down the stairs and stopped at Nicholas' side. "Thank you for bringing her to me." Madeleine tensed at the quiet threat behind the words.

He turned and entered the living room. Madeleine swallowed deeply and pressed her shoulders back, quietly preparing for his approach.

"Cassandra, make our guest some tea." He glanced down at the drips left by Madeleine's drenched skirt. "And perhaps she'd like a towel." He appeared more concerned about the state of his carpet than her comfort, but at this point, she didn't care. "Nicholas, go with Cassandra."

The young man's eyes screamed volumes at Madeleine as he walked away. But she had no idea what he was trying to say. She watched him leave, curious about the fear and warning that resonated through his body.

When she turned back, *he* was in front of her, staring down at her with glowing blue eyes and cool interest.

"How can I help you?" The question came out with no emotion, no real curiosity. Madeleine pressed her lips together in a tight smile. She hadn't made it through law school or corporate dinner parties by being intimidated by arrogance.

"And you are?"

A flicker of smug amusement lit his face. "I'm Stephen. This is my house."

"Oh." *Great. Offend the owner. Good move.* "I'm Madeleine Bryant." She offered him her hand. The move was automatic. Eight years as the perfect corporate wife had trained her for polite situations.

Stephen stared down at her hand but made no attempt to take it. Madeleine pushed her shoulders back and pressed her arm slightly forward. And dared him with her eyes. After a moment that bordered on rudeness, he reached out and took her hand in his. And she knew she'd made a mistake.

Heat exploded from the point of contact, spiraling up her arm and through her body. Madeleine stared at their hands, stunned that sparks weren't visible. It wasn't a handshake—it was a caress, subtle and small. Seductive. Her body began to melt.

She lifted her eyes to his. Triumph stared back at her. She snatched her hand away and pressed it against her stomach.

An enticing fire flickered in the depths of his eyes, calling to her.

"Again, Ms. Bryant, how can I help you?"

"I, uhm, I—" Images of Stephen and a woman rolling around naked on a satin-covered bed sprang into her mind—clear, stark pictures. Heat spread through her body. The woman in the fantasy tilted her head back to accept Stephen's kiss on her throat. Her face glowed with ecstasy. Madeleine gasped. It was her!

The image faded and she realized she was still staring at him. The right corner of his lip curled up ever so slightly, as if he knew what she'd been thinking. She felt her face flush.

This is ridiculous! She tossed her head back and tried again.

"I'm sorry. I lost my train of thought for a moment."

Stephen nodded. "Understandable."

"Yes. Well, as I was saying, I'm here to see Dylan."

Stephen stepped away and folded his arms across his chest. With slow deliberation, he looked down the length of her body, lingering briefly on her full breasts. She refused to let her eyes drop to see how tightly her wet blouse was clinging to her skin and resisted the impulse to cover herself.

His eyes made the return trip up her body to her face.

"You don't seem like Dylan's type."

"Maybe he's branching out."

"Unlikely. But it doesn't matter. He's not here right now."

"I'd like to wait." Very few people had the guts to actually throw someone out of their house.

"It could be hours before he returns."

"Nick said it would only be a few minutes." Madeleine smiled with false sweetness. The smile turned real when she saw Stephen's jaw tighten. "I don't mind waiting."

"Why do you want to see Dylan?"

"Why do you think that's any of your business?"

His eyebrows spiked at the sharp response. Madeleine pressed her lips together. *What are you doing?* she asked silently. She had never been the most tactful person, but she rarely pushed herself to the point of being rude. *Danielle.* She was doing this for Danielle.

And because there was something about this man. He inspired defiance.

He abhors weakness. The insight came to her in a flash. He'd use any weakness and destroy a person with it.

"Everything in this house is my business." The soft whisper sent another wave of shivers down her spine.

He took a step toward her. Instinct urged her to move back, away from his disturbing presence, but she wouldn't allow it. *Give no ground.* He stopped mere inches from her. *Close enough to touch.* The strange fantasy of Stephen and the satin bed flickered at the edge of her mind, and she felt her blush return. She looked up at him, refusing to be intimidated.

The light in his eyes caught her, and the world around her faded. A strange lassitude crept over her. She sighed. Why was she fighting him?

"Why are you here to see Dylan?" he asked again.

The smooth edge of his voice seemed to dull her senses.

"I'm looking for my cousin, Danielle," she muttered. The words slipped out without her permission.

This was important. She was supposed to watch him to see if he reacted to Danielle's name. She tried to focus, but the world blurred for one brief second and the moment was gone.

"Why would you think she was here?" he asked, his voice strangely distant.

"She's a friend of Dylan's."

She breathed in his warm scent and felt a response in the center of her body.

That's good, Maddie.

She heard the voice in her head. His voice. Belated internal alarms went off. She pulled her eyes away and stared at the muted red carpet on the floor.

"Maddie, look at me,"

Power filled his words and she clenched her fists as she resisted the strange urge to follow his command. She grabbed onto the name and used it as her anchor. No one called her Maddie.

"Look at me, Maddie." This time the pull was too strong. She raised her eyes to his. And fell inside. Light fragments the color of deep sapphires glittered around her, blocking out the world and guiding her to Stephen's gaze. His eyes, his warmth, his fire were the only safe place to be. He sought entrance into her soul and she opened to him.

Very good, Maddie.

The voice vibrated through her skull. Warnings crept from the back corner of her mind. This wasn't normal. Something was wrong. A warm glow settled around her, silencing the concerns. The seductive fantasy from a moment ago returned, flowing over her in hard sensations. Stephen, his mouth on hers, his lips against her throat. She sighed at the first warm touch. She licked her lips, the dream so real she could almost taste him.

"Madeleine." His voice was all there was, quiet and powerful. "It's time for you to go home."

A longing welled up inside her. *Yes, she wanted to go home.*

"Your cousin isn't here."

Madeleine shook her head. *No, Danielle isn't here.*

"You should—"

"Stephen, I—"

Madeleine jerked at the intrusion of another voice, the sound shattering the warmth and security that surrounded her.

She pressed her fingertips to her forehead and took in short, deep breaths, trying to slow her pounding heart. She was losing it. She gave herself a moment to recover before turning to greet the new arrival.

A tall man with blondish-brown hair stood in front of the kitchen door. He was well built, muscular, and had an open, friendly face that Madeleine immediately liked.

"I'm sorry." He apologized directly to Stephen, ignoring her presence completely. "Did I interrupt?"

Stephen shook his head. "Nothing that can't be continued later. Ms. Bryant, this is Dylan. Dylan, this is Madeleine Bryant."

Dylan smiled and nodded. "Of course. You're Danielle's cousin. I recognize you from her description."

He walked forward and offered her his hand. Tension slipped from Madeleine's shoulders. She'd found Dylan. He was handsome, charming. She took his hand. He had a firm grip and he smiled into her eyes as they shook hands— the perfect handshake.

With none of the strange heat she'd felt at Stephen's touch.

"How can we help you, Madeleine?"

Eager to push aside the darkly attractive man next to her, she kept her attention on Dylan. "Have you seen Danielle recently?"

Concern glowed in his eyes. "I haven't." He shrugged. "Not for days. She's not been home?"

"No," Madeleine answered.

"I've been busy lately. Stephen—" Dylan looked up. Whatever he saw in Stephen's eyes stopped him. "Oh, that's right. You didn't know Danielle, did you?"

"No."

"I'm sorry we can't help you, Madeleine."

Madeleine nodded. It was time to go. This had been a wild goose chase to start with. "Well, thank you. I'm sorry to interrupt your evening. If you do hear from Danielle, could you have her call home?"

"Can I give you a ride?" Dylan offered with a sympathetic smile. "Danielle said you didn't have a car."

Madeleine smiled. Her cousin seemed to have found one of the good guys.

"That would be nice."

"No." Madeleine and Dylan froze at Stephen's refusal. "Dylan, you have things you need to do." He paused. "Downstairs. I'll take Ms. Bryant home."

"Oh, sure." Dylan shrugged and offered his hand back to Madeleine. "I'll let Stephen have the pleasure of seeing you safely home. As Stephen said, I have some things that must get done tonight. If you hear from Danielle, please let me know. I'll worry until I know she's safe." He sounded sincere—and concerned. "It was nice to meet you, Madeleine."

She nodded. "It was nice meeting you."

Dylan stopped when he got to the kitchen door and looked meaningfully at Stephen.

"What about…"

She could have sworn Dylan's eyes flicked toward her.

"I'll take care of it."

Madeleine shivered at the quiet promise in Stephen's voice. The kitchen door swung closed with a quiet thump, and she was alone with Stephen. Again.

"Shall we go?"

"I'll call a cab." The protest felt good. Something

strange had happened to her independence a few moments ago, but it was coming back to her.

"I'll drive you," he countered as he crossed the room and opened a closet.

"No, I'd rather call a cab." She folded her arms across her chest. "I don't know you. Why would I get into your car?"

Stephen took a black raincoat out of the closet and pulled it on before answering. "Your cousin has gone missing. You've entered the house of a complete stranger, and you were willing to accept a ride from Dylan, whom you just met tonight. And *now* you're concerned about your personal safety?" He walked back to her and held up a second raincoat. "A bit late, isn't it?"

Madeleine glared at him. Stephen didn't seem to notice. He draped the coat over her shoulders and guided her out the front door.

Rain pounded them as they walked a short distance down the street. A black Jaguar sports car sat under a single streetlight. As they approached, the engine purred to life.

Madeleine jumped back and landed against Stephen's chest with a solid thud. His arms wrapped around her for a moment, the heat of his body warming her through the raincoat. A dangling key chain appeared in front of her face.

"Automatic start." His voice vibrated with humor.

"I know." She stepped away and glared into his amused eyes.

Stephen walked to the passenger side, opened the door, and helped Madeleine inside in one fluid motion. The car was already warming as the door snapped shut beside her. Stephen slid inside and turned the heat on high. Madeleine couldn't contain her sigh as the warmth burst from the vents.

She gave him directions to her apartment and then stared into the night. The close confines of the Jag didn't give her much to look at in the car besides Stephen, and she had enough fuel for her fantasies.

The trip was blessedly brief. If not for the rain, she could have walked the distance in about forty minutes.

"That's my building. Just pull over and I'll hop out."

He didn't even glance at her before ignoring her instructions and parking his car in the alley. Right in front of the No Parking sign. He climbed out of the car and walked around to her side as she unclipped the seat belt. She was struck again by the heat of his touch as he helped her out. She released his hand as soon as she was standing and forced a polite smile.

"Thank you for the ride home," she said politely, hoping he would leave her there. She wasn't surprised when he followed her to the dimly lit entrance of her building.

"Your car will get towed," she warned.

"No, it won't."

"It'll get stripped."

"No. It won't."

She stopped and turned to him. "I don't need you to walk me to my door."

He wiped the rain out of his eyes. "Get upstairs, Maddie," he sighed. Frustration lined his face.

She couldn't stop her triumphant grin as she walked away. It wasn't much, but for one brief moment she'd cracked his seemingly unbreakable control.

The fluorescent lights of the lobby stabbed at her eyes as she pulled open the security door that no longer locked. Stephen flinched against the glare and raised his arm to shield his eyes.

"Hey, Miz Bryant." Madeleine turned at the sound of her name. Bob, the building's maintenance man, sat in his customary position—cocked back in a wheeled office chair with his feet resting on his cluttered desk. He smiled as his eyes skimmed up the length of her body. They lingered on her legs and continued the journey upward, never making it to her face. They stopped at her chest, as if he could see through the raincoat's heavy material to her damp blouse underneath.

"Hi, Bob." Madeleine moved past, not wanting to get caught in a conversation with him tonight. His drawling voice stopped her escape.

"You know, there ain't no overnight parking available around here," he called out.

She stopped at the stairwell door and looked over her shoulder. "Pardon me?"

"If you're planning on having your friend here, uh, sleep over, well, there just isn't any place for him to park. Cars get towed if they're left overnight. For a slight fee, I can make sure that your car is still there when you leave tomorrow. 'Course, if you're just planning on a quickie, I won't charge you as much as if you was staying all night."

Before she could respond, Stephen turned and faced the maintenance man. Bob's lewd smile fell.

"Uh—uh. Never mind. You just take as long as you like. I'll make sure your car's there when you get back."

Madeleine tilted her head to look up at Stephen. He didn't look any different. What was Bob seeing that she wasn't?

"Let's go, Madeleine." Stephen put a hand on her back and urged her toward the stairs. The brief episode replayed in her mind as she climbed the three flights to her apartment. It made no more sense the second time around.

Exhaustion washed over her as she reached the top of the stairs. She glanced over her shoulder. He isn't even breathing hard, she silently groused as she stepped into the hall. Cracks in the walls formed a long, ragged arrow that ended at her apartment. She sighed when she reached her door.

She turned to Stephen. "Thank you, again, for the ride home."

"Invite me in."

His soft-spoken command wrapped invisible fingers around her heart. She didn't want him seeing her apartment. The walls needed paint and the cockroaches threatened daily to take over. And it was all she could afford right now. She opened her mouth to refuse. He cocked one eyebrow, taunting her.

She knew he was mocking her to prick her pride. She knew it and it still didn't matter. She wouldn't let him use this as a weakness.

The apartment was small and horrible, but it was clean, and it was her home for now. She wasn't about to let anyone condemn her for living within her means.

She straightened her shoulders and pushed open the front door. "Won't you come in?"

He wandered to the middle of her living room and stopped, his hands firmly fisted in his coat pockets.

She closed the door and waited. He scanned the living room with dispassionate eyes. Madeleine knew what he saw. The same thing she had when she'd first moved in— a small room with cracked and peeling walls and worn, ugly orange carpet. The ragged couch she'd picked up at a secondhand store formed the imaginary line between the living room and kitchen. An old, worn recliner sat at one end of the couch, with her tiny television on a cardboard box against the wall. The two doors that led to her bedroom and bathroom were closed.

Finally, he turned his gaze back to her.

"It must have been quite a come down to end up in something like this." The skin around her eyes tightened as she glared at him. "Pride got the better of you in the divorce, hmmm?"

"How did you know I was divorced? Did Danielle tell you?"

His lips curved into a slow mocking smile that didn't reach his eyes. "Very clever, Ms. Bryant. Was that supposed to slip me up into confessing I know Danielle? I've never met your cousin." He looked around the room before turning back to her. "It's obvious you recently moved here. And that it's somewhat *lower rent* than you're used to." Madeleine raised her eyebrows in question. "You're wearing a very well-made silk blouse and a rather poorly made polyester skirt. You seem too practical to spend money on luxuries when you're living in a place like this. I assume the blouse is part of your former life.

"Divorce is usually what sends a woman like you to a place like this. Pride won't let you accept alimony."

Madeleine blanched at his insight. That was what had happened. When she'd left Charles, she'd refused to take anything with her.

"I'd better be going."

That's it? Madeleine stared at his back as he walked away. He came inside to analyze her life and now he was leaving? She shook her head. It made no sense.

She followed him to the door. He paused, then turned back to her as if he'd made a decision. She looked up at him curiously. Her lungs grew tight, as if the oxygen in the room had been sucked out.

The daydream that had assaulted her earlier swamped her mind—her body twisted with Stephen's, his hands caressing her bare skin, his tongue tasting her. Heat pooled between her legs and the tips of her breasts tightened at the fantasy.

The reality stood before her. He bent his head and placed his lips against hers. The kiss was slow and warm, gentle, as if he were afraid of startling her. Reality mixed with the fantasy playing in her mind. She crushed the moan of pleasure that threatened.

His lips caressed hers, exploring their shape, learning their texture. His tongue licked her upper lip, teasing her with a light touch that made her hunger for more.

Open your mouth, Maddie. Let me taste you.

His voice resonated inside her head. He couldn't have spoken, but she'd heard him.

It didn't matter. She opened her mouth and he slipped his tongue inside. This time Madeleine did groan.

He tasted her. There was no other word for it. He lingered, moving within her mouth, licking slow lines around her tongue as if he were savoring each nuance, each unique flavor that was Madeleine. She leaned into the kiss. No one had ever enjoyed her like this. It went to her head and scattered her thoughts.

On this plane, only their mouths touched. In her mind, their bodies connected and the pleasure exploded. Her fingers dug into his coat, holding onto the one stable thing in her spinning world.

Abruptly, he lifted his head and stepped back. The strange fantasy evaporated but left a lingering desire.

He trailed one finger down her neck.

"Good night, Maddie."

And he was gone. The door clicking shut was the only sign he'd moved.

Madeleine stared at the empty space and brushed her fingertips over her lower lip.

What the hell just happened?

***

Stephen waited in silence outside her door until he heard the double click to indicate she'd locked herself in for the night. She thought she was safe behind her locks.

It didn't matter. She'd invited him in.

He would come back later and kill her.

Two

Heat washed over her body. Fiery heat that burst from inside, was captured, and made even hotter by the body pressed against hers. She moaned, the feeling too intense to be contained in silence. She dropped her head back against the satin-covered pillow.

"Beautiful Maddie. Sweet Maddie." The words circled through her mind. He was there. Even with her eyes closed, she could see him, see their bodies twined together, writhing to get closer, to become one creature. She had to fight him, had to stop this. Something wasn't right.

His mouth was a brand on her neck marking her forever. The pleasure and pain of his touch blended together until she longed for more of both.

"Look at me, Maddie." She struggled, knowing she would be lost if she looked into his wicked blue eyes. "Look at me," he commanded again. And she couldn't resist. She raised her eyes to his and gasped.

Loud ringing shattered the dream. Madeleine bolted upright. Her heart pounded in her chest and moved up to her throat and ears until all she could feel was the throbbing of her own pulse. She gasped a few breaths and looked at the clock.

The red illuminated numbers glowed back. 8:00 A.M. Damn. She was late for work.

She grabbed for the phone.

"Hello?" Her voice shook, her body still captive to sleep. The dream crashed through her mind and sensation flooded her body.

"Madeleine?"

She sighed with relief. *Scott.*

"Oh, good, it's you." She dropped back onto her pillow.

"Are you okay?"

Her ears no longer throbbed, and her heart didn't feel as if it was going to explode.

"I'm fine. I overslept. Weird night." Stephen and those strange erotic visions had danced around her head until sheer exhaustion had dragged her into sleep in the early morning. And he'd followed, haunting her dreams with penetrating eyes and seductive kisses. And his voice. Whispering to her.

She glanced again at the clock. It was too early for Scott to be calling. He was a cop who worked the late shift. She sat up slowly in the bed.

"What's wrong?"

"Madeleine…"

She'd known Scott for years—since law school before Scott had dropped out to join the force—and in all that time, she'd never heard him sound so grim, so serious. She dropped her elbows to her knees and let her head fall into her hands. Dread filled her heart. "Danielle?"

"We found her last night. She's dead, Madeleine."

"Oh God."

"I'm really sorry."

"What happened to her?"

"It looks like she was mugged and left for dead."

Her mind spun—racing to process the information. "Can I see her?"

"Madeleine, that's probably not a good idea. We can get someone else to make a formal identification."

"No, I want to do it." I did little enough for her in life, she added silently.

He paused for a moment, as if considering his options, and finally agreed. "Okay. I'll meet you at the morgue."

Mumbling a barely coherent reply, Madeleine hung up the phone. She lay still on the bed, her body frozen in time. The numbers on her clock clicked as they changed to 8:02. Only two minutes ago there'd been the expectation of finding Danielle alive. Now, there was nothing.

In a fog, Madeleine showered and dressed, drank some coffee to give her artificial energy, and called her office to tell her secretary that she wouldn't be in today.

Bright sunlight momentarily blinded her as she stepped onto the sidewalk. She paced in front of the building, waiting for the taxi she'd ordered. The sun blazed but the rest of the world clung to the storm. Leaves, wet with rain, molded to the sidewalk, the limp shapes forming decaying clumps. Earthworms drowned slowly in the tiny puddles that had lured them from the ground.

Madeleine rubbed her hand along her shoulder trying to get rid of the chill that lingered despite the warm morning air.

She stared without seeing the street. It was too early for the drug dealers to be out. The children in the neighborhood had already made the desperate dash to the safety of the local public school. A few workers were heading toward the bus stop. Madeleine would have been one of them if not for Danielle.

A lone man lingered across the street. He stood in the alley, his face hidden in the deepest shadows. She knew better than to stare. The rule of the street was to look at no one for long. But she couldn't look away. There was something familiar about his body. She couldn't see his eyes, but she felt them watching her from the dark of the shadows.

A honk grabbed her attention. She stepped back, dodging the soggy splash from the taxi's tires as it pulled to a stop. Climbing into the cab, Madeleine gave the address for the city morgue. She looked forward, ignoring the startled look on the driver's face.

Danielle's dead. Danielle's dead. She couldn't believe it. Just last night she'd been ready to lecture Danielle on safety and calling home and hanging out with strangers— now this. Madeleine closed her eyes and dropped her head against the back seat. All the things she'd planned to say seemed so trivial, so petty. And too late. Guilt lurked on the edges of her thoughts.

I should have taken better care of her.

The driver dropped Madeleine in front of the building. She stepped onto the curb and paused, gathering her courage before walking up the sidewalk. Scott met her at the door.

"How are you doing, Madeleine?" he asked, his gruff voice hesitant, as if unsure how to provide comfort at a time like this.

She tried to smile. "Fine."

"Are you sure you're up to this? We can do a photo ID."

Madeleine shook her head. "I need to see her."

Scott was silent, but he turned and led her through the double doors.

The antiseptic smell assaulted her senses. *It smells like a hospital, but they deal in death.* She followed him down bright white hallways. *Why white? Why not black to suit the visitors' moods? Or even gray?*

Her mind raced with nonsense questions. Anything to avoid thinking about why she was here. Scott led her down the long hall into an equally bright room. Madeleine kept her eyes on his back, not wanting to see what she feared would be around her. A huge window dominated one wall. A table stood in the room beyond the glass. A body rested on top.

A body. Not a person. The person is gone.

Madeleine stared at the sheet covering the body and waited, her mind surprisingly distant.

The cloth was pulled back. Danielle's pale face lay still against the shocking white around her. Madeleine nodded. A lump caught in her throat. She swallowed, trying to clear it.

The sheet fell and Danielle was gone. Madeleine barely noticed Scott leading her out of the room.

She sank down onto a bench that had been conveniently situated outside the door, her shaking legs finally giving out. A cup of coffee appeared in front of her blank, staring eyes. She took the cup from Scott without looking up.

"What happened to her?" She listened to the quiet, almost dead sound of her own voice.

"Her throat was cut."

"Where did it happen?" she asked.

He hesitated only a moment before answering. "We found the body in an empty warehouse. Got an anonymous tip."

"Convenient."

"Her money was gone. Her dress torn a bit. It looks like a mugging gone bad. Her body was dumped to hide it." Scott cleared his throat. "I know this is hard for you, Madeleine, but I need to ask a few questions about who might have wanted to hurt Danielle."

She looked up. "I thought you said she was mugged."

"It looks that way, but we have to check out everything." Madeleine nodded. "Was Danielle involved in anything that would get her killed? Was she doing drugs? Did she gamble?"

"I don't think so." Madeleine looked from Scott to her hands, back up to Scott. "I don't know. I would have said no, but recently—I don't know—she's been different." She took a shallow breath.

"You found an apartment for her in your building and helped her get a job?"

Madeleine nodded.

"I told her mother I'd look out for her. Guess I didn't do a very good job," Madeleine said with a self-mocking laugh. Tears began to form. She blinked them away, not allowing herself the luxury of sinking into the grief and guilt that threatened.

Scott squatted in front of her and took her hands in his. "This is not your fault."

Madeleine nodded. It seemed like the best answer.

Scott wouldn't understand. It was the difference between logic and feeling. Logically, she knew it wasn't her fault. But that didn't seem to make much difference with Danielle on that table.

"So you don't have any idea what she might have been involved in?"

"No. She was a nice girl, but she had bad taste in men." Madeleine froze as images of her strange visit last night returned. "Wait. She had some new friends. They aren't like the normal guys she hung out with." Her heart started to pound. She couldn't save Danielle, but maybe she could help find who killed her.

"Names?"

"Stephen and Dylan."

"You know them?"

"No, I just met them last night. I thought Danielle might be there, and I went over to talk with her. They said they hadn't seen her."

"Madeleine..." She ignored the warning tone of Scott's voice.

"Dylan seemed okay. Nice. Young. But the other one..."

"Stephen?"

She nodded. "There's something about him." She couldn't describe it. How did she explain that she'd been terrified and attracted by the same man? How did she explain she'd invited him into her home and kissed him?

"What?" Scott finally prodded.

"I don't know, but it was just something."

"And they knew Danielle."

"Dylan did. He was worried about her. Stephen said he'd never met her, but I'm not sure I believe him." Her mind searched for proof—something to give to Scott. She could do this. She could bring Danielle's killer to justice.

"Okay, I'll look into it." Scott snapped his notebook shut.

"I could help."

"Madeleine, let me handle it. It's my job. Do you have a way to contact them?"

"They have a house on State Street," she said with a sigh. If that was all she could do, then that's what she'd do. "I'll call you with it when I get home."

"Good." She stood and they walked to the front of the building, Scott carefully guiding her. He opened the door, indicating Madeleine should precede him. She turned and waited for him to follow her out.

"This has a price."

"What? You're selling me information?" Scott's incredulous look almost made Madeleine smile. Almost. She couldn't find the power to smile, knowing Danielle lay dead in that room—murdered, while Madeleine was supposed to be looking out for her.

"I don't want money, Scott. I want information. I want to be kept up to date on what you find out."

"Madeleine, you know I can't do that."

"Yes, you can. I'm not asking for privileged information. I just want to be kept in the loop. She was my cousin, Scott. I'm not asking much. Just keep me informed."

Scott sighed. "I'll do my best, but give me that address. And Madeleine, stay out of it."

***

"Scott, what the hell is going on?" Madeleine held the phone with one hand and the newspaper with the other. The article was small and the headline benign, but it still sent a pain through Madeleine's chest.

"Madeleine, I told you, yesterday and the day before that and the day before that—nothing is going on. It was a mugging." He spoke patiently and consistently, just as he had every other time she'd called. It wouldn't do any good. She didn't believe him.

"Tell me that's not Danielle they're talking about."

She found the relevant passage and started to read. *"The body of a young blond woman, not identified by the police, was found in an abandoned warehouse. The blood had been drained from her body."*

"Madeleine, we get a lot of homicides. Don't assume that story has anything to do with you. Danielle was mugged. She was in the wrong place at the wrong time."

"Did you talk to Stephen and Dylan?" she pressed.

"Yes."

"And?"

"And nothing, Madeleine. Dylan was Danielle's friend. Stephen had never met her. Besides having no reason to kill Danielle, they have alibis for the day of the murder." Scott sighed. Deeply. "Madeleine, it was a mugging. Let it go."

She shook her head even though Scott couldn't see her. "I don't buy that. You searched her apartment. Twice. If she was mugged, why would you care what happened in her apartment?"

"It was routine."

"Fine." Madeleine hung up the phone without saying good-bye. Scott was lying. He'd been lying since he'd reluctantly agreed to give her information.

She walked to the window and watched the night settle on the city. The pale pink streaks of the setting sun echoed through the haze of dust and smog. The streets emptied as people hurried home. She looked across the street. He was gone—the man who stood in the alley's shadows. She let the curtain fall and pushed the concern aside. It was probably nothing. In this neighborhood, people claimed a section of sidewalk as their own and then defended it with their lives. He was probably just some new drug dealer. She was getting paranoid.

She briefly considered telling Scott about him but dismissed it. If he was telling the truth and this was just a mugging, then the stranger on the street could have nothing to do with it.

She paced the length of the room, losing track of how many times she passed by the threadbare couch. She tried to mentally organize what she knew, but she kept coming back to the same place. She needed information.

Don't do it. Trust Scott. She exhaled sharply, her breath hissing through her teeth. *Yeah, right.*

She reached the short table she used for a phone stand and jerked open the cluttered drawer. Danielle's spare keys were somewhere in the pile.

Danielle had giggled when she gave them to Madeleine. "Be sure to knock," she'd said. "I might have Mister Right in there." Madeleine had smiled, thinking it was cute that Danielle was still looking for Mister Right.

Madeleine had thrown the keys in the drawer and forgotten about them. She pawed through the mess of old notes, bent nails, plastic silverware, and loose change until the bright red ring was shifted to the top of the pile. Grabbing them, Madeleine picked up her own keys and walked into the hall.

She hurried down two doors to Danielle's apartment. Police tape no longer barred the entrance.

She opened the door but hesitated. It was a dead person's house. Her fingers gripped the door frame.

Either go in or go home.

She took a deep breath and stepped inside. It looked like it always had—cluttered and frilly. Danielle had loved lace. Madeleine walked through the living room and glanced in the kitchen. Nothing seemed out of place, but then again, nothing seemed in place either. Danielle had had a fluid style of housekeeping, piles flowing into each other.

Madeleine grasped the handle of the bathroom door and stopped. *This is the point in horror movies when the unsuspecting neighbor finds a body hanging from the shower rod.*

"What are you doing in here, Miz Bryant?"

"Ahh." The yelp broke from her throat. Turning, she came face to face with Bob. She pressed her hand to her chest, trying to slow her wildly beating heart. "What?" she demanded.

"This ain't your apartment, Miz Bryant. I'm not sure you're supposed to be here."

Madeleine ground her teeth together, trying to hold back the words that threatened to burst forth. Adrenaline surged through her body. "Danielle gave me a key." Her voice shook. "Her mother asked me to clean out her stuff."

"Yeah, it's a shame about her. She was a looker. And she was a nice girl. 'Course it always happens. Them guys like that fancy fella of yours always get the good-lookin' ones."

Madeleine nodded, listening, as she did in any conversation with Bob, only partially. She opened the bedroom door. Bob's words registered. She spun around.

"Wait. Fancy fellow of mine? Who are you talking about?"

"That dude you were with the other night. Last time I saw your cousin she was getting into his car."

"Here? He picked her up here?"

"Yeah."

"And you're sure it was him?" she pressed.

"Yea-ah." Bob looked at her like she was stupid. "I keep up on the comings and goings of just about everybody around here. I especially noticed your cousin, if you know what I mean?" He gave Madeleine a knowing nod and wink. "She wasn't the kind of girl a man can ignore. I just didn't picture the two of you into sharing." A repulsive smile curled his lips. He took a step closer. "I kind of pictured you as the straitlaced, one-man woman type." He winked again.

Madeleine barely noticed. Stephen knew Danielle. He'd lied to her.

Shock moved through her body. She didn't know why
she should be surprised—why *wouldn't* Stephen lie to her?
But somehow she was disappointed.

"I was just coming up to see you, Miz Bryant." Bob's
voice stopped her as she stepped into the hall. "This
package was delivered for you this morning."

He handed her a large brown envelope.

"Thanks," she said absently, taking the envelope and
turning it over in her hands. It looked official. Her secretary
sometimes sent things to Madeleine's home, but it wasn't
her handwriting on the outside.

Bob cleared his throat as he took a step closer.
Madeleine almost choked on the smell of stale cigars in
his clothes. He ran a finger down her bare arm. "Don't I
get a tip?"

She slapped his hand and nodded. "Yes. Touch me
again and I'll break your fingers."

She didn't stop to see his reaction. She hurried to her
own apartment and snapped the locks behind her. She tore
the envelope open and gasped.

It was Danielle's autopsy report.

Madeleine stared at the report and felt her way to the
couch. She sank down and flipped through the pages. The
words blurred in front of her eyes. It told her nothing—
nothing she could understand. She flipped to the back page
and sighed with relief. The final opinion had been
highlighted.

*Cause of death was blood loss from a wound at the
neck. There was little blood found in the victim's body,
almost as if she'd been drained. Postmortem wound at
the neck indicates someone was trying to hide the initial
wound. Additional postmortem wound found in her heart
made by a nonserrated blade.*

She dropped back against the couch. What was going
on? Who'd sent this to her?

She looked at the outside of the envelope again. No

return address. Bob might remember who delivered it but as he'd said, it had been delivered this morning; she didn't think it was high on his priority list. Besides, she didn't want to think of the price she might have to pay for the information.

It had to be Scott. Only someone official could get this information. Maybe Scott was afraid he'd be reprimanded for giving her the information so he'd sent it to her anonymously.

It didn't really matter how she'd gotten it—she knew. Danielle was the girl in the newspaper article.

And she knew something else. Stephen had known Danielle.

Madeleine pushed herself off the couch and grabbed her jacket, moving before caution could stop her. Shrugging into the coat, she turned up the collar and stalked down the hall. The dim light outside her building provided barely enough illumination to see the street. She stayed in the light until she saw a passing taxi.

"Where to?" the cabbie demanded as she jumped inside.

Madeleine stared blankly at the back of the driver's head. Where *was* she going? And what was she planning to do once she got there?

"Hey, lady, where do you want to go? I'm not just sitting here all night."

"State Street. Take me to State Street."

"That's kind of a broad area. You wanna narrow it down a bit?" he grumbled as he placed the car into gear.

"I'll decide when we get there."

Sitting back against the stained seat, she watched the blur of buildings pass. Her fingers tapped on the filthy door handle.

What are you doing? She bit her lip and stared out the window, unable to answer her own question. She was going in without a plan. *I just want to see the house again.*

And Stephen.

A now familiar ache pierced her stomach. He'd invaded her thoughts throughout the week, distracting her at work, annoying her at home. The moment she'd relax, he'd be there—with his seductive voice and hypnotic eyes. Dreams haunted her sleep—erotic dreams. Initially they'd only been repeats of the first night's vision, but slowly through the week they'd evolved into full erotic fantasies.

"We're here." The cabbie's voice interrupted her thoughts. "Now where do you want to go? I go off duty here in a few minutes, and I'm not sitting around while you decide."

Madeleine looked out the window. They were about five blocks from Stephen's house.

"Here's fine." Without looking at the meter, she pulled out a twenty and handed it to him. "Keep the change." The startled look on the driver's face meant she'd overtipped him. Way overtipped him, but she didn't care. She had to get out of the cab and...and what?

She still didn't know what she was doing here, but Stephen and his house were the only clues she had. She shook her head.

Clues? Great, I'm channeling Nancy Drew.

The silence of the street weighed on her shoulders as night settled on the houses. Now that she was here, she had to do something. Hesitant footsteps moved her slowly toward Stephen's. Stephen had to be involved in Danielle's death. He'd lied about knowing her, and then there was Madeleine's memory of his house—the housekeeper's pale, tired face, Nick's fear, even her own strange compulsion when she'd met Stephen, though she was pretty sure she'd imagined that part of it.

Her steps slowed even further as she approached until she was barely moving. Two houses away, she could see his front porch. *Now what? Stand here and wait for a neighbor to call the cops? Go up to the door and demand that he tell her about Danielle's death?* She stared at the building as if it had answers to give.

The front door popped open and Dylan stepped out. He did a quick scan of the street, looking away from her, then turning back. She jumped into the shadow of the high stone fences separating two homes and pressed her back against the wall. She held her breath and slid deeper into the shadows. She watched the street and slowly realized what she was doing. She rubbed her forehead with tense fingers.

I really do think I'm Nancy Drew. If I'd just stayed on the street, I could have greeted him and kept moving. Or asked him some questions about Stephen.

Now, there was no way to explain why she was hiding in an alley.

Seconds passed. She waited. The air around her grew strangely still. The hair on the back of her neck stood up.

"Hello, Madeleine," a dark, masculine voice whispered from behind her. She spun around. A hand wrapped itself around her neck and slammed her against the brick wall.

"No!" She managed to scream before the bright lights that warned of unconsciousness swarmed over her. Bits of rock scraped her hands as she tried to catch herself against the rough stone. Her knees collapsed, dropping her to the ground. Stars swirled in front of her face.

"What is it that attracts you? Just like the others— can't stay away," her assailant growled. He grabbed the front of her blouse. She heard the tear of material as his hands jerked the edges apart. *Oh God, this can't be happening.* She opened her mouth to scream again. A pale hand flashed in front of her face, covering her mouth and muffling her cry. Between darkness and the pain in her head, she couldn't see the man's face—only a flash of dark hair against a distant streetlight.

Forcing her mouth open, she buried her teeth in the palm that covered her lips. A grunt of pain preceded her release. She knew only a moment of relief.

"Bitch." A violent slap across her cheek accompanied the curse, knocking her back against the wall. Another shower of pain fell on her body.

"No," she said again, trying to force the darkness away. Dizzy, she pushed at the hands that grabbed at her. But they were stronger. They pulled her forward until she was inches away from his face. Darkness still held him.

Madeleine weakened as the pain radiated through her body.

He raised his head as if he were listening to a distant sound. Lifting her by the flaps of her coat, he tossed her lightly against the wall.

"Until next time." And he was gone.

Released from the threat, her body shut down, collapsing against the bricks. The will that had kept her upright disappeared. Blackness swallowed her, and she fell to the ground.

***

Voices. In the distance. Angry voices. Unable to force her eyes open, Madeleine lay still and identified soft cushions beneath her cheek, a warm layer of material by her chin. Her head throbbed and her whole body ached. *What the hell had happened?* Then she remembered. She'd been in the alley and someone had grabbed her.

But where was she now? It didn't feel like home. The cushions felt too comfortable to be anything from her apartment. She slowly let her eyes drift open and immediately identified her resting place. *Stephen's living room.*

Well, you wanted another reason to get inside the house. Of course, a concussion wouldn't have been my first choice.

She pushed herself up to sitting. A few shallow breaths helped clear the swirling colors that invaded her eyes when she moved. Nausea welled in her throat. She froze and the wave passed. *Damn. Whoever hit me has a mean right cross.* Dark, dangerous images flashed across her mind. Hands pulling at her clothes, the dark hair—his voice. It seemed like she should recognize it.

She tried to imagine a face to go with the voice, but nothing came to mind. The only person who even vaguely fit the image was Stephen. Her heart started to pound. It didn't make sense. Why would he attack her in the alley? And then, why bring her here? The throbbing in her head overwhelmed her thoughts, and she pushed the concerns away for later. Right now, she had to deal with the pounding headache.

She touched the back of her head with light fingers and gasped as pain shot through her body. The voices behind the kitchen door had dropped to a low rumble. She thought about calling out to let someone know she was awake, but the idea of raising her voice, even just a little, made her head pound even worse. She'd walk over there quietly and tell them *quietly* that she *really* needed some aspirin.

Standing was easier than she thought it would be—walking was the challenge. Each step inspired an additional throb in her skull. After three steps, she rested against a high-backed chair and took a heart-calming breath.

"I can't believe you brought her here." Stephen's voice resounded from the kitchen.

"What was I supposed to do? Leave her lying in the alley?" Nick asked.

"Yes."

Madeleine froze.

"When are you going to understand that you don't get involved with humans?" Stephen demanded.

Humans? Like we're alien creatures? Madeleine smiled. They had to be joking.

"I'm human," Nick insisted, his voice firm, defiant—and with a hint of pleading.

Silence filled the space. Madeleine was afraid to move. She waited, and Stephen answered quietly, "No, you're not."

It didn't sound like a joke.

Her fingers dug into the back of the chair. She had to get out of here, but she couldn't make her feet move. She waited for Nick's response.

"I couldn't just leave her there," was all he said.

"Fine." Stephen's voice had turned logical, but the edge was still there. "You brought her here. She's perfect. Do it."

"No."

"Nicholas." Darkness and warning filled Stephen's voice. "She won't feel a thing."

"No! Why do you keep pushing me?"

"Because, damn it, you're starving. I can see it in your eyes. I know what it's like. You need blood. Fresh, human blood. And there's a body in the living room with plenty of it."

The throbbing in her head faded as her heart moved to her throat. She took tiny pants of silent air to keep the panic at bay.

"I drink it now."

"From a blood bank. Nicholas, that will sustain you for a while, but you need to complete the conversion and drink fresh human blood."

Her jaw dropped open.

"I'm not ready."

"You're a vampire. You'd better get ready."

Madeleine gasped, and the silence between the two rooms changed. She could feel it—the heavy weight of an invisible force, searching for her, stalking her.

She backed away, moving as quickly as she could and still maintain the silence she knew was vital. Her heart pounded. The scrape of a chair across hardwood floor sounded from the kitchen. They were coming! She spun around and raced for the door, silence no longer her goal. She burst onto the street and ran.

Madeleine! Stephen's voice echoed through her head and followed her down the street. She pumped her legs faster, sure that any moment he'd be behind her. Tears flowed down her cheeks, her sobs draining valuable breath.

Later, she couldn't remember how she got home. The city streets were blurred, the memory of her run filled with panic and terror. No one followed her, but his presence lingered. She stumbled into the brightly lit lobby of her building and tore up the stairs, ignoring Bob posted near the door.

Her hands shook as she tried to unlock her apartment. With a clatter, the keys fell to the ground. She sobbed and knelt for them. On her knees she reached up to open her door. The key slid into the lock and with a sigh of relief she tumbled inside. She slammed the door shut and clicked the lock.

Oh my God. Oh my God. Vampires! Her breath came in panicked gasps.

She crawled to the phone. Her shaking hands could barely dial the number, but finally she heard the ring on the other end. She wrapped one arm around her waist and rocked back and forth until Scott picked up.

"Lambert," he answered after the fourth ring.

"Oh my God, Scotty."

"Madeleine?"

"They think they're vampires. That's why there was no blood in Danielle's body. They think they're vampires!"

Three

Stephen stopped in his doorway and watched Madeleine race down the street. Damn, he should have been listening for her. She'd been unconscious when Nicholas had carried her inside. He'd assumed she'd be out for a while.

He started down the steps. He would catch her before she got home. Madeleine was about to become another victim of random city violence.

Light shimmered at the bottom of his steps. Stephen tensed and waited for the person to materialize. He relaxed only slightly when he saw it was Gayle.

Gayle rarely left Death's Door, the nightclub he owned. With the sun just set, it was prime hunting time, so why was he here?

"Hello, my love." Gayle draped his arm over the stone ledge in a pose of elegant exhaustion. "I haven't seen you for days." Gayle rarely asked direct questions. He made statements and waited for others to fill in the blanks. Which they usually did.

"I've been busy."

"So I hear."

Stephen straightened. Of course Gayle had heard. There was little that didn't move through the gossip mill at Death's Door. It would have been too much to hope Madeleine and Nicholas would have gone unnoticed. "I brought something for you."

"Not now. I've got to attend to something." He shouldered past Gayle and was surprised when Gayle's hand landed on his arm.

He held up a newspaper. "Read this morning's news?"

"What do I care what the human press reports?"

"Because it looks like familiar handiwork."

He slapped the newspaper onto Stephen's open palm. The article was small. He skimmed it quickly. "Damn."

"Just what the Community needs. Bad press on top of three dead Council members."

Stephen snapped his head toward Gayle. "Three?"

"Well, there are only two officially, but rumor has it that Mikel the Lesser was found dead in his lair."

Stephen felt his jaw tighten. *So, they found the third one.*

Gayle gave a delicate little shudder. "Death by silver dagger. Sounds horribly painful, doesn't it? Just the thought makes my skin crawl." He flicked his fingers like he was waving away fairy dust. "Everyone is saying that Mikel was one of your least favorite Council members." He pursed his lips. "Not that I think you have a favorite."

"No," Stephen agreed.

Gayle was a great source of information. The challenge was not to give any away while he was supplying it.

"I take it you know something about this." Gayle pointed to the newspaper. "And that's why the Council wants to see you." He gave a negligent shrug in response to Stephen's glare. "They came by my place looking for you."

"Shilling for the Council now, are you?"

Gayle's eyes narrowed, and he snapped, "I was just trying to help. I thought you might want some warning, but you obviously don't need any assistance. Good night." He swirled away and disappeared.

Stephen stared at the newly vacated space. *Now I've pissed off Gayle.* He tapped his fingers on the stone wall. He didn't have that many friends left. He couldn't afford to alienate any more of them. Gayle was one of the few vampires Stephen actually trusted—as far as he trusted anyone these days.

He looked down the street. Madeleine was gone. He'd take care of her later. Right now, he had to deal with the Council. It would be easier for everyone if he showed up under his own power. He didn't think they were ready to arrest him, but they were working up to it.

Besides, facing the vampire leaders would give him a chance to find out how much they knew. They obviously didn't know it all, or he'd have been dragged before them in silver chains already.

He walked up to the bedroom he kept on the third floor. He never slept here, only using the room as a closet and a retreat—a small semblance of a human's existence.

Stephen slapped his hand on Nicholas' bedroom door as he walked past. The door opened and the fledgling walked out, pulling on his coat.

"Follow her," Stephen commanded, though it was obvious Nicholas was already headed in that direction.

Nicholas nodded but didn't move. Stephen stopped on the next landing and waited. He could feel the young vampire gathering his courage.

"Yes?" he prompted.

"You're not going to hurt her, are you?" The fledgling's voice was soft with the tiniest quiver.

Stephen slowly turned to face him, giving him time to fear.

"Why do you ask?" He bared his teeth slightly. Nicholas had been working up to this for days. "Yes?" Stephen asked darkly when the fledgling didn't answer.

"Well, she didn't do anything," he blurted out. "And she doesn't know anything. She was just worried about her cousin, and I don't think that's a good reason to end up dead."

Stephen strolled down the steps, giving Nicholas ample time to back away. The young man tightened his fists at his side and visibly braced himself, but he didn't step back. Stephen hid the small flicker of admiration.

"She does know something. She heard us talking." He kept his voice quiet. "She heard us talking because you brought her here. I will deal with Madeleine. Watch her."

Nicholas nodded glumly.

"Don't get too attached," Stephen warned. "She's not going to survive this."

Nicholas tensed, and Stephen waited to see if he was going to make another run at it. After a moment, Nicholas sighed and moved toward the stairs.

Stephen folded his arms across his chest and stared at Nicholas' back as he walked away. He's going to have to lose his squeamishness for death, he thought.

The fledgling froze two steps down.

"Uh, Stephen?"

Two indistinct shapes glittered and swayed in front of him, solidifying as they floated up the stairs. Bodies began to take shape. The long cloaks they wore identified them as Council Guardians.

Stephen's eyeteeth extended, and his lips curled back in an unconscious snarl. How dare they enter his home?

"Go on, Nicholas," he commanded. The young man hesitated for a moment before plunging down the steps.

A vague, disembodied voice filled the room. "You have been called before the Great High—"

"I got your *request* earlier, Antonio." His words were slightly blurred because of the length of his teeth. "Go back to your masters. You aren't welcome here." He waved his hand and the shapes disappeared.

Stephen growled at the empty house and stalked the rest of the way up the stairs, stripping off his shirt as he went. He dropped it on the floor and took another from the closet. In moments, he was changed. He had no mirrors, but two hundred years had taught him to dress without seeing his own reflection.

He focused his thoughts, his irritation, on the Council. They ruled the vampire community like a City Council, only vampire politics tended to be a bit more violent. The only way a person left the Council was by dying, and there were only two ways for that to happen—self-destruction and execution. Most of the members had been a part of the group since its creation more than two hundred years ago and had no intention of leaving. Stephen smiled. The best laid plans...

They left Stephen alone for the most part. And he ignored them in return.

To summon him in such a manner—it was the height of rudeness to enter a vampire's house without invitation. The messengers couldn't have done anything—not even solidify—until he gave his permission, but it didn't matter. They'd entered his home.

And they'd seen Nicholas. Stephen tensed for a moment, hoping that in their vaporized state they hadn't recognized the significance of that. It wasn't likely. Unless they knew what to listen for, Nicholas's heartbeat would sound normal, human. Only someone with experience could distinguish the minor differences and know he shouldn't exist.

Five minutes earlier and they would have found Madeleine. A human draped across his couch would have been something to report. The Council left him alone, but they also kept a watch on him. With his history, they would never fully trust him. No human had entered his house for years, with the exception of his human companions. Certainly no one like Madeleine.

The line of his lips flattened out as he faced reality.

I should have just killed her.

She was trouble. He'd known it when she'd appeared on his doorstep. He'd stood on the stairs and watched her, defiantly determined in soaking wet clothes, and known she was trouble. Bulldog tenacity was a dangerous trait in a human. When a human showed up at a vampire's house looking for a lost relative, things were usually starting to fall apart.

She obviously wasn't going to let this go. Convincing the human police to let the case drop hadn't been difficult.

Madeleine wasn't going to be as easy. If he were lucky, the attack in the alley would scare her away. But his luck hadn't been going that way for the last few months. No reason to think it would change now.

Under any other circumstances, at any other time, she never would have left his house alive that first night, let alone gotten free of him the second. He'd let her live on instinct. The same instincts that had kept him alive for two hundred years, years when many vampires had faded or died or gone insane. He'd learned to trust his instincts. He wasn't going to ignore them now.

Unfortunately, Madeleine's arrival at his house tonight and the newspaper article had changed things. Instinct was subject to the laws of logic. And logic said she was too much of a risk to let live. Too much had happened recently. She was a distraction he couldn't afford. He stared down at his hand and curled the fingers into a tight fist.

Madeleine was just the latest addition to the web that was being woven. Did she belong to the weaver or was she just another fly caught in the threads? He was too close, too trapped in the web himself, to know.

He pulled on his coat and left the house. The Council would be waiting for him, watching him. No one ignored an official summons. The thin wisps of the Guardians hovered behind as Stephen walked down the street. He could use his preternatural strength and appear at the Council Chambers in minutes. Or he could drive at normal *human* speed and arrive in a little more than an hour. He smiled and climbed into his Jag. They could wait.

He drove by Madeleine's apartment. Nicholas lingered in the shadowy corner across the street. He straightened when he saw Stephen's car, but he didn't make any attempt to contact him. It hadn't been the first time Stephen had come by Madeleine's.

Caution and curiosity had drawn him back the second night. And that set the pattern for the rest of the week.

Each night he'd stood in the dark and watched her silhouette undulate against the curtains as she moved through her apartment preparing for bed. Alone. Her shadow flickered against the curtains, teasing him—her hands opening her blouse and sliding it off her shoulders, slipping her skirt down her legs. His mind filled in the rest. Two hundred years had given him one hell of an imagination.

It had also given him boundless self-control. Which seemed to have disappeared since Madeleine's arrival into his life.

He glanced up at her windows but didn't slow the car. *She's just a human.* But there was something about her that intrigued him. Tempted him.

It had been years since any female, and decades since a human woman, had interested him. Females of both species turned out to be more work than pleasure. *Maddie would be all pleasure.* His eyeteeth grew at the thought.

This strange attraction was the only explanation for his behavior the night they met. He should have killed her. Instead, he'd kissed her.

It had been a logical move, Stephen insisted quietly in his mind. Human females were much easier to control when passion was involved. The seduction scene he'd fed into her thoughts would surface again. And again. He didn't doubt that she'd been dreaming of him. His body clenched at the thought.

Damn. This can't be about sensation. It's about control. The more tightly they were bonded, the easier she would be to manage.

Stephen drove to the edge of the city and turned down the winding road leading to the Council Chambers. Their arrival in America two hundred years ago had been followed by an immediate land grab. The Community moved each generation, and individual members came and went, but the Council retained their chambers. The location was far enough out of town that visitors at odd hours went mostly unnoticed. Stephen arrived at the Chambers and parked a distance away. The final walk would do him good—give him a moment to regain the control that had slipped.

His amorphous escorts hovered nearby. Having been in that state, he knew the senses were dulled almost to the point of blindness. It was an uncomfortable form for vampires, having grown used to the hypersensitive abilities that came with their conversion.

Two huge guards blocked the Chamber doors with their bodies, arms folded tightly across their chests. They stared straight ahead, ignoring Stephen as he approached.

The doors behind them swung open.

"Stephen, thank God you're here."

The guards stepped back, opening a space for Thomass, Council Member and all-around model vampire. Stephen and Thomass had been raised together—given to Joshua when their conversions were completed—but never were two creatures more different. When a seat on the Council had opened up, unanimous consent inserted Thomass into the slot. Now, Thomass was a leader in the Community and Stephen a self-imposed outcast.

Through all their years, Stephen had never liked Thomass much, but he was the closest thing Stephen had to a friend on the Council.

Thomass grabbed his arm and pulled him inside. He slowed when they were away from the guards but not quite in the main chamber.

"Things are not going well, Stephen." Thomass glanced around nervously before continuing. "I don't like it. There are so many rumors going around, unbelievable statements. About you. You've never been a favorite of the Council—"

"For obvious reasons," Stephen interjected.

"Well, yes. But now, even those sympathetic to you

are starting to question your loyalty."

Stephen didn't answer though Thomass paused long enough for him to do so. There was nothing to say. They'd never earned his loyalty, and he'd never given it.

"Be careful when you go in there. I know you don't like them or respect them, but some of them are very clever."

Stephen nodded. Thomass was right and he'd do well to remember that.

"Is there anything happening I should know about?" Thomass asked

Stephen raised an eyebrow. "Like what?"

"I don't know. Anything unusual. Anything out of the ordinary. Anything." He repeated the furtive glance up and down the hall before dropping his voice. "I think one of them is having you watched. I can't be of help to you if I'm surprised by what I hear. So, is there anything I should know about?"

Stephen scrolled down the list in his mind. *An illegally created vampire, a tenacious family member, and a physiological change that could threaten the whole community.*

He shook his head. "No."

A glimmer of disappointment sparked in Thomass' eyes, almost as if he knew Stephen was lying. Stephen brushed the disturbing thought away. He'd spent years learning to control his physical responses. But then, Thomass had been with him during those years. If anyone was going to recognize the signs, it would be him.

"Ready?" Thomass asked and waited for Stephen's nod. He shook Stephen's hand and stepped back. "Okay, let's go."

Stephen let Thomass precede him, the vampire's anxious fluttering grinding on his nerves. He'd face the Council, leave, and go kill Madeleine.

And at some point, he had to apologize to Gayle. He'd

only known Gayle for a dozen years, but he knew the other vampire could pout for that long, or longer.

He added it to his mental list of things to do before dawn and entered the Council Chamber.

The room was lit entirely by candles, ostensibly because of sensitive vampire eyes. Stephen knew it was for atmosphere—*the better to intimidate you with, my dear*. The low light created shadows deep enough to hide the creatures that entered the Chamber.

He walked to the center of the room and waited. Sound slowly faded as he began a deliberate scan of the Council members.

He let the anger and memories flow into his eyes as he moved from person to person. It had been years since he'd seen most of them. He passed by the new members and lingered on the original Council. Some looked away. Stephen waited patiently until they looked up and met his eyes.

They'd created him. They could damn well acknowledge his existence.

Silence prevailed until he reached the last Council member.

The Leader, Simon, sat at the top of the half circle that formed the Council table.

"Stephen, we asked you to come here tonight—"

"You entered my house without permission," he interrupted.

Simon had the courtesy to look embarrassed. "As to that, we apologize for the rudeness of our messengers. They were overzealous in extending our invitation."

"Invitation?" The corner of his lip curled into the mockery of a smile. "Then I'm free to leave?"

"Well—"

"Of course he's free to leave," Thomass interjected. "This isn't a trial, is it? We wanted him here to answer questions, nothing more."

Simon acknowledged Thomass with a nod and then turned back to Stephen. "As Thomass has stated, you are free to leave. We hope, however, that you will stay and speak with us."

Stephen nodded. He wanted to hear their questions, wanted to see how much they knew. And how much they suspected. He decided to push a little to see what came out.

"I hear you lost another one," he taunted, silently thanking Gayle for the information. He looked again at the table behind which the Council was seated. Three chairs were empty. "Joshua, Bernard, and now Mikel. Some people might consider being a member of this Council hazardous duty."

"Murderous bastard!" Robertson bolted to his feet, sending his chair clanging to floor. "Chain him to the field. Let the sun have him. We all know he's the one."

Stephen ignored the ranting vampire and continued to stare at Simon.

"You're well informed," the Leader acknowledged.

"I like to keep up on things."

"Then you probably know the rest. He was found in his lair…"

"Death by silver dagger," Stephen finished.

Simon nodded. "Three vampires, all killed at night with silver daggers. We have to look at—" He paused. "All options." *Suspects,* Stephen mentally substituted. "Anyone who might have a grudge against this Council."

"And you suspect me? I'm honored."

A low hum of voices vibrated across the floor. The Council was used to being respected, feared at the very least. Simon held up his hand, and the grumbling slowed. Anger flushed the faces of several vampires. Shoulders hunched, teeth were bared.

Stephen felt his own eyeteeth extend, his body preparing for attack.

"This is ridiculous." Thomass' voice rang clear over the rumble of voices. He stood and opened his arms wide, hands uplifted. "Unless Stephen has suddenly developed an immunity to silver, and I'm assuming he'd tell us if he did..." Several vampires around the table smiled at Thomass' sarcasm. "He isn't the one."

"Whoever's killing us is using a human," Robertson said.

"Stephen doesn't like humans," Thomass dismissed.

"He seems to have developed a taste for one or two." Robertson's smug tone indicated he knew something.

So, they know about Madeleine. And Nicholas. Thomass was right. They had been watching him. Stephen held himself still, crushing any reaction.

"We've all seen the paper." Robertson held up the same article Gayle had shown Stephen earlier. "There's more to the story. I spoke with the fledgling Stephen *volunteered* to raise for our community." Robertson was one of the Council Members who had disagreed with Stephen taking on Dylan when Joshua was found dead.

"I don't see what the problem is," Thomass said. "Yes, it was sloppy, but these things happen. Bodies do get found."

Stephen felt the approval of several members as Thomass finished. He shifted his shoulders, trying to loosen some of the tension that had crept up his back. Yes, one body had been found. His hope was the other three would stay where they were supposed to—dead and buried.

"This isn't just a question of tidiness, Thomass." Robertson held up the paper. "This woman was staked and her body found on your friend's property—now, she's got a cousin who's asking questions. And it looks like she's turning to Stephen for the answers."

One by one, each set of eyes turned from Robertson to Stephen. It wasn't an official rule—the Community had few official rules—but it was an unspoken one. Any family member who appeared looking for a victim was eliminated. Immediately.

The survival of the Community depended on myth and legend—on the disbelief in the supernatural by the general human population. One human who knew the truth could cause problems that would rock the vampire world across the planet.

Madeleine.

Stephen ignored the heated stares and looked back at Simon. They were looking for proof or protest. Something from Stephen to say he was innocent. He would give them nothing.

"Stephen?" The Leader turned his name into a reprimand.

"Yes. The cousin has been to my house."

"On more than one occasion," Robertson added, his voice dripping with sarcasm.

"Why haven't you destroyed her?" Simon asked, his voice turning logical. "You, in particular, understand the danger of allowing family members to search for the lost."

Stephen pulled his lips back at the reminder but kept his voice steady. "Yes. She won't be a problem."

"Why haven't you destroyed her?" Simon repeated.

Stephen stood silent. He didn't have an answer. Didn't have one to satisfy himself and certainly didn't have one that would satisfy the Council.

"Because of the press, of course," Thomass said. Stephen as well as the entire Council looked toward Thomass. "If Stephen had killed the cousin so recently after the death of the woman, we'd have press swarming this case. You know how the media loves a good multiple murder."

Members seated at the table nodded in agreement.

"I'm sure that as time goes by, Stephen will address the issue. Right, Stephen?"

Stephen nodded. It was all so simple. A little too

simple.

"But how many of us will die before he decides to kill the woman?" Robertson shook his head. "Whoever has been killing vampires is using a human to help." He pointed to Stephen. "He's always hated us, he's got a *family history* of silver daggers, and now he takes up with a human. Interesting coincidence."

"But I thought the woman just came onto the scene when her cousin died." The voice of reason came from Charles, one of the newer Council members. Stephen had no feeling for him at all, but he was pleased someone had asked the question. Logic among the Council had to be encouraged.

"That's what he'd like us to believe. I think we should talk to the fledgling he's been raising." Before anyone could stop him, Robertson nodded to the guard, and a side door opened.

Dylan stumbled into the room. He looked young and scared. Stephen was amazed at the lack of sympathy he felt for the fledgling. It struck him again how unusual the choice was for Joshua. If Joshua was going to convert a human, why Dylan? They didn't seem like a good match. Joshua had believed in truth and tolerance. Dylan was too smooth. No, they weren't a good match. So why?

Dylan looked at Stephen as he walked by. "I'm sorry," he pleaded.

"Fledgling, speak to me." Dylan turned to face Simon. "Tell us what you know about this situation." He tapped the newspaper article.

"It was nothing, really."

"Tell us."

"Well, I was friends with this girl, Danielle. A human. I was going to make her my human companion when I moved out of Stephen's house. I came home one night, and she was there. But she wasn't right. There was something wrong with her." His voice sped up to a hysterical pace. "And Stephen said he'd take care of it. I left to go feed—" He glanced at Stephen and looked like he was about to apologize again.

Stephen watched dispassionately. He wasn't about to become part of Dylan's little show. The lies were clever and close to the truth. Close enough that explaining the subtleties would be a waste of time.

With one more pleading look, Dylan turned back to Simon.

"When I came back, Danielle was dead and her cousin was there."

"Had you ever seen this cousin before?" Robertson asked. "Maybe she was one of Stephen's friends," he prompted.

"No. I mean, I knew about her." Dylan shook his head. "No. I know what you're thinking, and it isn't possible. I'm sure Stephen didn't know Madeleine before that night. I'd swear to it."

He sounded so earnest, so sincere—so unbelievably loyal that it became obvious to Stephen, and probably everyone in the room, that Dylan would lie to protect him. Stephen could barely contain his sneer. Dylan was setting him up. Why? And who was pulling Dylan's strings?

"Stephen? What do you have to say to this?"

"What would you have me say? You said this wasn't a trial, yet you bring out witnesses. If there is an accusation to be made, do it now."

Gazes fell and turned away as he boldly looked back at the Council set on condemning him. They were just two hundred years too late.

"The disposal was a mistake," Stephen continued. "I admit to that. I will handle the cousin when it is appropriate."

"It's been enough time. We will send someone after her," Thomass announced.

"No!" Stephen felt his teeth extend at the threat to

Madeleine. "She's mine. I will handle it."

Thomass laughed—a gentle, warning laugh. "It's no problem. Let one of us do it." Stephen could see pleading in Thomass' eyes.

"I will handle it," he repeated.

"You'll eliminate her?"

"She won't be a problem."

"See that she's not, or we *will* take care of it," Simon said. "Stephen, we don't know who is responsible for these recent deaths, but you do hold a history with this Council. We will do whatever is needed to protect this Community."

He couldn't fault Simon's desire to protect his people. "I expect nothing less." Stephen turned. It was time to leave. He had what he needed. They didn't seem to know any more than he did. Less, really. They were of no more use to him tonight, and he had things to do before dawn.

"You'll excuse me."

He didn't wait for permission. He turned and headed for the door, pausing as he walked by Dylan. The young vampire flinched. Stephen didn't bother to look at him. "You're no longer welcome in my house."

Stephen walked out, stopping only when he'd reached his car. He replayed the scene in his head.

Two things were obvious.

He was the target. The Council was the weapon.

The answer he didn't have—who was behind it?

And why? Stephen allowed himself a grim smile. With his history, it wouldn't be difficult to find enemies. He'd spent two hundred years bound to those he hated the most. Maybe someone had decided it was time to end it.

"Stephen!"

He tensed at Thomass' call. He didn't want to deal with the other vampire right now.

"Wait."

Stephen released his grip on the door handle and turned around.

"Do you see what I mean?" Thomass asked as he approached. "Robertson is leading the charge, but the others are right behind him."

"I'm not worried about them."

"You should be," Thomass snapped. "They have a lot of power on the Council."

"The Council has no power over me."

"They do if they grab you and stake you out with silver chains." He waved his arm toward a distant hill. It faced east, ready to catch the morning sun. "That's what they'll do, Stephen. With just the slightest provocation."

Thomass stared at Stephen, clearly looking for a response he wasn't getting. "And why didn't you tell me about this woman? I could have helped."

"She's not your concern."

"Stephen, you don't have to deal with this alone." Thomass shook his head. "I've known you longer than anyone." He smiled. "We were cellmates, remember? I know you have nothing to do with this, but please, keep your head down. For once, do what the Council wants."

"I said I would deal with her."

"Fine." Thomass capitulated. "You'll have to deal with Dylan as well. He's very upset. He's afraid he might have given them the wrong impression."

Stephen laughed without humor. "Yes, lying will do that."

"I'm sure he didn't mean to lie. He said you kicked him out of your house." Thomass placed a fatherly hand on Stephen's shoulder. "Please, talk to him. Let him come home. Out of respect for Joshua."

"Joshua was your mentor as well. You take his fledgling." Stephen pulled his car door open.

"Can I at least bring him by for his stuff?"

"Make sure I'm not there when you do," Stephen growled.

He started the engine and drove off, leaving Thomass

standing in the dark.

He should go to Madeleine's. For once he agreed with the vampire leaders. Enough time had passed. It was the perfect opportunity to stage a suicide by the distressed cousin. But tomorrow would be soon enough. His mood wasn't suited for a delicate death.

Instead, he drove to Gayle's club. The huge, black building sat back from the street. A tiny sign with the words "Death's Door" in red-black letters hung by the entrance to the gate. During daylight, it looked like a southern mansion, painted black by some madman. At night, it was dark and menacing, the home of the dead—or the undead. Just the look Gayle had been going for when he built it.

The entrance was dimly lit—for effect and to accommodate the eyes of the less lively patrons. To enter Death's Door, visitors had to navigate a pitch-black maze that led to the actual bar. The squeals of laughing fright proved Gayle's theory—humans loved a little terror with their nightclub.

Stephen nodded to the doorman-parking attendant, who checked every vehicle that came through. Stephen was known here. Not always welcome. Gayle had told him on more than one occasion that he was bad for business—he scared the humans and the vampires.

Avoiding the maze, he slipped in through a side entrance. The bar was divided into two sections, one side with tables and almost no light, the other an open area with a dance floor and enough light for human eyes.

Stephen stood near the back of the darkened side and looked out at the small crowd, humans and vampires mixed together. It was a game—one the humans didn't know they were playing.

He waited, knowing Gayle would find him. Moments later, Stephen sensed a presence behind him. He slowly turned. Gayle leaned against the back wall, his arms folded over his chest.

"Come to apologize?" he asked with excessive casualness.

"Yes."

"Good." With that, their relationship returned to normal. Stephen wasn't quite sure what that meant. He'd never had a friend like Gayle. Gayle tossed his mane of blond hair over his shoulder and strolled to Stephen's side. "You look pale. Have you dined?"

Gayle was *nouveau*-vampire. While other vampires "hunted" and "fed," Gayle "made reservations" and "dined."

"I'm fine."

"You need to keep up your strength. Word on the street is you have a new pet."

Stephen whipped his head around and nailed Gayle with his eyes. "Male or female?"

Gayle leaned back. "Pardon me?"

"What do the rumors say? Is it male or female?" Stephen demanded through tight teeth.

"Male. Which is why I was pretty sure you'd deny them outright." Gayle glanced quickly over Stephen's shoulder. His eyes widened briefly before he smiled at Stephen. "You have one of each? You are a busy boy. What's her name?"

"You're not asking about him?"

Gayle shook his head. "No. If it's male, it's not a pet." The term "pet" in the vampire community had a sexual connotation. "Hmm. Was she the one who ran from your house tonight? Tsk, tsk. That's no way to woo a lady."

"I'm not trying to woo her."

"What's her name?"

"Maddie, uh, Madeleine," Stephen corrected instantly. "And it's business. She's not a pet." He couldn't see Madeleine as anyone's pet. A pet needed to be compliant, submissive, malleable—none of which could be applied to Madeleine.

Gayle looked vaguely disappointed. "Too bad. You could use the distraction. As I recall it's been a while since you were *distracted* by anyone. Let alone a human."

"I've never been one to play with my food."

Gayle chuckled and snapped his eyes to the corner of the room again.

Stephen looked at his friend. He had no reason to trust him. Gayle was flip and flirtatious and sometimes irritating as hell. But he was loyal. Or at least he appeared loyal. And more importantly, he gathered information like an anteater on a feeding frenzy.

"I need a favor." He hated to ask it, hated to bring anyone near to the situation, but he needed information. "Keep me up on what you hear."

"About you or everything?"

"Anything to do with me, dead vampires, or silver daggers."

"So, you want only the best gossip," Gayle teased.

"Yes." Stephen cocked his head to the side. "Why do you keep looking over my shoulder?"

"Matthias is here."

"Ahh.*" Just what I need tonight.* "And you'd like me to leave."

Gayle winced. "Well, things tend to get violent when the two of you meet."

"I have that effect on people lately."

"Yes, well, my insurance costs skyrocketed after the last time you two were both here. And it took some doing to convince the police that you were just actors rehearsing and that you didn't really have fangs."

Stephen nodded. Matthias was the last person he wanted to see tonight. "Don't worry. I'm leaving."

When he arrived home moments later, the house was silent. Dylan was gone. Nicholas was watching Madeleine, and Cassandra was downstairs asleep. Her heartbeat pounded in his ears but he felt no desire to feed. It was probably time to release her. Things were going to get dangerous.

Stephen climbed the stairs to his room and walked to the wall safe hidden in his closet. He spun the dial until the lock clicked open in his hand. A single black case sat in the gray lined vault. Stephen tensed and opened the box.

Slashes of silver rested against the dark black velvet. Silver daggers given to him by his father. The father who'd believed in vampires.

The case held slots for ten silver daggers—only seven remained. Stephen smiled at the irony of it.

After two hundred years, his father's knives were being used for the purpose for which they'd been designed— killing vampires.

Four

"This is insane."

Madeleine looked up from her place on the edge of Stephen's couch. Scott had repeated the same sentiment several times this afternoon. She was a little tired of hearing it. He paced the opposite side of the room beneath the curved staircase.

She glanced out the window. The sun was beginning to set.

Cassandra, the housekeeper, had let them in and hadn't objected when Scott showed her the search warrant he'd obtained. She'd stepped aside and let them search, asking them only to keep things as tidy as possible. She didn't look as exhausted as she had last week, but the same pale skin made Madeleine wonder if Cassandra wasn't part of the club.

When the police had left and only Scott and Madeleine had remained, Cassandra had been polite as she'd offered them coffee and told them Stephen would arrive shortly after sunset. Staying true to nature, Madeleine thought as she rolled her eyes.

"Maybe you misunderstood him."

Madeleine ground her teeth together and resisted the urge to growl. They'd been through this several times as well. But her temper wasn't Scott's fault. She hadn't slept well. Even though she knew Stephen was crazy, he'd still followed her into her dreams—more seductive and daring than before.

She took a deep breath and forced her lips into a tight smile. "It's a little hard to misunderstand when you hear people talking about drinking blood."

"It doesn't make any sense."

"It makes perfect sense," Madeleine corrected. She ticked off each item on her fingertips. "There was no blood in Danielle's body. She had a cut on her neck and a stab wound in her chest. Maybe they thought they'd turned her into a vampire and had to kill her. They stake vampires, right?"

Scott spun toward Madeleine. "How do you know that?"

"I watched horror movies as a kid."

"No. How did you know about Danielle's wounds?"

Madeleine rocked back at the anger and shock on Scott's face.

"You told me about the wound on her neck, and I read the autopsy report for the rest of it."

"Where the hell did you get the autopsy report?" He stomped forward, stopping in front of her.

"Someone sent it to me. I thought you had."

"Why would I send you a confidential report?"

Madeleine shrugged. She'd thought he'd been trying to help. So who'd sent her the report? And why?

After a few moments, Scott sighed. "Okay, we'll fight about that later. Go over this with me one more time."

She sighed. "I was here. They were in the kitchen talking."

"And you're sure they didn't know you were listening? Maybe they were playing a joke on you."

Madeleine wrapped her arms around her chest to ward off a chill she couldn't seem to shake. "It was no joke. They think they are vampires. If you'd heard this conversation, you'd almost believe it, too."

***

Stephen pulled the Jag into a narrow parking space and climbed out. The sun was just below the horizon. The sounds of the city murmured around him. He took a moment to savor the muted noise, then extended his hearing, focusing the sound and turning it from a dull hum to distinct echoes.

Voices sharpened from inside the homes, laughter, tears, the slither of a bicycle tire across the sidewalk. And a heartbeat. Nearby.

He turned his head. Nicholas stood silently in the shadows.

"What are you doing here?"

He cocked his head toward the house. "*She's* here."

"Madeleine?" Stephen couldn't quite keep the surprise from his voice.

Nor could he control the physical reaction. The changes were startling and immediate. His teeth extended, stretching, straining for the need to pierce her flesh. Lower down, remnants of his human flesh began to lengthen and grow hard. He traced his tongue over the sharp points of his eyeteeth, briefly enjoying the spike of pleasure that jolted his body. More surprised because it had been years since he'd had any kind of sexual reaction to a human. Or to anyone. He'd thought the human desires had left him, as they did some vampires of a certain age. He hadn't regretted the loss much. He hadn't formed any particular attachments, and seducing a human was too simple and typically a waste of time.

Somehow, he didn't think seducing Madeleine would be either easy or a waste of time. The images he'd implanted in her mind flooded back on him and his body tightened, preparing to act out the fantasies. *Yes, Madeleine would do nicely.*

Now that he knew she was near, he focused on her heartbeat—the familiar, distinctive rhythm. She was tense and irritated.

And she wasn't alone.

"Who's with her?" Stephen asked.

"A cop. I think his name's Lambert. They searched your house."

Stephen nodded. He'd convinced the police to discount his role in the situation. Until Madeleine brought them back.

The corner of his mouth kicked up into a smile. He

had to admire her tenacity. It took a lot of persuading to convince the average human, let alone a cop, to search for a vampire. But she'd managed to do it.

Stephen nodded to Nicholas. "I'll deal with Madeleine." He wasn't worried about the cop. He was rather concerned about the Council. They'd almost assuredly have someone watching.

"I'll wait for her here."

"No. You won't need to watch her tonight."

Regret washed across the fledgling's face, but he didn't say anything.

Good. He's learning.

Stephen turned away.

He hadn't expected Madeleine to be able to move this quickly, but caution had saved him. Just before dawn, he'd decided to sleep elsewhere—too many people had taken an interest in his actions—and he'd returned to Death's Door. Gayle had installed a vault below the club that he let his friends use.

A light breeze ruffled Stephen's hair. He stopped inside his front door and ran his fingers through the wayward strands, putting them back in place.

"Good evening, Detective," he drawled as he wandered down the hall and turned the corner into his living room. "Find anything interesting?" Tension clung to Lambert like a tightly wound spring. *I wonder what it would take to set him off.*

Comparatively, Madeleine looked calm seated behind the coffee table. Her eyes locked on Stephen as he entered. With any other human he might have expected her to look away, drop her eyes. Not Madeleine. She steeled her spine and stared him down.

"Good evening, Cassandra," Stephen acknowledged when she came in from the kitchen, her hands clenching and unclenching nervously at her sides.

"You said I should let them in if they came." The

confession broke from her mouth.

Stephen bowed his head. "So I did. Thank you. Will you bring our guests some tea?" She nodded and returned to the kitchen. He stepped to the edge of the coffee table, blocking Detective Lambert from Madeleine's view. "Good evening, Madeleine." He dropped his voice to a low, seductive whisper. Her hands tightened in her lap. And shivers ran down her spine.

"I invited Ms. Bryant because she is—" Stephen could almost hear the detective's mind searching for the right word. "Involved."

Stephen kept his focus on Madeleine. "Yes."

She lifted her chin a little higher and stared defiantly into his eyes, daring him. He could feel the tension bind her body. She was fighting the most basic animal instinct—to run in the face of a predator. She was being hunted. But unlike most animals, she forced herself to remain still, knowing that if she ran or showed fear in any way, he'd be on her.

Very good, Maddie.

She flinched at the sound of his voice in her head but didn't drop her gaze. She pressed her shoulders back even farther.

Stephen closed his eyes for a brief moment, creating an image in his mind, then returned to Madeleine's gaze. *Think of us, Maddie.* He sent her his mind's latest creation.

She gasped. Her heart started to pound as the brief fantasy played through her thoughts. The sound of her tight breath reached his ears. She was waiting for him, preparing for his touch.

The points of his eyeteeth drilled downward, anticipating the penetration of her body, the glide into her warm flesh. He wanted her. Wanted to fill her, enter her in every way.

"Mr. Smith?"

Stephen pressed his lips together. He'd forgotten about

the detective. And now his teeth were fully extended. He closed the flaps of his jacket to hide the evidence of human arousal and kept his lips closed.

He glanced at Madeleine. She stared at the carpet, her chest rising in short, shallow breaths. A faint tinge of red covered her cheeks.

Stephen turned to face the detective. "Yes?" He had to speak carefully until his teeth retracted.

"I asked if you mind if Madeleine stays while we talk." His body tightened at her name. "That's fine."

While he fought to regain control, he strolled to the far end of the sitting area and lowered himself into a high-backed chair. From there he could watch Madeleine and Lambert.

Madeleine's fingers twisted together in her lap. She hadn't quite recovered from their mutual foray into fantasy. Stephen felt a strange sense of satisfaction at that. His body was slowly releasing the tension, and everything was shrinking to normal size.

I should have fed before coming here.

He'd decided to wait, knowing he would be going to Madeleine's tonight. Some perverse part of his mind had wanted to delay feeding until he was with her—the taste of her, the feel of her trembling would be a sharp spike to a hungry body.

That had been a mistake. He could have at least eased the physical hunger. Then maybe Madeleine's scent wouldn't be so tempting, or the steady beat of her pulse so intriguing. Strangely, he found himself angry at Madeleine. He'd never struggled with controlling his hunger, not since the first time. Until *she'd* entered his life.

"Mr. Smith?"

Again Stephen looked up. *Damn. That was twice.*

"I apologize. My mind is off on other things." He gave the apology with no true feeling. He propped his elbows on the arms of the chair and formed his fingers into a loosely constructed tent. "You said you had some questions."

Through the weave of his fingers, he looked at Madeleine. She'd regained her control and with its return had come a temper. The skin around her eyes was tight with anger. She seemed to sense his covert examination and turned her gaze to him. The defiance was back. She pressed her shoulders back and straightened her spine once more.

"Mr. Smith." Lambert stepped into the corner of his vision, trying to capture and hold some of Stephen's attention. "You have a lot of vampire information around your house." Lambert paused, waiting for an answer.

Stephen glanced to the side of his hands. "That's a statement. Not a question. And I have no idea how you want me to respond."

Madeleine was poised on the edge of the couch, back stiff, knees firmly clenched together, eyes boring into him, watching him for any reaction. Stephen almost laughed at the questions he could see swirling through her mind. *She* wouldn't have started the interrogation in such a nebulous way. She would have walked in and accused him of being a vampire and dealt with the consequences.

His admiration grew another step. She was proud, defiant, gutsy. *It's almost too bad she's human.*

"Do you believe in vampires, Mr. Smith?"

Stephen tapped his fingers against his lower lip as he thought about the answer. "As in how? Do I believe there are dangerous men dressed in long black capes, stalking helpless virgins, and drinking their blood? No. But I find the concept of vampires fascinating. The idea of living forever but paying the price for it is…interesting to me. What kind of creature would desire life so much that he would sacrifice his humanity for it?" He looked over his hands and drilled Madeleine with his gaze. She swallowed convulsively, understanding the threat to his words.

"Do you think you're a vampire?" The detective's abrupt question startled Stephen, though he was sure no sign of his surprise had shown on his face.

So, Maddie doesn't actually believe in vampires. She thinks I'm crazy. Stephen momentarily thought about his answer. Honesty seemed appropriate.

"No, I don't think I'm a vampire," he answered, throwing the proper amount of scorn into his voice. I know I am, he added silently in his mind.

"You have two large wooden boxes in your basement," Lambert continued. "They have dirt in them. What are they?"

"The ones that look like coffins?" Stephen asked with a slight smile. "Window boxes."

"Those are awfully large window boxes," Madeleine interjected. Stephen looked up from his hands. A shiver assaulted her body as their eyes met.

"I have awfully large windows," he said, daring her to contradict him. "At my other house," he explained. She scowled back at him. *You can't win. I've been playing these games for two hundred years. You can't win.*

It was time to end this. As entertaining as it was to tease Madeleine, he didn't need the hassle of human police in his life right now. With so many other things happening, this one could be eliminated. Madeleine's presence in his home was sure to be noticed.

"Do you want to talk about gardening now, Detective? How about you, Madeleine?" Irritation created an edge to his voice.

"Mr. Smith, can we keep to the subject at hand?" Lambert asked with polite firmness.

Madeleine tensed under Stephen's accusing glare, refusing to look away. *Uh oh. He's getting cranky.* Fire flashed in his eyes but she held firm. She wasn't going to let him intimidate her. Still, her breath released in a sigh as he turned his heated glare from her to Scott.

She continued to watch Stephen, looking for some sign that he was as crazy as she thought him. Unfortunately, he seemed way too sane.

As if he knew the image it would create, as if he knew how to best display the power and control of his body, he slowly placed his hands on the arms of the chair and pushed himself to a standing position. Power, intimidation, and anger radiated from his body with each deliberate movement.

Chills ran over Madeleine's arms and turned into tiny fires in the pit of her stomach. She squeezed her lips together to contain her gasp. *How can anyone make standing up seem sexy?* There was nothing sexy about his movements. He was pissed. That didn't stop her body from responding. His strength and power called to her.

She closed her eyes for a moment and willed her body to relax. Now was not the time to sink into another erotic daydream. The one earlier had hit her with such force. And it had been a new dream. Stephen and her, still together, different bed. The fantasy had begun at the precise moment of Stephen entering her body. She opened her eyes to see Stephen move fluidly across the room.

"I thought you were investigating a death, Detective. Why you question me about vampirism is beyond my comprehension. If you're that fascinated with the subject, I have several good books I can loan you."

Stephen's hands curled briefly into fists, clenching for a moment before relaxing and hanging comfortably by his side. Madeleine watched each movement. He hadn't threatened Scott, but the implication was there.

Scott leaned away from Stephen's approach.

"I think that's about all I need," Scott announced. Madeleine felt her mouth drop open. Scott was going to give up. *But...but there are so many more questions to ask.*

She jumped up, no longer able to remain quiet. "Do

you drink blood?"

Stephen turned his glare from Scott to her. She forced her body to stay standing in the face of Stephen's anger. Gone was the man who had arrogantly coerced entrance into her house. In his place stood a powerful, dangerous creature who, on a bad night, Madeleine *could* imagine drinking the blood of his victim.

"What?"

"It's a simple question." Madeleine took a step forward.

"It's an insane question," Stephen shot back.

"One you still haven't answered. Do. You. Drink. Blood?"

"Maddie, you're obviously not getting enough sleep at night." Stephen brushed off the question with the right amount of disgust and mockery. A thin line of tension traveled through his body so quickly she almost thought she'd imagined it. Then she saw the fire in his eye. She folded her arms over her chest and stepped in front of him. He hadn't answered her question and she wasn't moving until he did. He sighed. "No, I don't drink blood."

"I heard you talking to Nick last night."

"Is that what this is all about?"

A cynical half smile curled his lips. His brief, mocking laugh didn't fool Madeleine. He was completely controlled, giving no indication that he was anything more than amused by her accusations. Still, something didn't sit right. Something about the way he carried himself screamed "I'm lying!"

"I see, now, Detective, the curious line of your questioning." Stephen stepped around Madeleine and walked to the window. He smiled as he leaned against the frame. "Madeleine was able to convince you I'm some kind of monster that feeds on the blood of sweet, young virgins." He glanced at her for a brief moment. He didn't need to say anything—she could tell what he was thinking.

She'd never been a sweet, young anything. Stephen ignored her glare and addressed Scott.

"Did Madeleine tell you she'd been hit on the head last night?" Stephen folded his arms across his chest and waited. He looked arrogant and powerful. Sexy.

A solid punch of desire tightened in her stomach. She pushed away the hollow feeling and tried to focus on the conversation.

Scott shook his head.

"Yes," Stephen continued. "She was mugged not far from here. Nicholas happened to be out walking and came to her rescue. She was unconscious when he brought her inside." He raised his eyebrows and looked from Scott to Madeleine. "I don't know that much about head wounds, but I believe they can cause hallucinations."

"Madeleine, is this true?"

"Well," she turned to face Scott, but she kept Stephen in the corner of her sight, unwilling to let him get fully behind her. "Yes, to a point. I did get attacked." She looked over at Stephen. "Call it a mugging if you want." Her gaze bounced back to Scott. "And I did hit my head, but I know what I heard." She spun around to face Stephen again. "I was not hallucinating."

I wish they were on the same side of the room, she thought. *I'm getting dizzy.* Her head still hurt from the night before, but she decided *now* would not be a good time to mention that.

"I apologize," Stephen offered. Madeleine had to fight to keep her sneer contained. He sounded so contrite, so penitent she wanted to scream. "I didn't mean to suggest that you were hallucinating. I merely think that in your confusion, you might have misunderstood something that was said."

"How do you confuse drinking blood?" Madeleine demanded. She looked to Scott for support but saw only skepticism on his face. "Scott, I heard him."

"I don't doubt that you did," agreed Stephen. When both Madeleine and Scott looked at him, he shrugged. "I might very well have been discussing this topic with Nicholas. I honestly don't remember." He spoke past Madeleine to Scott. "I was concerned with Madeleine's welfare, you understand." His arrogant courtesy made her skin itch.

"If you were so concerned, why didn't you call for help? Call an ambulance."

Stephen directed another condescending smile her way. "You seem to have recovered quickly enough."

"So, you *were* discussing vampires and blood," Scott interrupted.

Madeleine crushed her irritation and watched Stephen, hoping to see something in the way he reacted, something in the way he moved that would give her the truth.

"Yes, but you must realize the context." He went to the coffee table and picked up a magazine. Below it lay another *Vampire Warrior* comic book, similar to the one Madeleine had seen on her first visit. Same vampire, same blood, no woman. Stephen picked it up. "Nicholas is a comic book artist. Every month, he produces another exciting episode of *Vampire Warrior* for the thrill and edification of America's youth. He and I often discuss plot lines and story problems. It's quite possible Madeleine overheard one of these conversations while she was recovering and misinterpreted what she heard."

Madeleine felt her neck muscles tighten as she listened to him. He was lying. She'd heard him. And he hadn't been talking about the plot of any comic book. She turned to protest to Scott. The look on his face stopped her. He didn't believe her. He would never believe her now. He'd made up his mind.

The kitchen door burst open. Cassandra backed through it carrying a wooden tea tray.

"Fine, let's go," Madeleine announced with a frustrated

toss of her hands. She walked to the hallway and waited for Scott to finish his apologies to Stephen.

"I'm sorry if we've caused you any undue annoyance, Mr. Smith," she heard him say.

"It's no problem. I'm sure she truly believed what she heard. And she can be very convincing when she tries."

"Thank you for your time." Scott stopped at the front door. Madeleine stood on the steps waiting for him. "Mr. Smith, I don't believe you're a vampire, but I'm not altogether sure you didn't have something to do with Danielle's death. Don't leave town."

"I hadn't planned on it, Detective." Stephen followed them to the door. Resting against the door frame, he watched them walk away. The streetlights barely illuminated the darkened sky. *I'll see you later, Maddie,* he whispered.

She paused as the quiet voice reached her ears. Scott didn't stop. *As if he hadn't heard it.* She looked over her shoulder. Stephen still watched them—a dreadful light flickering in his eyes.

Madeleine hurried after Scott as he stalked toward the car, his shoulders taut with anger. Without speaking, he savagely cranked the key in the ignition and pulled onto the street. Madeleine buckled her seat belt and waited.

"Why didn't you tell me about being hurt?" he snapped moments later.

"It didn't seem relevant."

"Didn't seem relevant?" Scott alternated between watching the road and glaring at Madeleine. "You were mugged and hit on the head. Then you come to me with a crazy story about vampires, and you didn't think it was relevant?"

"I wasn't hallucinating," Madeleine bit out. "And I don't think I was mugged. I think he was waiting for me." She didn't remember it all. A voice—*talking to her, calling her by name?*

"A comic book artist," Scott continued as if Madeleine hadn't spoken. "His roommate draws comics for a living. How am I going to explain this to my lieutenant when he asks what we found? 'Well, sir, we found a couple of boxes. They looked like coffins, but you know, it's okay. In the end it was nothing. Call off the National Guard. Just some gardening tools.' And the rest of the search crew. They all thought we'd found a coven of vampires…"

"I don't think vampires form in covens," Madeleine said with a shake of her head. "I think they move in packs, like wolves."

"Whatever!" Scott shouted. He stared straight down the road. "I'll just have to tell them it isn't a true gaggle or pack or whatever it is of vampires. Just an eccentric comic book artist and *his friend* who hopefully won't decide to sue us."

"Stephen's lying," Madeleine protested. "He wasn't talking about a comic book. I heard him."

"When, Madeleine? When did you hear him? What were you doing?"

"I told you. I was in the living room, and they were in the kitchen."

"Was this just after you were unconscious?" Scott sighed. "There is no connection whatsoever between Stephen Smith and your cousin, except that his roommate used to date her."

Madeleine sat up straight in her seat. "What about Bob? He told me he saw Stephen pick Danielle up at our building a few nights before she disappeared."

"No, he didn't. I talked with Bob today, and he said he'd never seen Stephen Smith until *you* brought him home."

Madeleine felt her jaw fall open.

"He's lying. He told me…"

"What, Madeleine, is everyone lying? Bob's lying, Stephen's lying. Everyone is lying except you. You know all the answers."

Madeleine watched Scott's profile as his agitation grew. She wasn't going to change his mind. Stephen had already done that.

"I wasn't hallucinating." Her voice was calm, quiet. She had no energy left to fight. "And I know Stephen knew Danielle. I'd bet on it."

"Well, it looks like I already did. I'll have to find a way to explain this to my lieutenant."

Anger filled the car. Madeleine concentrated on keeping her breathing steady. She had to get home. She had to be alone. Someplace where she could scream.

Scott's car pulled up in front of her building. He stopped at the curb and waited for Madeleine to climb out.

Stephen walked to me to my door, Madeleine thought, holding back a hysterical giggle.

"Good night, Madeleine," Scott said in a neutral voice.

"Good night, Scotty." Madeleine got out of the car and watched Scott's taillights disappear into the dark. She might have ruined a friendship over this.

The need to be inside, under bright lights and behind the safety of her locks, hurried her into her building. She took the elevator up, something she rarely did. Stepping into the hall, she clutched her keys in her fist and walked slowly toward her door. She was alone, but another presence hovered about her. She shook her head to clear it. She was going to end up as crazy as Stephen if she wasn't careful.

Sounds of imagined footsteps followed her down the hall. Her hands shook slightly as she inserted the key in the lock. Panic welled up in her throat. She looked left, then right. She was alone. She jiggled the key, willing the door to open.

Finally, the lock gave. With a sob, Madeleine slipped inside.

She slammed the door behind her, leaned against it and stared into the dark apartment. Each labored breath calmed her pounding heart. The realization that she was home safe settled into her body and her mind, allowing her muscles to relax. She shook her head and smiled at her vivid imagination. Pushing away from the door, she stepped toward the kitchen.

Something stopped her. Like a wall of black air, surrounding her.

She couldn't see it, but she could feel it. She stepped back. It was behind her. Around her. Frozen, unable to move, barely able to breathe, she opened her mouth.

A hand reached out from the dark and grabbed her throat, cutting off her scream.

"Maddie, you've been telling secrets."

Five

By the dim light from the street lamps outside, Madeleine stared into Stephen's eyes, inches from her own. Barely banked fires of anger glittered back at her. For a moment his eyes looked red. Blood red. She gasped, trying to force air through her constricted throat. His hand relaxed enough to allow her to breathe. She swallowed and reminded herself to inhale while she had the chance. He stepped closer, his body trapping her against the wall.

"How did you get in here?" she whispered, hoping he wasn't real, wasn't inside her apartment.

"You invited me."

She opened her mouth to protest. The hand tightened.

"Don't scream, Maddie. I can kill you before anyone even thinks about coming to your rescue." His voice was the same husky whisper that had haunted her dreams. Tonight, his goal was clearly not seduction.

He eased the grip on her throat but didn't step away. His body lightly brushed hers, holding her captive by its presence and power. His fingertips caressed the line of her throat, a subtle reminder to keep silent.

"You went to the police, Maddie. I'm very disappointed." His deep voice whispered close to her ear. "Do you know what kind of difficulty my friends and I could find ourselves in if people started to believe our little secret?" One fingertip circled the pulse point at the base of her neck. The teasing touch clouded her instincts, lulling her, soothing away the terror she knew she should be feeling.

"Have you ever had your house searched, Madeleine?" He asked the question casually as his seductive fingers continued their fluttering exploration of her throat. She gave a quick shake of her head. "It's very intrusive," he whispered. He bent his head to her neck and placed a gentle, lingering kiss on the pulse, now beating out of control. "I can't let you tell anyone else, Maddie."

Tears pooled behind her lashes. One escaped over the edge and trickled down her cheek.

"I won't tell anyone," she promised, her voice a strained whisper.

"I know."

His words wrapped around her heart like a fist. He was going to kill her. Is this what had happened to Danielle? Had she stumbled into this bunch of crazies and been killed because of it?

Reacting, with only a flash of thought before she moved, Madeleine lifted her hands and shoved with all her strength against Stephen's chest. Simultaneously, she sent her knee in the general direction of his groin. She connected with solid flesh, and Stephen grunted in response.

His hands fell away. Madeleine lunged for the door.

Her hand reached the knob as his landed on her shoulder.

Madeleine yelped at the painful grip. She struggled but couldn't break his hold. With seemingly no effort, he spun her around and pressed her back against the door. He stepped in front of her, once again caging her body with his own. His hand returned to the base of her throat but with none of the tenderness of the previous caresses.

Her heart pounded. From rage and fear. Grinding her teeth together, she lifted her eyes to his. She forced herself not to flinch at the fury in his gaze.

"Don't mess with me, Maddie," he growled, his words thick around his tongue. His fingers tightened for a moment.

Then the hand that held her throat relaxed. Madeleine sighed with relief. A clean breath of oxygen did little to calm her pounding heart. She turned her head and stared at the tiny room behind him, her entire body vibrating with fear and rage. She tensed, waiting for the blow that would end her life.

But capitulation wasn't in her nature. Even as she prepared for the end, she fought against it. She tried to think of a plan, some way to escape, but her mind refused to cooperate. Panic and something else—something strange and lingering in the pit of her stomach—blocked her mind from thinking beyond the fear. And the knowledge of his touch.

Stephen's fingers caressed her skin as if apologizing for the bruises they'd caused. The tension in her shoulders began to ease. She rested against the door behind her.

No, this isn't right. Fight him, her mind commanded.

He cupped her jaw in his hand. There was a gentle pressure, telling her silently he wanted her to look at him. She resisted and kept her eyes averted. The memory of her dream and the dark, dangerous power of his gaze flashed through her mind.

He slowly bent his head and placed a light kiss on the column of her throat. A shudder ran through her body, a shudder that had nothing to do with fear. Of course he'd go for the neck, she thought with a silent, delirious giggle. He opened his mouth against her skin, warm and damp. He tasted her as he moved up the length of her throat. The movement was slow and seductive. Madeleine pressed her lips together. The deep, physical portion of her thoughts swelled, quieting the fear.

Very good, Maddie.

She shook her head to clear it. The strange fog that had been subduing her mind eased.

Stephen straightened. "Don't fight it." His lips brushed against her ear. He placed his hands on the door behind her, trapping her, caging her.

"Look at me, Maddie." It was just like her dream. Over and over, night after night, she'd been wrapped in Stephen's arms. Night after night he'd commanded that she look at him. And night after night, she'd obeyed. Unable to resist, and knowing it would lead to her doom, she responded as she'd done in dreams every night since she'd met him.

She raised her eyes to his.

His pupils were contracted until only a pinprick of black was centered in the midnight blue. Her heart pounded and her breath came in struggling, intermittent gasps.

"Relax." His voice filled her ears. "Just relax. This won't hurt. That's it. Relax. Breathe deep..."

The litany of words continued, drawing Madeleine away from her fear and deeper into his eyes. The world around her faded until she was boxed in by deep sapphire-blue crystal walls. The walls surrounded them—she and Stephen, alone. Her body began to listen to his quiet commands and ease. This was where she should be. With Stephen.

Warnings rushed through her mind. Something was wrong. She should be able to fight. She should *want* to fight.

The glitter of his eyes and the steady drone of his voice kept her captive, clouding her understanding until she saw his lips move, but no recognizable words came from them. Her eyelids drooped to half-mast, blurring her vision. Sounds that didn't seem to come from his lips swirled and resonated in her head. Words circled, commanding her submission. Her fear faded.

Resting against the door, Madeleine tilted her head to one side as his sweet, seductive lips lightly brushed her forehead. Words of praise and encouragement flowed through her mind. She turned her head and placed a light kiss on his palm as it cupped her cheek.

That's it, love. He kissed her eyelids closed. Even behind her closed eyelids she saw the deep blue. The color seemed to move through her body, a warm internal caress that sent heat to her center. *So beautiful.* He teased the lobe of her ear with his teeth. Her mouth opened, aching for his possession.

"Please," she whispered, surprised at her ability to speak. She knew she shouldn't want him, but she did, and all the erotic fantasies locked in her mind since she'd met Stephen were freed. She couldn't control them. Each image more tempting than the last. Warm, naked bodies wrapped around each other. Hot, open-mouthed kisses. His strength around her, inside her, hard and deep.

The first soft touch of his lips tantalized her. She'd spent the week trying to avoid thoughts of Stephen's kisses. Now his mouth was all there was. His mouth gently melded to hers, soothing and tempting her. Slowly, ever so slowly, he licked the crease of her lips, seeking entrance into the warm depth of her mouth.

Open for me, love.

It registered that he couldn't have spoken those words aloud. The concern drifted away as his lips pressed deeper into hers. She opened her mouth, wanting his taste. Stephen teased the inside of her mouth, not demanding or taking, but asking for a deeper caress. The silent request was too much for her to resist.

She tried to recall her own warnings, but the thought disappeared before it was fully formed, leaving only Stephen and the sensual, seductive web woven around her. Her only craving was for more. More of him. Her body begged for it. The soft silk of his hair brushed the back of her hand as she placed her arms around his neck. The strange compulsion was gone. She no longer saw the glowing blue walls. The cracked paint of her apartment was again visible. Instinctively, she knew she could escape—could break free of his touch—but oh, she didn't want to. She wanted to sink deeper into the fantasy.

His mouth touched hers but it wasn't enough, wasn't deep enough. She needed him to fill her. He rubbed one hand down her back, pulling her closer, pressing her against the hard line of his body.

A delicious ache started at the apex of her thighs and

inspired tiny fires in all corners of her body. A picture of Stephen easing her need, sliding into her body, filled her mind. She wanted him.

She groaned softly as his thigh slid between her legs as if it were the most natural place for him to be. *Yes.* This was what she wanted. She arched her hips against the subtle pressure and was rewarded with more mental praises and a groan of pure pleasure from Stephen.

Feel me. Tell me what you want.

She pulled her lips from his and drew an unsteady breath.

"More," she whispered.

Yes.

His mouth returned to hers as if he couldn't bear to be away from her taste. The warm, teasing kisses disappeared in a rush of heat and light. She immediately welcomed his tongue inside, sucking lightly on it, seduced by the hot male flavor of him. She rocked her hips against his muscular thigh. The fiery coil that was forming deep in her center tightened, and she couldn't stop the groan that escaped her throat.

She took control of the kiss. She slid her fingers into his hair and held him captive for her pleasure. His moan vibrated through her body, and she felt a spike of triumph. One hand slid down her back, pressing her against his leg, setting a rhythm that spread tension through her body.

She cried out as he pulled his mouth from hers. He planted sharp kisses along her jaw. His hand rested against her cheek. She turned and scraped her teeth along his palm, needing some way to convey the violent ache centered between her thighs. The hardened tips of her breasts brushed against his chest with the rapid rise and fall of her tormented breath.

She couldn't be passive; the need was too great. She leaned forward and placed a hot, open-mouthed kiss at the base of his neck. He straightened as if electricity had shot through him. He pulled her mouth away.

"Too much," he muttered.

She shook her head. "More."

He kissed her again, a little harsher, a little deeper, a little less controlled. Satisfaction shimmered through her. She dropped her head back against the door, surrendering to the pleasure of his lips high on her neck. Any remaining caution evaporated.

The violent rhythm of her heart pounded in her throat and was echoed in the unsteady beat between her thighs. She arched her neck, offering herself up for more.

"Please," she whispered, her body consumed with need, not knowing what she was begging for.

Yes.

He opened his mouth against her neck. A brief stab of pain was lost in the flow of pleasure that washed over Madeleine. He sucked the soft skin of her neck, seeming to draw her life into his body. Her world became concentrated, centered on two points—the draw of his mouth on her throat and the steady press of his thigh between her legs. She clutched Stephen's arms, begging him silently to end the torrent of pleasure. It was too much and not nearly enough.

She moaned. Her body battled on one front to hold the pleasure and, on another, to end it, seeking a final completion she knew was just beyond her.

The ache in the center of her body grew. Madeleine swirled her hips hard against his thigh.

He jerked his mouth away from her neck. She cried out at the violent loss.

"No!" It was a plea and a command. He couldn't stop. She needed him. Without thinking, responding only to her body's desires, she pulled his mouth back to her throat. She was so close. The need for release surged through her body, obliterating all thought. His mouth on her neck and the hot pressure between her legs would satisfy her. She needed him.

He hesitated. Interminable seconds passed. She hung in anticipation.

"Please."

With a harsh moan, he placed his mouth on her skin and began to suck. Madeleine gasped. His hands cupped her bottom, urging her hips in a fast, delicious rhythm that matched the pull of his lips. This was what she needed. Her fingers dug into his shoulders—holding him as the one solid object in her glittering world of pleasure. The fire that had been building inside her exploded, spinning wildly, until it shattered, sending jolts of pleasure to the far reaches of her body.

Warmth spread through her limbs. Her only strength was the power to cling to his shoulders. The haze over her mind thickened. She vaguely acknowledged that he'd stopped the seductive caresses to her throat, her need no longer desperate. His voice, filled with disjointed sounds, circled through her head. Scattered words reached her. None made sense.

" ...belong to me...your secret...knowledge is yours alone...mine..."

Her lips curled into a satisfied smile. She opened her dazed eyes and looked at him. A trickle of blood dribbled down the side of his mouth.

Darkness covered her as she sank to the floor.

***

Stephen thrust all ten fingers through his hair, forcing it away from his face and holding it there for one brief moment. He jerked his hands down and continued pacing. He stopped at the end of the couch and looked down at Madeline. Her lithe body lay draped across the tattered cushions. The pounding of her heart vibrated through his ears and shook his whole body. The scent of her arousal was sweet and so strong he could almost taste it. Her body was warm and open. Waiting for him.

He wanted her. Still. Again.

He bared his teeth in a silent snarl and walked to the far end of the small room. The movement brushed his trousers against the bulge still waiting in his pants. He wasn't supposed to get hard. And he sure as hell wasn't supposed to *stay* hard. He'd gotten what he wanted. He should be satisfied.

Unfortunately, his eyeteeth hadn't retracted either. He wanted more.

He'd taken too much already, and he wanted more. He wanted to bury himself in her body, absorb her heat. He found himself back at the end of the couch. Her head was tilted to the side. The tiny wounds were already starting to heal. By tomorrow they would have almost faded.

Unfortunately, the bruise wouldn't. *Damn.* He curled his hands into fists. He hadn't lost control like that since he was a fledgling. He should have taken more care, but the pleasure of entering her body, the rush of her life force flowing into him, had melted the control he'd learned so long ago.

And maybe beyond carelessness, there had been the need to mark her, to claim her so all could see—human and vampire.

He'd taken too much from her. He should have stopped. He didn't need much to sustain himself, and the mere act of biting her would have bound her to him. But he'd continued on—lost in her taste, lost in the feel of her body, lost in her need for the pleasure he could give her.

What was wrong with him? Other human women had found pleasure at his touch—it had never lured him beyond his limits.

Only Madeleine. He'd finally managed to regain control and leave her, but she hadn't let him go—hadn't let him leave until she'd been satisfied. He smiled. She would be a demanding little lover. That thought led to others—Madeleine over him, demanding her pleasure, her plea for "more." His body tightened at the image.

He should have killed her. The Council was expecting it. No one in the human world would even be surprised, not after the police told them about her vampire delusions. It was the logical thing to do. Her mind was quick and strong. She'd push the limits of the block he'd put on her, and he'd have to reinforce the blood connection to keep it strong.

She's going to be trouble. Just kill her.

He tensed at his own thoughts.

He'd killed before. Often. She was just another human.

She was just worried about her cousin, and I don't think that's a good reason to end up dead. He heard Nicholas' voice in his head. Oh, the fledgling was wrong. That was precisely the reason she should end up dead. Families were dangerous things to vampires.

But the question remained—what had brought Madeleine into his life? Was it coincidence or design? There was too much at stake for him to assume she'd stumbled into his life at this time. He needed to know. Before he killed her.

The slow, steady beat of her heart began to change, increasing as she struggled back to consciousness. Stephen looked around and finally dropped into the only other chair in the room. He grabbed a book off the shelf, not bothering to look at the title, and opened it, purposely creating the picture of casual. He crossed one leg over the other, hiding his persistent arousal. His teeth were still extended, but that would help add to her fear.

He stared at the words on the page, not seeing them, focused on the subtle changes in Madeleine as she made the transition to wakefulness. He could almost feel the soft flutter of her eyes as she came to. When he was sure she was awake, he looked up from the book and glanced in her direction. She smiled for a moment before the greeting turned to confusion, then confusion evolved to horror.

"Oh my God. You really are a vampire." She sat straight up. Her eyes glassed over, and she swayed in her seat. Stephen was beside her before he commanded his body to move. He placed a stabilizing hand on her back.

"You need to move slowly."

"Don't touch me!" She pushed away from him, ignoring his advice. She hurled her body off the couch and put the heavy piece of furniture between them. Her fingers gripped the fabric as she used the armrest to keep herself vertical. Stephen rested against the back and waited for her to regain her equilibrium, his body tense, preparing to catch her if she fainted again. Not Maddie. After a few deep breaths, she raised her eyes to him. She slapped her hand against her throat. "You bit me!"

"Yes."

"I can't believe you bit me."

"It was necessary. Now would you please take a seat before you fall down?" He stood and stepped away from the couch, giving her space to feel safe. "Having you swoon in my arms was enjoyable, but once a night is plenty, don't you think?"

"I didn't swoon," she muttered, but she stepped around the end of the couch and slowly lowered herself onto the cushions. She might be terrified, she was definitely pissed, but his Maddie was nothing if not practical. She lowered her head into her hands as if the weight of her skull was too much. "I never feel this bad after giving blood."

He felt a tiny shaft of guilt. The mere thought of it shocked him into silence. He hadn't felt guilty about anything in years. It was a useless human emotion. Still, he was causing Madeleine some discomfort because of his loss of self-control.

"Yes. I apologize for that." He hadn't been prepared for his own apology but was glad he'd said it. "Normally, you wouldn't have even noticed."

She raised her head and looked at him, the thought of "are you insane?" clearly on her face. "I think I would have noticed if someone *bit* me."

He shook his head and wandered into the small kitchen. "No. You might have felt a slight twinge but no pain, no lingering aftereffects. The teeth marks typically fade by morning."

The mark he'd left on her throat wouldn't fade that quickly, but he didn't tell her that. He wasn't sure he wanted to be around when she figured out he'd given her a hickey. He opened the refrigerator and pulled out some orange juice. It was strange. He'd never taken care of his victims afterward. He'd told her the truth. Most didn't notice they'd been bit. Those who did ended up dead.

He poured a glass of juice and carried it to her. She took it without a word. She was obviously still too fogged to fight him. She drank the juice and stared into space. The truth of it all would hit her soon.

The urge to comfort her crept up inside him until he found himself walking toward her. He stopped when he reached the couch. He couldn't do this. He couldn't let her mean anything. She was a means to an end. Unfortunately, he didn't know where this would end.

"I'll contact you later." He pulled on his coat and headed toward the door.

"Why didn't you kill me?"

He stopped at her quiet question. The easiest answer was to tell her nothing, let her worry. For some reason he didn't want that. He settled on the truth.

"Because I have a feeling someone wants me to do just that."

She blinked. "And you just feel like being contrary? That's the only reason I'm still alive?"

"I don't like being pushed into things. Especially when I don't know why or who's doing the pushing."

"Why me?"

Stephen shrugged. "I have no idea. I doubt it has anything to do with you. You just got caught in the middle."

"Danielle." Madeleine eased herself to standing, using the couch for support. "This started with Danielle, didn't it? She got mixed up in this and one of you...did you kill my cousin?"

"No."

"Who did?"

"I won't tell you that."

"Why the hell not? I have a right to know."

Stephen laughed without humor. "You don't have *any* rights in this, Madeleine. Your cousin is dead. Let it go."

"I can't. Someone has to be punished for it. Humans have a thing called justice."

"We have a different definition of justice in my world. Your cousin chose to join that world, and she lost playing by human rules. Don't make the same mistake."

"Aren't you afraid I'll tell the world about you?"

"No. You're bound to me now. You won't tell anyone anything I don't want you to."

If sarcasm could be expressed in a smile, that was what curled Madeleine's lips. "I hate to break it to you, but making out for a few minutes doesn't connect us for life."

"Yes, it does. You're marked as mine." He could see her tense up, preparing to fight him. "Look at me, Maddie." She struggled every inch, but slowly, unable to resist, she turned her eyes to him. "Come to me."

Her steps were slow and laborious. She was strong, but he was stronger. He moved to meet her when she came within reach. He bent his head and covered her mouth with his. She tasted so sweet. He relaxed the mental lock on her and was pleased that she didn't struggle. She sighed and relaxed into the kiss, accepting and returning each lingering caress. He cupped her head in his hands and ate at her mouth.

Yes, Maddie.

She jerked back as the words filled her mind. She pushed on his chest, and he released her.

"Stay away from me," she commanded.

"You don't want that." He leaned against the doorjamb. "Been dreaming about me, Madeleine?"

"You bastard. You're messing with my mind," she accused.

"Stay inside after dark." He ignored her comment and opened the door. "And don't invite anyone into your home until this is all over."

"Fine." She said the word so quietly he wasn't sure she'd been listening.

"I'm serious, Madeleine." He didn't know what would happen over the next few days. He didn't have time to worry about her. "A vampire has no power over you in your own home unless you invite him in. Don't invite anyone in."

"I heard you the first time. I'm not stupid."

"You invited me in."

She grimaced and finally looked up at him. "Good point." She wrapped her arms around her stomach. "How will I know when it's over?" she asked, stopping his departure.

"Pardon me?"

"You said I shouldn't invite anyone into my home until this is over. How will I know?" She looked at him. He waited. He heard the skip of her heart and saw the understanding creep into her eyes. "You're going to kill me when it's over."

He had no other answer to give her. "Good night, Madeleine."

Six

Madeleine stared at the mismatched pile of books, movies, and implements. Three different store clerks in three different locations now thought she was nuts. From the video store where the manager followed her around after her ill-fated attempts to say "vampire movies" to the supply warehouse where she asked for garden stakes sturdy enough to go through someone's chest, she was pretty sure she wasn't welcome anymore.

And it was all Stephen's fault. Frustration was fast becoming a familiar emotion. Whatever he'd done to her, however he'd done it, he'd managed to lock the word "vampire" into her throat. She could think it, mentally scream it, but she couldn't say it. She couldn't even write it down—her hand wouldn't shape the letters. Nothing worked. Her own mind defeated her.

But she wasn't letting it stop her. She finally had it all—garlic, wooden stakes, holy water, a cross, and a bad attitude. Now, she just needed a little time to prepare before—

"I'm going to think you don't want me around."

Madeleine yelped and spun around to face the amused man behind her. Her breath forced itself out of her lungs, and she glared up at Stephen. "How did you get in here?"

"You invited me." His whispered reply sent the memory through her body.

"No, how did you get in here tonight?"

"Surely you didn't think a few locks would keep me out?"

"What would?"

"Nothing."

He said it with such definitiveness. And she knew it was true. He was in her home, in her life, for as long as he chose.

The thought probably should have terrified her, but

she'd spent the last twenty-four hours contemplating the strange reality that had become her life. The knowledge that she was going to die, and that it would be soon, had settled into her brain—blocking all attempts to panic the way any reasonable person would have. She knew how, she knew why. The only question left to answer was when.

"So, is this it? Have you come to kill me?" Madeleine asked.

The flash of surprise in his eyes inspired a tiny flicker of triumph. He expected the world to tremble before him, and she didn't doubt that it did so on a regular basis.

"No. I've come to talk to you. You obviously had other plans." He reached past her and picked up a garden stake and the mallet. "Going to use this on me, Maddie?" He offered them to her. "It takes a certain kind of person to kill another. Even when you know he's a monster."

Moving mechanically, she took the wooden stake from his hand.

"Just take it, hold it against my chest, and drive it into my heart."

She couldn't pull her eyes from the stake. Could she do it? Could she actually hurt him? Kill him? She lifted the stake—it shook in her hand—and tried to move forward, tried to point it at his heart.

She took a deep breath and looked up. Stephen watched her, no emotion showing on his face, none glowing in those haunting blue eyes. There was no dare, no prodding. He seemed completely willing to stand there while she killed him.

She tossed the stake onto the couch.

"Maybe later."

A sad smile curved his lips. "Yes, maybe later."

Madeleine ignored the shiver that moved down her spine.

"What about the rest of this stuff? Does it work?"

"Holy water? No. Garlic. Sort of. It's a physical

allergy, but it would require you chasing me around with a peeled garlic clove. I doubt even you're that desperate."

She saw amusement sparkle in his eyes and felt her chest tighten. Dark and dangerous—he was stunning. When the darkness faded from his eyes and he smiled, he was irresistible.

She straightened her spine, drawing her energy tight into her body and crushing all erotic thoughts. *The man is planning to kill you. You simply cannot be attracted to him.*

Physically, there was little she could do. That black hair and those blue eyes matched her description of physical perfection. There was no way she could get around the attraction. Or she hadn't found one yet. But physical was just physical, and she didn't have to act on it.

"So, what did you want? I have a lot to do tonight."

He scanned her vampire repellents again. "Yes, I can see that you do." Shoving his hands into his pockets, he strolled across the room. Though he looked around, she had a feeling he wasn't seeing the faded walls and orange carpet. "What brought you to my house that first night?"

"I was looking for Danielle."

"How did you find my address? What did Danielle tell you?"

She propped her rear end on the back of the couch, folded her arms over her chest, and tracked him as he walked to the window.

"Why do you want to know? What exactly happened to Danielle?"

"I'm not going to tell you that."

"Then I'm not going to tell you anymore, either."

"Madeleine…" He infused her name with warning, but Madeleine ignored it. What could he threaten her with? He'd already told her she was going to die. What was a little fright before death?

"No." She shrugged. "If you want answers, you'll have

to do some talking yourself."

She watched Stephen suck in his cheeks as if he was trying to stop another smile. She had the distinct impression no one had defied him in a long time.

"Fine. But I won't answer questions about Danielle."

"But—"

His upraised hand stopped her protest. "I could force you to answer my questions, you know." Madeleine tensed. She hadn't forgotten the strange compulsion to come when he called her last night. It was horrible, that loss of control. And the threat was enough to make her agree.

"Fine. I found Dylan's name in Danielle's address book."

"Dylan. Did Danielle ever mention—"

Madeleine shook her head. She wasn't going to be left out. It wasn't an interrogation.

"What can kill you?" Stephen cocked an eyebrow in question, and she said, "You want information, so do I." She struggled to feel as bold as she sounded. She was shaking inside but she'd never let him see it.

"Sunlight." He nodded toward the garden tools. "Stakes. What did Danielle say about Dylan or me?"

"Nothing. She didn't want to talk about you guys."

Now I know why. Madeleine chewed the edge of her lip. What would have drawn Danielle in? Madeleine looked over at Stephen. Besides the obvious. Danielle had liked her men strong, powerful. Those were the words Madeleine had used to describe Stephen. The same things that Danielle would have found attractive. Stephen had said he didn't know Danielle, though Madeleine no longer believed that. How well had he known her?

But he wouldn't talk about Danielle.

"How old are you?"

"I was eighteen when I was converted." She waited. He knew that wasn't the information she wanted. "I was converted over two hundred years ago."

Two hundred years? She squinted, trying to see some sign of it on his face. He looked young but he didn't look eighteen—there was too much maturity in his face. The age in his eyes warned he was older than he appeared. But two hundred years? She'd been lusting after a two-hundred-year-old man?

An arrogant light flickered in his eyes as if he could read her thoughts. While she watched, he lowered his gaze to the base of her neck. The tip of his tongue made a long slow trail across the inside edge of his lips. The center of her stomach fell away, leaving a desperate ache. The force of it weakened her legs, and she clutched the back of the couch to keep from tipping over.

She drew in a sharp breath and struggled against the pulsing pleasure that seemed to radiate from the mark on her neck and slide through her body to the warm place between her legs.

"Whatever you're doing, stop it."

"Just wanted to remind you who you're dealing with."

"I'm not likely to forget."

But she was lying. It would be easy, way too easy, to forget who and what he was.

He carried himself with an innate style and charm that was difficult to ignore and harder to resist. The erotic dreams she'd lived with for the past week hadn't helped. She had no idea who was real—if the Stephen in her dreams was reality or some fantasy made up by her own mind to satisfy her lust.

With him in front of her, the slide into fantasy was simple, and the memory of the hard press of his mouth on hers was too close to ignore. She licked her lips, tasting him as if only moments instead of a day had passed since they'd touched. Her eyelids fluttered, and she realized she'd let her eyes drift closed. She snapped them open. It was too much to hope Stephen wasn't watching.

Before she could move, he was in front of her, and the

98 T. L. Sinclare

feel of his mouth on hers was no fantasy. She sighed as his tongue slipped between her lips. It was soft and gentle and filled with his heady male taste. Time faded as she wrapped her arms around his neck and reveled in his leisurely exploration of her mouth. It was so sweet. The long curl of his tongue wrapped around hers, heating the core of her body. She stepped closer, needing the feel of him, wanting to be filled and surrounded. She brushed against the hard line of his erection. And captured his groan in her mouth.

Then he was gone. He stepped back and placed Madeleine away from him.

"I'll be going now."

She nodded. She couldn't speak. If she did, heavens knew what she would ask for. *More.* She'd beg for more.

She steeled her spine and watched him walk toward her door.

"Why did you become a vampire?" she blurted out as his hand touched the doorknob. He stopped and looked over his shoulder. A furious blaze ignited in his eyes then was quickly extinguished. The muscles in his jaw tightened and for a brief moment, Madeleine was sorry she'd asked. She forced herself to press on. This was important. Knowledge is power, and she needed power right now. "Why did you choose to become—how did you describe it—the kind of creature that would desire life so much that he would sacrifice his humanity for it?"

"I didn't."

The sharp answer stunned Madeleine into silence. He hadn't chosen to be a vampire? Her heart leapt with compassion. Images of a tormented existence quickly flooded her mind.

Stephen's mocking voice intruded. "Don't let your sympathy overwhelm you, my dear. I didn't choose this life, but the fact is, I'm a very good vampire."

He seemed to know what she wanted to ask but didn't

dare—what makes a good vampire?

"You have to be willing do anything to survive, anything to protect the Community."

Even kill. He didn't say the words. He didn't need to.

"Good night, Madeleine." With those simple words, he sent a line of fear through her body. He'd said "good night" but she knew he meant—*I'll be back.*

Her hand gripped the edge of the couch as the door snapped shut behind him. She looked down. The stakes lay scattered across the tacky cushions.

Do anything to survive.

She could do it. For a short while, she would think like a good vampire.

***

Stephen stopped in the hallway. If his heart could have raced, it would have been matching the beats of Madeleine's. *Damn. What was that about?*

He'd come by tonight to find out what she knew, to determine how and why she'd come into his life—was it truly chance or some exotic vampire plot? The coincidence of timing was too much to ignore, but if she knew anything beyond what she'd told him, she hid it well.

He shook his head. No, she wouldn't have been able to hide it. Her body reacted to every question with subtle changes his hypersensitive hearing picked up. She hadn't lied to him. He'd have felt it. He came searching for information, but in the end, he'd revealed too much. She went to his head—her defiance, her poorly disguised fear. It would do neither of them any good for him to get attached. The end result would be the same. He would do what needed to be done. And that meant killing Madeleine. He'd told her the truth. He was a good vampire.

So, why did you leave her alive once again? He ignored his own question as he exited her building, not wanting to look too closely at his motives.

Stephen crossed the street to where Nicholas huddled

in his favorite corner. The fledgling glared at him as rain dripped off the overhang. Nicholas hadn't forgiven Stephen for what he knew was going to happen to Madeleine, but the young man had agreed to stand guard over her.

"Miserable night, isn't it?" the fledgling asked. His shoulders shook with cold and damp.

Stephen nodded. "Anything interesting?"

"A couple of guys stopped and stared at her window. I think they were just looking." *Like you.* Nicholas didn't say it, but Stephen heard it behind the words. He indicated a shadow on the opposite side of the street. "I thought I saw something move over there, but then…nothing."

Stephen stared, trying to penetrate the darkness but nothing moved. "Leave me a message." He started to walk away and turned back. "And be careful."

The human sentiment seemed to startle Nicholas almost as much as it did Stephen. The fledgling's eyes widened for a second, and then he nodded. "Uh—okay."

Stephen left him huddled in the rain. Nicholas needed to be careful. No, he needed to complete his conversion. Until he did, he was a risk to the Community and to himself. If others found out about him—realized what he was— they'd stake him just for safety's sake. His state of half-conversion gave him the strength of a vampire but none of the weaknesses. The Community would never allow that.

Nicholas was fighting his final conversion, struggling against it with a strength that didn't seem human. Stephen grudgingly acknowledged the admiration he felt for the young man. He knew from experience the dangerous hell Nicholas was in. He wanted him free of it. And there was only one way for that to happen.

Stephen let his thoughts wander as he walked through the town. He could have driven one of his many cars but decided a rainy night was an appropriate atmosphere for a restless vampire. He considered going to Death's Door. Matthias would probably be there. He could burn off his excess energy fighting with him. He smiled. Gayle wouldn't approve.

It was late when Stephen finally turned his steps toward home. Dawn was an hour away. He'd killed the night walking the streets.

Stepping inside, he shook the rain from his hair and sat down in his living room, absorbing the house's sounds. Cassandra was gone, sent away with a hefty severance package and a minor memory loss. He'd contemplated attempting the procedure with Madeleine but rejected the idea. Madeleine would never submit, and she'd fight the block for the rest of her life. If she managed to break the mental hold he had on her, she'd tell the world. *And damn, if anyone could convince the secular, cynical world of today that vampires existed, it would be Madeleine.*

Madeleine.

He dropped his head against the back of the chair and stared into the dark. Her mind was open to him but still strong. The temporary block he'd put on her last night would have to be reinforced by a blood connection. His eyeteeth pressed against his lower lip as the thought and the memory blended together in a sweet fantasy. Even as he savored the dream, he growled, his body tightening.

Pushing aside his physical cravings, he renewed his resolve. He'd wait a few more days. Let the Council wonder. And then he'd finish Madeleine.

Until then, he was staying away from her. He nodded into the darkness. Far away.

Three nights later, as he sat in that same chair staring, he brooded on his failure to do just that. Each night he'd woken from his daytime death, felt his resolution crumble, and before the night was half over, found himself standing in her living room.

What was it that drew him to her? She was mouthy, opinionated, and entirely too bold. He smiled into the darkness. Maybe that was it. She wasn't afraid of him.

No, he mentally corrected. She was afraid, but that hadn't stopped her. She'd faced him anyway. Too many times this week he'd found her watching vampire movies or reading books on the undead, unrepentantly trying to find a way to break free.

It was pointless, of course. The only way he would leave her life was by death—his or hers. He'd offered her the chance that first night, knowing she couldn't do it. Perhaps, if she knew the truth, she might be willing. She might then decide it was worth it.

It was times like these when he longed for human senses—wished he could drink alcohol and feel its effects. Something to blur the edges just a bit, make the memory of her taste a little less sharp. He licked his lips. Her flavor lingered. And with good reason. Only thirty minutes ago he'd had Madeleine pressed against her bedroom door— her blouse unbuttoned, her lips swollen from his kisses— and her throat releasing soft sighs of pleasure. He wanted those sighs—wanted them to be screams.

He dug his fingertips into the arms of the chair until he felt the wood crack beneath his palms. Damn, he wanted her, but he hadn't—wouldn't—take her. He shook his head at his own reluctance. He didn't want to make love to her, then kill her. He didn't need the memory. He silently mocked his own reluctance. It was almost human.

"You look dreadful, if you don't mind my saying so." Gayle's droll comment was a welcome distraction. Stephen had invited the blond vampire over for company and to act as the voice of reason. He shut his eyes. A sure sign his life had spun out of control—Gayle as the voice of reason.

"You haven't been feeding." Gayle tapped his finger on his lip. "Hmm, what could it mean? The pet, what was her name? Madeleine, isn't it? She's taking up all your interest." He winked as Stephen lifted his head to glare at him. "And none of the sweet young things who visit my place will do?"

"I'm fine."

"You're pale." Gayle poured himself across the chaise lounge, the personification of stylish boredom. But there was an intelligence in his eyes that stopped Stephen from believing the appearance. Gayle was more than he seemed. "When did you feed last?"

"I said I'm fine." Stephen didn't want to have this discussion. He didn't need a mother hen. So, he hadn't felt like feeding. No one interested him. Not even for a quick bite. He'd last fed when he'd bitten Madeleine four nights ago. His body throbbed with the hunger, but the thought of taking one of the young women from Gayle's bar held no pleasure for him.

A bite didn't have to be sexual. In most cases, it was methodical and prosaic. If his frame of mind were right, he'd simply satisfy the physical requirement. But his thoughts were scattered. He wanted Madeleine. Wanted her not only as a blood source but also as a lover.

"Where's Cassandra?"

Stephen looked up, shocked that Gayle even knew her name. He'd always done his best to keep his household inconspicuous. "She's gone."

"That's uncomfortable."

"I'll find another when this is all over." It hadn't been difficult to send Cassandra away. She'd been convenient, nothing more.

"How will you know when it's all over?"

Stephen tensed. Madeleine had asked him the same question.

"When it's finished." *When vampires stop dying. And Madeleine is dead.*

The time he'd spent with her over the past four nights hadn't revealed any secrets. At least none that helped. He'd learned much about Madeleine, but nothing that indicated she was anything more than she appeared—a human who'd accidentally found a vampire's lair. It didn't happen often.

But with each night, with each new human secret, he learned how dangerous she really was.

"You told me to listen to rumors, and that's what I've been doing."

Stephen glanced up, hoping he looked casual. "And?"

He'd tried investigating the Council deaths on his own, but his history with them closed more doors than it opened. It wasn't that he cared about the Council being killed off one by one, but whoever was doing it had decided to frame him. And as the chief suspect, no one was prepared to trust him with their secrets—like which vampire was working with a human. It had to be a human. He looked at his own hand. The alternative was too frightening to contemplate.

"You're the topic of most of the latest gossip," Gayle drawled. "It gets more outrageous as the days go by. That you beat Dylan. That you're working with this human pet—"

"Madeleine is not a pet," Stephen snapped.

"Well, that would be a little more believable if you were a little less defensive. Mostly, they want to know why you haven't killed her."

Stephen nodded. It was time. He had no reason to allow her to live. And his future sanity dictated he break free of her—soon.

"Pass the word. It's done tomorrow."

He could feel Gayle's eyes watching him as he stood up.

Gayle followed him seconds later, taking Stephen's hint that it was time to leave. They stopped in the doorway. The rabid curiosity that usually lived in Gayle's eyes was muted, suppressed by a concern that Stephen chose to ignore. He had to focus on what needed to be done.

"Come see me." Gayle's voice was a whisper. "After you've done it."

Seven

"So, what's with the sudden fascination with the undead?"

Madeleine flinched, sending a long blue streak across the paper she was signing. She stared at the ruined page for a moment before looking up at Charlotte, her secretary.

"What do you mean?" Madeleine asked, hoping she sounded curious instead of cautious.

"You've been hauling in a new stack of books every day." Charlotte slapped her hand on today's pile. "I thought maybe we got a new client—Count Dracula."

"Uh, uh—" The words locked in Madeleine's throat. As they had for four days now. Four days of mentally shouting "vampire!" and having only stuttering silence come out of her mouth. For some reason, she could say it to Stephen, but to anyone else, the word froze in her throat. She could almost feel the hand on her neck, ready to squeeze at the slightest indication that she might reveal one of the "secrets" Stephen was so intent on keeping.

I'm going to kill him. It was a threat she'd made a number of times in the past four days. At first, it was the normal societal threat of saying, "I'm going to kill him," but not really meaning it.

Madeleine was moving past that stage, frustration and the humming in her head changing it into a real desire to *kill him.* If only she could figure out how to do it without actually hurting him. The feel of the stake in her palm and his emotionless voice directing her on its use were stark memories that haunted her. She'd tried again last night, picking up the stake and imagining herself putting it into Stephen's chest. The memory turned her stomach.

"Just an interesting topic," she finally answered when she realized Char was still waiting. Charlotte nodded, but she didn't look convinced.

Don't ask, please don't ask any more questions. She

didn't have any more lies to tell.

"Well, if you're going to start advertising, just remember 'defender of the undead' will take up a lot of space on the business cards."

Madeleine laughed but it sounded forced. Needing a quick change of topic, she handed the ruined signature page to Charlotte.

"I messed this one up. Can you print it again?"

Charlotte nodded, her eyes flaring with concern as she walked away.

As soon as she was gone, Madeleine dropped her face into her hands and growled. Dating a vampire was hell on her life. She straightened. *Not dating. We are not dating.*

We're just spending lots of time together.

And making out at the end of each evening. Damn, it sure sounded like dating to her.

That first night had set the pattern for the following three. Each night, she went home and tried to ignore that she was waiting for Stephen to appear. She'd almost managed to convince herself the strange flutter in her stomach was fear, but she knew it wasn't. It was anticipation.

The nights flew by, filled with Stephen—in reality and in dreams. The dreams continued their strange evolution. They still left her breathless and aching in the morning, but now she saw him smile. The darkness had faded and left behind a warm touch and seductive power.

She stared at the document in front of her. Her eyes saw the words, but her mind was too busy and too tired to comprehend their meaning.

It should have shocked the hell out of her—spending all her free time with a vampire. Instead, the thought of him sent a tingle of pleasure through her body. Madeleine took a deep breath and tried to smother the feeling. She didn't know why she kept trying to suppress it—it hadn't worked yet. But she had to do *something* to stop from getting more involved. This wasn't some nice boy next door. This was a vampire with fangs and mental powers. And really nice shoulders. And very talented lips.

Even the cries of protest from the voice of logic were fading, slowly silenced by the rest of the noise in her brain. She clenched the pen tightly in her fingers.

It had started the morning after Stephen's second visit. Faint and hissing, each day the noise had increased until it was a tiny roar, like a thousand voices whispering to her. Madeleine opened her mouth to release the tension in her jaw and neck. Her concentration was gone, and her work was stacking up.

Madeleine. The sound vibrated just above the hissing in her ears.

She tilted her head and listened harder. The buzzing became more distinct, her name a clear cry within the mumbling.

Great. Now the voices in my head are calling me by name.

A clean signature page appeared on her desk, and Madeleine focused on making her hand work properly. Charlotte waited silently and took the page away when she was finished.

Madeleine lifted her hand unconsciously to the two puncture marks at the base of her neck. It had become a habit in the last four days—at first, because she couldn't believe they were real and then because it reminded her of Stephen. His mouth on her skin, the sweet touch of—

She dropped her hand. She wasn't going to think about him. She crushed the tiny flame of rebellion in her body, the one that longed to relax and luxuriate in the fantasies that tempted her.

She'd allowed herself to be distracted by the small flicker of light in his eyes. Somehow over the past four nights, she'd found herself wanting to fan that flame and help him push the darkness back. She'd tried to ask him about his "conversion" again, but he'd refused to answer her questions. And he wouldn't talk about Danielle. Any time the questions got too personal or too near to emotion, he'd refuse to answer.

He may be a vampire, she thought, rolling her eyes upward. *But he's still male.*

Tonight would be different. Tonight, she was going to get some answers. About Danielle and about vampires. Tonight she wasn't going to let him distract her from her mission. No more hot stares or long lingering looks. No more soul kisses that left her hungry for more.

Still hungry. She glanced down at her blouse. The thick lining of her bra helped hide the fact that her nipples were tight, the memory of his touch too close to the surface for her body not to respond.

She pounded her fists on the desks.

I don't have time for this at work!

"Madeleine, are you okay?"

Oops. "Yes. Sorry. Carpal tunnel exercises." Char's eyes squinted, and she opened her mouth as if she was going to ask a question. Madeleine had to stop that. She smiled and laughed, hoping Char would think it was a joke.

Madeleine. Come...

The muscles in her neck tightened. That was the other item to put on her list. Ask Stephen how to get the voices out of her head. It was irritating enough with just the humming and buzzing, but now that they'd actually started on words she could understand, she wanted it stopped. Her one saving grace was that the whispering in her head stopped after sunset. Just another reason to anticipate the coming of night.

It was almost a relief when the alarm clock on her desk released its loud, annoying ring. That was the sign the sun was about to go down.

"Time to go home," she called to Charlotte.

"Madeleine, we've got work to do. Lots of work."

"I know, but it can wait until tomorrow. I don't like you out after dark." Madeleine had made up a story about a pack of wild dogs running through the city at night. Char hadn't believed it, but she'd finally agreed to be home before dark each day. It wasn't much, but it was the only protection Madeleine could give her. The weirdness that had become her life would not—*would not*—spread to her friends.

"Does this have anything to do with those books you're carrying around?"

Madeleine shook her head, unwilling, unable to answer. "Please. For me. Just for a little while longer." *I hope.*

She had no idea how long this would last, how long until Stephen came for her.

Char sighed. "Okay. I'll go lock myself in my house until sunrise."

"And—"

"And not invite anyone in. I've got it. It's weird, but I've got it." Char didn't understand and Madeleine couldn't explain. Not yet. Probably not ever.

Charlotte pulled her raincoat off the tree stand in the corner and draped it over her arm. The sun had left its mark on the day, and it would be a hot, sticky ride home. "That guy's out there again."

Madeleine felt a familiar tickle of anticipation, then stopped. The sun was still up. It wasn't Stephen.

Nick.

"I'll talk to him."

She'd noticed him the morning after Stephen had bitten her, when her mind was still cluttered with the previous night's revelations. Nick had been open about his presence. He followed her to and from work. At night, she could see him in the shadows across from her building, his eyes bright against the darkness. He never approached her, never threatened, but if he was making Charlotte nervous, Madeleine would tell him to back off.

But why was he watching her? Was it for Stephen? Or someone else? There had to be other vampires in the city, but she'd never met any of them. Except Dylan. And Nick, but she wasn't sure he was really a vampire. If Nick was a vampire, why was he out during daylight? According to Stephen, all the books she'd read, and movies she'd watched over the past few days, sunlight was a definite no-no for vampires. The rest of the legend varied from movie to book to Internet article. She could find out the truth. She had a real live vampire to ask, but she wasn't going to do it. Stephen would no doubt offer her the stake again. She wasn't quite ready for that.

"Well, good night."

"'Night," Madeleine called as the door closed behind Char. She had to get home as well.

In the silence, the noise in her head returned, louder.

Madeleine. Madeleine growled, finding the sound comforting and loud enough to make the whispering fade. Sundown couldn't come soon enough. Only two things worked to dull the noise in her mind during the day—conversation with a real person and fantasies about Stephen. The conversations she'd been a little short on, but not the fantasies.

She absently fingered the bruise on her neck. Random thoughts rushed through her mind—vampires, Stephen, sex, voices, Stephen, sex.

She needed to talk to him, really talk to him. Right after he told her how to get rid of the voices in her head, she'd tell him to stop with the fantasies. They were intriguing but very distracting. A nagging voice warned her the fantasies were her own creation. Stephen had somehow implanted the first ones in her mind, but they'd changed since then. She'd never had sexual dreams before. But then, she'd never met someone like Stephen before.

A quiet knock on the door jerked her from her introspection. Nick filled the open doorway.

"It's getting dark. You need to get home," he announced.

Madeleine was struck by the age in his eyes. He looked tired, weary. Haunted.

They reminded her of Stephen's eyes but without the power.

"I was just leaving." She smiled, trying to give him some small comfort.

"You don't want to be out after dark." His voice echoed the warning in his words.

"I know."

"And you might want to get some silver."

She stopped in mid-gather on her desk and looked at him. "What?"

He lifted his chin toward the stack of books on her table. "Silver. It actually works." His eyes searched the room as if looking for another presence. "Get some." He spun around and walked away.

Silver?

She finished cramming everything into her briefcase and raced to catch up with him. He was waiting for her outside. Hands shoved into his pockets, he turned with her and started down the street. She'd stayed too long tonight and missed the bus. It would be a long walk home.

Nick walked with her, his eyes scanning the street. What was his connection with Stephen? Why did he look like he was in pain? And why had he told her about the silver?

She thought about grilling him for information. The tight press of his mouth warned her he wasn't inclined to talk, but she'd gotten into this situation by being pushy. Maybe she could find a way out the same way.

"So, have you known Stephen long?" Nick's jaw tightened, but he shook his head. "How long?" He shrugged and sped up, forcing Madeleine to stretch her legs. "Come on, Nick, give me something. Help me get out of this."

"Even if I knew a way out, which I don't, I can't help you. Stephen would—" He stopped and shook his head. "He's dangerous, Madeleine."

"I figured that out when he bit me."

"No, it's worse than that. He's hard and cold. I don't think he's afraid of anything or anyone."

He didn't fear death. She knew that from experience. "So, he's a bad dude among the vampires," she said, trying to sound casual.

"Dylan's gone."

"What?"

"Dylan used to live in the house. Now he's gone. Stephen just threw him out, and who knows what will happen to him now."

"Isn't Dylan a vampire?" She'd somehow assumed that they all were in that house.

"Yes, but he's young. Young vampires are very vulnerable."

"Like you."

Nick spun around on his heel, his lips pulled back in a snarl and a spark of red illuminating his eyes.

"*I am not one of them!*" It was difficult to tell who was more startled—her or Nick. His shoulders drooped, and his hands came up, curling and opening, as if not knowing how to plead his case. "I'm so sorry, Madeleine. I don't know what came over me."

Her heart pounded in her throat. "Don't you?" she asked quietly.

Nick raised his chin and continued to stare at her, defiance turning his eyes stone cold.

"You were turned without your permission, weren't you?"

Nick looked away, finally dragging his gaze from hers.

"Who?" As Madeleine asked the question, possibilities popped into her head. *Stephen? No.* There had been a grim hopelessness in Stephen's eyes when he'd told her he hadn't chosen to be a vampire. He'd never convert someone else. "Who converted you?" It shocked her that she was using the language Stephen had taught her, but after only four days, it flowed off the tongue easily.

"I don't know. They wiped my memory."

"And Stephen took you in."

He glared at her. "I'm not some orphan off the street, Madeleine. He took me in so I could finish the conversion." Madeleine shook her head, not understanding, and he explained, "It works like this. You get converted by drinking a vampire's blood, but you stay a half-vampire until you die or you make your first kill."

You need blood. Fresh, human blood. And there's a body in the living room with plenty of it. Stephen's words crowded her memory.

"That's what Stephen wanted you to do that night." Her voice was dazed. "I was supposed to be your first kill."

"Yeah."

The answer shocked her into reality and how close she'd been to death. All gentle thoughts of Stephen faded. It was too easy to forget what he was.

"Don't worry about me. Be careful around Stephen." She barely heard his words.

"Nicholas?"

Nick tensed beside her as a new voice intruded. He took a step closer, his body crowding hers, covering her.

"Nick, here." Slowly, they turned at the quiet call. Dylan stepped out of the shadows.

"Oh, Dylan, you *don't* want to be here," Nick warned. "If Stephen finds out, he'll kill you."

"With what? He's no threat to me." The young man smirked. His faced turned sweet when he looked at

Madeleine. "How are you doing, Madeleine?"

His voice was so gentle, so concerned. So different from everyone else since this started that she felt tears well up in her eyes. Dylan put his arm around her shoulders and gave her a quick squeeze.

"I'm sorry you got caught up in all of this." He shook his head. "I tried to get you out that first night, but Stephen had already laid claim. I'd like to help now but I'm not sure I can." He glanced over his shoulder. "It isn't wise to fight Stephen. He's dangerous."

That was the second time in a very short while someone had warned her Stephen was dangerous.

"What happened to Danielle? Who killed her?" The questions were out of her mouth before she knew it was even in her mind. Stephen would tell her nothing about her cousin.

"I can't say. It wouldn't be wise." He looked away, his jaw tightening as if he fought revealing some secret. "I'm sorry about your cousin. I brought her into this. I didn't understand what would happen. She was fun."

His smile was gentle, reminiscent. Madeleine nodded, feeling like a mourner at a funeral listening to an old friend talk.

"I didn't know Stephen would take an interest in her." Dylan slammed his fist down into his open palm. "I shouldn't have left her alone. I thought she'd be safe. Stephen sent me out for something, and I left her there. I came back, and she was gone."

Madeleine felt the air rush out of her lungs. Stephen and Danielle? Had Stephen killed Danielle? He'd denied it, but then he'd lied about knowing her at all. She hadn't let herself think about the possibility.

"Oh, Madeleine, I've upset you. I'm sorry. I just wanted you to know—" He stopped. "I don't want to say too much, but Stephen was ordered to kill you, and he hasn't."

Madeleine flinched. It had been easy in the past few days to forget the ultimate outcome of their relationship. Hearing another person say it made it that much more real.

"I'm afraid he's planning to use *you* now that Danielle's gone."

"What?" She shook her head. "I don't understand."

"Vampires he doesn't like have been turning up dead. Staked. I don't know how he's doing it, but somehow he's killing vampires."

Stephen? Killing vampires? She didn't believe it. Or maybe she just didn't want to believe it.

Dylan continued, "However he's killing them, it's something he can't do on his own. He needs a human's help."

He let the statement linger and finally Madeleine lifted her eyes. "I don't know what you want."

"Has Stephen done anything or talked about dead vampires? If you can give me something, maybe I can get the Council to back off. Let you live. Killing vampires might seem like a good idea to you, but in the end, you'll still end up dead. Look what happened to Danielle."

It was too much to take in. Her overburdened mind couldn't assimilate all the information, but that didn't stop the questions. Had Stephen used Danielle, then killed her? Was he planning to do the same with her? He'd handed the stake to her and urged her to use it. Maybe it had been a test. But had she passed or failed by refusing?

Dylan put his hands on her shoulders. "I don't really know what's going on, just that he's dangerous and somehow you fit into his plan." He looked over his shoulder. "I have to go. It isn't safe. Be careful, Madeleine."

Before she could respond, he disappeared. She stared at the empty space and listened to the rapid patter of her heart. Dazed, she stumbled behind Nick as he silently urged her home. The sun was fully set. It was the first time since it all began that she'd been outside after dark, but even fear couldn't penetrate her thoughts. Was Stephen using her? Planning to use her to kill other vampires? It didn't seem possible, but then none of this was possible.

She barely noticed entering her building or Nick waiting patiently while she unlocked her door and slipped inside. The flurry of her thoughts precluded any conversation.

She left her briefcase by the door and dropped onto the couch. Slowly, her exhausted mind began to sort through Dylan's statements, and none of it made sense. Questions streamed by her, one right after the other. She needed answers, and the only person she could get them from was Stephen.

That strange overwhelmed sensation faded, slowly dissolving into anger. And with it the return of her resolve.

Tonight, she was getting her answers.

She just had to wait for Stephen to appear.

Eight

He entered through the crack in her window. Even in his vapor state he could feel the waves of emotion emanating from her. She was furious. She lay staring up at the ceiling, her fingers tapping violently on the bed covers. Moving to the darkest corner of the room, he re-formed and sent his thoughts to her, willing her to sleep. She fought it, but finally true exhaustion and his influence won, and her eyelids fell shut. He listened in the darkness, tuning in to the rhythm of her breath, the sweet sound of her heart sliding into the relaxed pulse of sleep.

He eased out of the shadows and stood beside her bed.

His tongue slipped along the bottom edge of his lip, remembering her taste. So sweet. Sexy. His fangs were half extended—a regular occurrence lately.

She curled on her side, her hand bunched up under her chin. She looked sweet. Innocent. Safe. Stephen shook his head. Lightning flashed outside the window. She didn't move. The heat from the day had called another storm. Rain would come soon.

She'd waited for him. Stephen rubbed the tips of his fingers across his forehead—a gesture from his human days, a mortal affectation that had no meaning. He didn't get headaches. Still, the action seemed to help. She'd waited for him—and that's why he'd stayed away.

Four nights indulging in Madeleine and he'd found himself addicted—to her taste, her smile, her wit, her strength.

Something strange was happening to him. He'd spent four nights with a human, and he hadn't bitten her, hadn't seduced her. They'd talked or fought. He felt the corner of his lips curl up into a smile. It was fun to fight with Madeleine.

She was so full of life.

And it would end tonight.

It would be simple. She wouldn't feel it. She would drift off and never wake.

And now she slept, unaware of the danger that waited for her.

He wandered around the room, still hesitant. Waiting for her to sink fully into sleep. He grimaced in the dark. He was stalling. *How human.*

He turned and forced himself to Madeleine's side. His weight rolled her toward him as he sat on the edge of the bed. She grumbled in her sleep, and her forehead crinkled in complaint. He smiled. She didn't like being disturbed.

He drew in a deep breath he didn't need, inhaling her scent. His tongue slipped out and brushed the inside edge of his lip. She shifted. Sleep eased the tension from her body, but her mind wasn't resting. She sparkled with mental energy as she snuggled down into the blankets. He wondered briefly if the dreams were still haunting her. She hadn't complained about them in days but that didn't mean much. Maddie was changeable and might have decided to enjoy them. Or maybe she'd found a way to ignore them. Stephen felt the edges of his eyes tighten. He didn't like the idea of her ignoring him—even if it was just in a dream.

A lock of hair fell across her forehead. He automatically moved to brush it back.

The slow half smile that seemed to hover over his lips whenever he was around her returned as he watched her sleep. She made him smile. She was so tough, so proud, and yet so vulnerable.

The morning crept closer and still he didn't move. It did him no good to remember that he hated those he was protecting, or that Madeleine had done nothing wrong, nothing worth dying over. He had a responsibility to the Community.

He ground his teeth together and placed a hand on the mattress behind her hip.

He bent over and opened his mouth against the warmth of her neck. The throb of her heart pounded through his ears.

The air was filled with her scent—warm, sweet, and sensual. She shifted underneath the thin blanket, her restless movements brushing against his leg. He tensed and endured the almost painful pleasure of touching her.

He dropped his jaw and positioned his teeth over her pulse, preparing for the sharp spike of pleasure as he entered her body.

The image hit him like a bullet, plowing into his thoughts with deadly force.

Madeleine naked on a bed, this bed. Writhing beneath his touch. Her throat arched back, open to him, begging for his mouth and the pleasure he could give her. She wanted it. She grabbed his head and pulled his mouth to hers.

Stephen straightened and looked at Madeleine. She twisted under the sheets, her body reacting to the dream that had captured her mind. The warm, delicious scent of her arousal reached him. He forced himself to stand and slowly backed away. This wasn't supposed to happen. It couldn't happen. Humans couldn't transmit.

Her lips slowly caressed the column of his neck, imitating the long, teasing kisses he'd given her. She opened her mouth and nipped the taut flesh with her teeth. He threw back his head and allowed a groan to escape. She smiled against his skin, thrilling in her power. She sucked lightly on the base of his throat, twirling her tongue over the pulse point, teasing it until he was begging, pleading for the gentle bite of her teeth. Her nipples grew hard as she tempted him. She rubbed them lightly against his chest, loving the sweet friction.

Eyes trained on her sleeping body, he backed away. He stumbled over a small bump in the carpet and fell back against the wall. The strength of his legs betrayed him, and he sank slowly to the floor. Madeleine's form no longer held the sleep of the innocent—she twisted in slow movements, seductive, her body unconsciously seeking sensations, needing his touch. His hands clenched convulsively, wanting to provide what she sought.

She rolled onto her back, and her hand skimmed across her stomach. A tight band wrapped around his chest as he watched her hand against her pale skin.

This was no dream he'd given her. She'd created it. And somehow, she was giving it to him.

Another wave hit him. He tensed and let the scene play through his mind.

"Please, Stephen, please," she begged. And he was there, sliding into her warmth, filling her. She groaned at the joy of holding him inside her. He raised his head and their eyes met. Glowing with power and love, he began to move inside her.

Stephen closed his eyes and groaned quietly. He wanted the reality. He could have her. He could create the dream she envisioned. Except for the love. The man in her fantasy loved her—she trusted that and loved him in return.

Her body tightened under the slow steady assault of his thrusts.

Locked in her mind, Stephen's body responded. Each pleasure she felt, each touch she experienced, he received—the shudders, the need, the ache. Stephen clenched his jaw, too caught to seek an escape.

She needed more, just a little more pressure. He moved in sync to her unspoken commands, filling her. The sweet tension between her thighs began to build. She couldn't find the words, but they weren't needed. He knew what she wanted. He moved inside her. She couldn't stop. She had to have it. It—

The picture evaporated, ripped from the screen in his head.

Madeleine came awake and sat up, staring into the

darkness. Her heart pounded, her body empty and crying for release.

Stephen sank farther into the shadows. His fangs were stretched to their painful limit, and he could feel his eyes glowing. If she saw him now, she'd see the vampire from movie nightmares. He wanted her. Wanted the flesh. His body was hard with arousal. He could have her. She was needy and aching.

But the reality wouldn't be her dream. He was too gone, too far from control to get near her. New images filled his mind, these of his own creation—a broken, bloodied body, eyes staring sightless at the sky. *Madeleine*.

He came here tonight with a purpose—to kill her.

But not like that.

She shook her head and looked into the shadows. She couldn't see him but she was too close, too tempting.

He closed his eyes and dissolved his form into a fine vapor, the mist indistinguishable in the darkness. He shifted, heading for the window, but found he couldn't resist one final touch. He circled her body, twining himself around the curves and angles.

As he slipped around the corners of her flesh, Madeleine tensed as if sensing his presence. His muffled faculties recognized her distress and he comforted her, sending soothing thoughts to ease her. Slowly, her body began to relax, though need still hummed through her veins—a need he couldn't satisfy. Even in his vapor state he could sense it. It was too much.

He forced himself from her body, from her room, and left her alone and wanting.

Tension encased his body as he eased into his corporeal form a few blocks away. Away from temptation. He released a quick laugh. He'd never escape the temptation of Madeleine.

He stalked down the street, burning the energy that shimmered through his body. It felt good to move. *Not as*

good as moving in Madeleine would have felt. The thought
reignited the fires in his body, and he growled into the
quiet street.

He had to talk to someone. Someone who might know
what the hell was happening. How could Madeleine have
sent him her thoughts? And how could he receive them?
Even vampires couldn't transmit to other vampires—a
vampire's mind was too protected, too shielded for others
to implant thoughts. Joshua's opinion had been that it was
an evolutionary development designed to protect them so
no vampire could control another the way humans were
controlled. Joshua would have known. But he was dead,
and there was only one other vampire Stephen trusted.

Within moments he was standing inside Death's Door.
He slipped in the back again, not wanting the attention. If
Gayle's comments were true, the rumors were going fast
and furious. And too damn close to the truth. He stepped
to the edge of the light, watching the mass of bodies
scattered at tables around the dimly lit dance floor. A few
patrons looked up. Some nodded. Some dropped their
gazes and whispered to companions. Gayle wasn't on the
main floor, but Stephen waited. Gayle's innate awareness
of his club would send him over soon.

"It looks like someone's taking up where your father
left off."

Stephen tensed at the snide comment from behind him.
He turned slowly and stared into the dark corner, a corner
so black that none but the eyes of a vampire could pierce
the darkness. Even with his hypersensitive sight, Stephen
could barely make out Matthias' face.

"What?" Stephen snapped.

"My best guess is it's you."

Stephen's lips curled back in an involuntary snarl.
Emotions hummed through his body—frustration, anger,
desire. He'd spent days denying himself what he wanted
most. The feelings wanted some release.

"Gentlemen..." Gayle appeared and placed himself between them. "No trouble. You both promised."

"And I don't know why you'd trust him. He's been waiting two hundred years for this," Matthias sneered.

With a few notable exceptions, Stephen had done his best to avoid Matthias in those two hundred years. Matthias, after all, had good reason to hate him.

But tonight, he wasn't willing to play Matthias' games.

"Matthias, if I were going to start killing vampires, don't you think I would have started with you?"

A flash of white from Matthias' fangs and the glowing orbs of his eyes illuminated the dark corner. The blackness moved as Matthias stood. Stephen bared his teeth, one predator responding to the threat of another.

"Boys." Gayle's singsong voice pierced the tension. "As intriguing as it is to see this macho display of power, you're starting to scare the humans, and that's bad for business."

Neither vampire reacted to Gayle's comment. Stephen took a step toward Matthias' corner. Gayle's body blocked his next step.

"Why are you here?" Gayle asked.

"Is that any way to greet a friend?" Stephen didn't look at Gayle. He kept his focus on Matthias.

"I love you dearly, you know that, but you make people nervous."

"Good."

"Stephen—"

The warning in Gayle's voice was strange, tense. Unusual enough that Stephen took his eyes off Matthias and stared at his friend.

"Not tonight," Gayle whispered. There was a plea behind his command.

"Why not tonight?" The question seemed to throw Gayle off kilter. Stephen raised his eyebrows and waited. "What's so special?"

"You can't afford the press."

"Why?" It was true he'd never been a favorite, but there had always lingered enough sympathy among the Community to allow him some security.

"Rumors are they found another one."

Stephen straightened. "What? No—" It wasn't possible.

"It's just rumor, but the Community's tense. Dylan's been talking, reminding everyone about your past. You're everyone's favorite suspect tonight. And then with your pet..."

"She's not a pet."

"It doesn't matter what you call her. The Council wants her gone, and you're protecting her." Gayle glanced around the room. Stephen didn't look back, but he could feel the eyes on them. "You won't find a lot of friends here tonight."

"That's nothing unusual."

"I think you have more friends on a regular basis than you think."

"But not tonight."

"No. Can I encourage you to leave?"

"I need to talk to you first."

For a moment, Gayle looked as if he would refuse, but then he nodded. "I've got to go pull Mitch off that sweet young thing and come right back. Want to wait by the bar?" He moved in that direction, trying to herd Stephen with his body. Stephen stepped to the side. He was prepared to keep the peace for Gayle's sake, but he wasn't going to walk away. Not with Matthias staring daggers at his back.

"I'll wait here."

Gayle flashed him a look of warning before he left.

Stephen turned and faced Matthias. He was easily twice Stephen's age, though he looked no older. Two hundred years had made them familiar with each other. *Know thy enemy.* Stephen almost smiled. Matthias had no idea what he was facing.

Then it hit him. There was something different about Matthias tonight. Stephen stared blatantly into the dark, trying to find it. Hatred marred the arrogant face that looked back at him, but that was nothing new. It was something else. A kind of smug confidence glowed behind Matthias' eyes. As if he had a secret. Or he knew one.

"Well, I guess I'll go." Matthias strolled out of the darkness, walking toward Stephen. "I don't much care for the clientele this place attracts." Stephen refused to react to the childish taunt. He stepped back, giving Matthias room to pass by. Still, Matthias stopped in front of him. "It's time, you know."

"What?" Stephen wasn't interested in cryptic riddles.

"It's time. I've waited over two hundred years for just the right moment." His eyes flared as he looked at Stephen. "And just the right woman. She'll do nicely."

Fear and fury enveloped Stephen. He bared his teeth and grabbed for Matthias, but the older vampire was gone, his body disappearing in a puff of smoke. Stephen stood in the place Matthias had occupied and stared unseeing at the club.

Matthias knew about Madeleine. She wasn't safe.

He had often wondered when Matthias would come for him. Matthias had made it clear he hadn't given up his desire for revenge. And he was right. Madeleine would be perfect.

"Damn," he whispered in the noise of the bar. Had this been the plan all along? Was Madeleine part of an elaborate revenge plot? It seemed impossible— improbable. But Matthias had had two hundred years to plan.

"Sorry, I had to make sure Mitch didn't forget the new rules," Gayle said, brushing his long blond hair away from his face.

"New rules?"

"Yes, the cops were getting irritating, so from now

on, no dead bodies in the club." He winked. "Except for the ones walking around. So, how can I help?"

Stephen considered asking Gayle about Matthias but decided against it. If Matthias was involved, he would be a dangerous enemy, and Stephen didn't want to burden Gayle with that. And the truth was, he didn't know if Gayle might be involved already. There were too many variables. Trust had never come easy. Now, with so many questions, it was almost nonexistent.

What would Gayle do with the information Stephen would give him tonight? Could he trust him? He had no choice. He needed a vampire's knowledge.

"Have you ever known of a vampire who could receive a human's thoughts?" The noise of the club served as an excellent buffer for their voices, so Stephen wasn't worried about being overheard. Matthias had marked this corner of the club as his. Most patrons knew enough to stay out of the area. Stephen looked out across the nightclub. It was easy to see why Matthias liked this corner. It provided an excellent view of the whole room. He could see who was trying to listen.

"You mean read minds?"

"No, just have thoughts transmitted. Like you would send your thoughts to a human."

Gayle thought about it for a moment. "No. Is—"

Thomass, with Dylan in tow, started toward them. Stephen looked at Gayle and shook his head to warn the other vampire. All tension left Gayle's body, and he lounged against the solid wood table. Stephen took his cue from his friend and leaned against the wall, his arms folded across his chest. They were the picture of casual, *private* conversation. That didn't stop Thomass from interrupting.

"Stephen."

Stephen didn't have to fake the irritation at Thomass' concerned greeting. Gayle twirled one strand of blond hair around his finger, pointedly ignoring Thomass' approach.

"Is it wise for you to be here?" Thomass asked, his voice low and secretive.

"Why shouldn't I be here?" Stephen returned the question with as much innocence as he could fake.

"Well, with all the rumors..." Thomass let his voice trail away.

"I'm not concerned." Seeing Thomass and Dylan together, Stephen realized they were quite alike—they even looked alike. It gave Stephen some insight into why Joshua might have converted Dylan—he was just like Thomass. He needed a few more years to perfect the smooth façade, but Stephen had no doubt that's what the fledgling would do. *Just what the vampire world needs—another Thomass.* "No one really takes those things seriously. It's just gossip." Stephen drilled his gaze into Dylan and had the satisfaction of seeing the young man retreat one step behind his mentor.

"How dare you?" Gayle flipped his hair over his shoulder. "Gossip is my lifeblood."

Thomass' upper lip curled up in disgust as he watched Gayle, and Stephen found a reason to smile for the first time tonight.

"Yes, well, I never listen to it myself," Thomass said. "I just wanted to check on the *situation*. The Council meets tomorrow night. They'll want an update."

"It's fine."

"It can't be that fine." Gayle and Stephen turned in unison to face the sneering fledgling. Dylan's eyes grew wide as they focused their glares on him.

"What do you mean?" Thomass asked.

Dylan straightened. "Madeleine's still alive," he said confidently. That confidence vanished as Stephen shot his arm out and snagged the young vampire by the throat, choking off his words.

"How would you know Madeleine's current condition?" He dragged Dylan forward, his fingers squeezing tighter. The young vampire's eyes bulged as Stephen pulled up, raising Dylan to his toes.

"Stephen, let him go."

"No, Thomass. I want to know when he saw Madeleine. And why?"

"It's nothing to get upset about. I sent him to watch her." Thomass' voice returned to its standard, conciliatory tone. "The Council wants her dead. The whole Community knows about her and your strange fascination with her."

Stephen thought about protesting but realized it would be worthless. And a lie.

"I thought if I set someone to watching her, we could prove she wasn't involved," Thomass went on. "I should have said something. I'm sorry. I trust your instincts, but you have to understand, Robertson is pushing the Council."

They were the right words, but Stephen found no comfort in them. Matthias' involvement had changed everything.

Thomass stepped closer, his words for Stephen alone. "Robertson almost has them convinced that you and Madeleine are working together. I was able to pull them back tonight, but I don't know how long that will last." His voice dropped even farther. "Another vampire is missing and they've sent to Europe for information on your father's daggers. They're doing research into silver daggers and you know what they'll find when they do."

Stephen kept his face impassive. Thomass couldn't know. Stephen opened his fist, and Dylan dropped to the floor, clutching his throat. Deep red bruises in the shape of Stephen's hand were already forming on Dylan's pale skin.

"Keep out of my way, Thomass. Tell the Council to do the same. Madeleine's mine." As he said the words, he realized they were true. Madeleine belonged to him.

He stepped over Dylan's body. Gayle did the same and followed Stephen outside.

Once in the distant corner of the parking lot, Stephen rolled his shoulders, trying to free some of the strain. It wasn't helping. His body was wound too tight for any minor easing. He needed release—he needed Madeleine. *Mine.* He'd never felt possessive about a human before. He used them and let them go—taking only what he needed and sometimes a little sex. But not Madeleine. The craving for her blood was strong, almost overpowering at times, but it was more than that, and he wanted more than a little sex from her.

"So, ignoring what just happened," Gayle began, pointing one elegant finger toward the nightclub, "and I'm not really sure what just happened—go back to this thing about you receiving a human's thoughts?"

Stephen quickly told Gayle about the strange dream Madeleine had transmitted to him. He didn't go into the details—just that there was a dream. He finished and waited for Gayle's response. For once, his friend was silent. Finally, he smiled.

"I have *got* to meet this woman."

"Gayle..."

"Really. Bring her by before you kill her. She's tormenting you in the most wonderful fashion. Is it intentional, do you think? Or is it just blind, human luck?"

"Somehow I doubt she finds knowing me to be all that lucky."

Gayle shook his head, the light of laughter flashing in his eyes. "The sex must be incredible for you to be going through all this."

Stephen grimaced before he thought to hide the reaction.

"Do you mean you haven't even..."

"No."

"Why not?" Gayle sounded truly offended at the idea.

Because she'd settle herself into my heart. "It didn't seem right," was all he said.

"I see. Don't want to sleep with her and then kill her. I guess I can understand that. But I'd definitely say sleep with her. You'll be a lot less cranky, and we'll all be a lot happier."

"Gayle..."

Sometimes he forgot exactly why he considered Gayle a friend. He could be damned annoying when he tried. And he was trying tonight.

"And if you don't want to kill her afterward, let someone else do it. I'll do it if you're squeamish."

Stephen's eyeteeth extended and he growled in Gayle's direction. "You'll stay the hell away from her."

Gayle wasn't intimidated. He laughed. "Oh, you have it bad. This is just too wonderful. Bring her by."

Without answering, Stephen turned on his heel and walked away, Gayle's laughter following him across the parking lot. The pressure built as the sun began inching toward the horizon. It was time to be home. He welcomed the need to sleep and a day's existence without thoughts and dreams.

He stepped inside and walked down the short hallway to the great room, his mind on Madeleine. And Gayle's words—*you have it bad*.

He turned into his living room and stopped. Something wasn't right. A presence. Gone, but something lingered. He sniffed the air. A scent? Familiar but too vague to identify.

He knew the sights and smells of his house. Someone had entered his home. He wandered through the living room. Nothing triggered. It was familiar. He should recognize it, but somehow he didn't.

He glared into the darkness. Too many questions, too many possibilities. He needed to start eliminating problems.

And his first one was upstairs.

Those damn knives. The safe they were kept in was

lined to block any vibration from the silver. But someone knew about the knives. How long before that was made public? He should get rid of them. Or at the very least move them.

Instead, he turned and headed downstairs to his vault. The knives were safe at least for one more day. The scent, the presence he'd felt wasn't human. No vampire could touch those knives. Unless...

He closed the heavy door of the vault, engaging the security lock that he usually left undone. He'd relied on Cassandra and Nicholas to stop any casual visitor from wandering in. But Cassandra was gone. Nicholas was watching Madeleine. And Stephen was trusting no one.

The pull of the sleep was heavy upon him, and he crawled into his coffin. He struggled against the dawn, stretching the limits, enduring the pain to see it through the sunrise. He knew the precise moment when the sun rose. His blood sang with agony. Stephen fought the need to sleep, pushing the pain away with the thought of his knives and dead vampires.

The killing wasn't over.

There were fifteen members on the Council. Stephen had ten knives. The question wasn't who would die, but who would be left alive?

Nine

"He'll *stake* me."

Madeleine felt some sympathy for the wide-eyed and pleading young man in front of her—but not enough to stop her.

"Don't worry, Nick. Stephen will know it wasn't your fault."

She'd waited all last night, and Stephen hadn't come to her. So she was going to him.

Nick looked into her determined eyes for a long moment before he sighed. "Fine, but if I get nailed to the wall…"

He left the threat hanging. Madeleine smiled at his back as she followed him outside. He was too young, too sweet, to come up with a credible threat anyway. He led her one block away from her office and stopped beside a black sedan.

She looked at the car, then up at Nick.

"Stephen won't let you drive the Jag, huh?"

"No."

She tried not to smile as he pouted. She couldn't really blame him. The sedan was nice, but it wasn't a Jaguar. She climbed into the front seat and stared out the window as Nick drove through town. The world blurred before her.

She'd waited for him all night. Anger turned to irritation when she thought about it—irritation at herself mainly. She'd let the last week and all its strange events happen to her. Well, now she was going to make something happen.

She'd mulled over Dylan's strange warning. Her mind still didn't know what to believe. She knew Stephen was dangerous, but she couldn't imagine him killing another vampire. She hadn't let herself dwell too long on the theory that he'd killed Danielle. Thinking about it wouldn't change the truth, and that's what she was seeking tonight—

the truth. Stephen couldn't walk out on her if she was in his house. At least that was the idea.

The sun was at the horizon, ready to plunge the city into darkness, when Nick pulled up in front of Stephen's house. Rain clouds had hovered all day, waiting, she supposed, for the night. She shivered as she climbed out of the car. *Nothing like going to a vampire's house on a dark and stormy night.*

The house was silent as they walked in, the normal sounds missing.

"Is Cassandra going to pop out of somewhere and offer me tea?" she asked with a smile, wanting to fill the oppressive silence.

"She's gone. Stephen will wake soon. He'll know you're here."

With no farewell, he stalked up the steps, leaving Madeleine alone in the living room. He obviously didn't want to be around when Stephen arrived. She couldn't blame him. Stephen wouldn't be thrilled to find her there.

She wandered alone through the living room. Now that she knew him better, she saw it fit Stephen perfectly— neat, elegant, suitable for conversation, and filled with books. The coffee table had been tidied recently. All the magazines neatly stacked. Just like before.

Where is Cassandra?

Icy fingers raced up her spine, and she shuddered. People had a way of disappearing around Stephen. It made Dylan's warning a little too real.

She sat down on the chaise lounge and picked up a magazine, hoping to look calm and serene when Stephen walked in. The second book down was one of the vampire comics she'd seen before. Too tempted to ignore it, she started to read.

Rain poured down on a woman standing at the door to a dark castle. The light from a window illuminated a tiny corner of the page, a man's shadow etched in the glass.

Madeleine quickly found herself caught up in the story of a young woman stranded in the middle of nowhere with only the eerie house for shelter—and the dark, dangerous creature as her host. As she turned the pages, she felt the woman's pain and the vampire's fear. He fought against who he was—but the battle was lost. Sympathy for the vampire welled inside her.

The vampire's mouth opened, his long white incisors moving toward the column of the woman's throat.

The air around her changed. Madeleine tightened her grip on the comic and slowly raised her eyes. Stephen watched her from the far corner of the room.

"Why are you here?" His voice was tight, made rough by the clenched line of his jaw.

He looked haunted, as if demons had chased him there and now held him captive. All the reasons she'd thought of during the day, all the crimes she was prepared to lay at Stephen's feet, vanished as she stared into the hollow centers of his eyes. The light she'd grown used to, the laughter she'd teased to life, was gone.

She couldn't—wouldn't—give him any answer but the truth. "I wanted to see you." Her anger, her questions faded from her mind. She'd missed him last night. Had wanted his presence to comfort her and keep her safe. The erotic dreams and passionate kisses they'd shared flooded her senses. She wanted him, wanted to see the light return to his eyes.

He made no move to approach her, but his gaze followed the line of her body as she stood. Knowing he watched her movements, she walked around the coffee table and started toward him. For a moment, she thought he was going to back away, but he didn't. His fingers curled slowly into fists, as if he was fighting the urge to reach for what he wanted.

Female power ignited in her body. He wanted her. The glow of his eyes told her that, and more.

"You shouldn't be here."

"Why not?"

"Maddie, it's not safe." He said the words so quietly she could barely hear them.

"You won't hurt me." She spoke with a confidence she wasn't sure was real, but the words flowed from somewhere inside her.

"Oh, but I will."

It should have frightened her. The reminder should have been enough, but still she walked forward. This was why she was here, she realized. To see him. To be with him.

Stephen tensed as Madeleine came closer. He'd woken up with the pounding of her heart in his ears and the scent of her heat inside his house. The sensations had lured him upstairs, even as the remaining trace of his humanity hoped it was a dream. She couldn't be here. Not now. Not tonight.

Desperate hunger clawed at his throat. Her dream was too recent. His control was at its limits. He wanted her. And she offered him the one temptation he couldn't fight—her welcome. He could see it in her eyes. She would accept him, take him into her body, just as she'd done in her dream.

No woman had ever held more power than Madeleine as she strolled across his floor. He'd have dropped to his knees and begged if she asked it. The only thing keeping him upright was pride. And maybe some latent honor that lingered from his human days.

"Madeleine, I'll have Nick take you home."

She shook her head, and the sweet smell of her hair washed over him. "I'm not ready to leave." As if someone had lit a match against his skin, he felt every whisper of her husky voice move across his body and into his soul.

Wise thoughts of retreat tried to reassert themselves, but they were lost in the smile on Madeleine's lips and in her eyes. Moving slowly, giving her one chance to get away, to pull back, he took her hand and brought her to him.

Still waiting, still hoping, for her sake and ultimately for his, that she would stop this. His body protested his delay, his resistance. He wanted her, wanted her now. The thin line of his control was bending under the weight of desire.

He had to have her. The thought blocked all others, allowing only desire and need to be heard. He covered her mouth with his, sinking his tongue deep inside her warmth, giving her no prelude, overwhelmed by the need to be inside her in all possible ways.

Just a taste, he promised himself, though he knew it was a lie. The primal instincts that fed his hunger howled with possession. She was his.

His hand slid into her hair, cupping her head and holding her to him, afraid she might escape before he could fully taste her. But she wasn't trying to escape. She was moving forward, moving her lips with his, pressing her body against him. He knew then that he wouldn't let her go. Not tonight.

Not ever.

He created a mental picture of their bodies entwined and flashed it into her thoughts. Madeleine groaned as the image hit her, but she jerked back and glared at him. A flurry of confused emotions hit him.

"No. If we're going to do this—" She waved her hand between their bodies. "We do it for real."

It was the perfect excuse to leave—mock her human emotions, human need. Self-protective instincts that had guided him for two hundred years told him to escape now. Madeleine would settle into his soul, creating new tears in the scarred fabric of his mind.

He gripped her shoulders, ready to put her aside. Then she moved—with all the honesty that was Madeleine— she stood on tiptoes and placed her mouth on his. It was a light touch, a mere connection of their mouths, the sweet rush of her breath against his skin.

He resisted for a moment, found a strength he didn't

know he possessed to hold back, but years of indulgence crumpled his will. He couldn't resist the offering, couldn't fight the temptation to have all that he'd craved. With a groan, he caught her to him and returned her kiss, teasing her lips, licking her, entering the warmth of her mouth.

And she responded with all that she had—strength, courage, passion. Unafraid as she was to challenge him, she didn't hide her desire. Her lips returned each caress. Her tongue tangled with his as he tasted her, clouding his mind with sensation until all he could feel was her.

He dragged his mouth from hers and placed warm, lingering kisses along the length of her neck. The fading mark glowed against her pale skin. She had no idea how erotic the bruise on her neck was to him. It was a sign of his possession. A vampire's bite became sensitive to the vampire's touch, always seeking to reestablish the connection. His teeth ached, longing to penetrate her flesh and feel her flowing around and through him. But he held back, thinking he might be able to resist that one temptation. He circled his tongue around the tiny bite marks. She melted, sighing as her body sagged against his.

The touch of her hand on his thigh obliterated all thought. This was what had filled his dreams—Madeleine, her touch, her pleasure, her warmth. Images clouded his mind, his own dreams returning, welling up inside him. Madeleine, naked on his bed, clad only in moonlight, covered only by his body, her lips begging for his kiss, her legs wrapped around his waist pulling him deeper inside.

He moved without thought, responding to the need to absorb the warmth of her body. The runaway rhythm of her pounding heart filled his senses.

He reached down and tugged her skirt up, baring her legs to his touch. The warm press of her skin against his hands weakened his knees. *So soft.* He lowered her to the rug and followed her down, easing his body over hers,

hungry for a deeper touch, the feel of hot flesh against his
skin. Madeleine twisted beneath him, her breath coming
in long slow draws, as if she wanted to slow the sensations.
He growled. She was his—he wanted her open to him, his
to pleasure and own, unable to resist his touch.

His hands slid up the insides of her legs, spreading
her thighs, creating a cradle for his hips. Slowly, he lifted
his head and stared into her glowing green eyes. He held
her gaze, wanting her thoughts only of him, her senses
filled with him. As she watched him, he pressed his hips
forward, deep between her legs, their only connection the
steady pulse of his erection against her femininity. Even
through the layers of their clothes, he could feel her heat.

Her breathless gasp filled the room. Triumph and
pleasure swept through his body as she moaned and
clutched his arms, her hands tightening on the taut muscles
that held him above her. He arched his hips again,
massaging her sex with steady pulses of his hips, preparing
her for his penetration. He rocked against her center and
listened to the increase of her heart. He had her. She
belonged to him.

He leaned forward and kissed her, drawing her breath
into his body, filling himself with Madeleine. And still he
moved his hips against her. She whimpered, and the echo
vibrated down his spine.

Her mouth slipped away from his, down the tight line
of his throat. He almost stopped her, knowing it would be
too much, but the silk-soft touch of her lips on his neck
was a lure he couldn't resist.

She swirled her tongue over the slow pulse point, a
counterpoint to the rhythm of his hips against the warmth
of her sex. His body tightened. He couldn't move, too
captivated by her touch. Her lips curled into a smile against
his skin, and she purred as she licked a single line up the
length of his neck.

"Maddie." Caught in her web, he could do nothing

but feed his own desire and hers. She opened her mouth on his skin and played—she tasted him, licked him, sucked him. He turned his head to the side, giving her more access, silently pleading for her to continue. She set her teeth against the muscles of his throat and bit. The tiny nip was too much. Stephen shivered and released the ragged groan he'd been fighting. Her unsteady breath and rapid heartbeat pounded through his veins. Another wave of desire flooded his already heightened senses. He threw his head back, arching his neck and feeling his eyeteeth lengthen.

Madeleine smiled. It was an intensely female smile, the smile of a woman who knew her mate's weaknesses and knew her own power. She moved again, as if to return to that sweet spot on his neck, knowing she could drive him beyond control. He caught her cheek in his hand and pulled her back up to his mouth, stopping any future torment.

Witch, he whispered into her thoughts. Her lips smiled against his.

He pulled her sweater up and over her head, tossing it out of his way. His hands quickly worked the front catch of her bra. She sighed as the heavy weight of her breasts was released and his hands cupped them. Her nipples were erect and pressed hard against his palms as he smoothed the warm flesh.

He wanted to linger, to learn all her curves and hidden corners, but he needed more, needed all of her. He tugged at her panties and felt them separate in his hands, the warm scent of her arousal drugging his senses. He slid one hand down the warm flesh of her stomach, skimming through the soft hair that protected her most feminine place. He replaced the pressure of his hips with the light, delicate caress of his thumb.

Stephen! Her mental cry filled his head.

Yes. Mine. Primitive possession racked his body.

He would give her the pleasure, would please her as

no other. She arched her hips, urging him to deepen the touch. He kept his touch light, wanting to draw it out, fill her, until only he existed.

Her cries echoed in his ears and her jumbled thoughts resounded in his mind. Last night he'd been concerned by her thoughts in his head—tonight he reveled in them. Her mind centered on one thought—more. More of him.

He drew himself up and rested on his heels. She lay before him—wet, open, wanting. Her bra was spread open, baring her full breasts, her skirt hiked up around her waist. She was beautiful in her passion, her eyes clouded with a hunger he recognized as a mirror to the one in his soul.

His being cried out to be inside her, in every way, but he held himself still. His hunger was too strong. He would take too much—his control would snap. His eyeteeth were extended and aching, matching his erection.

Fill me.

Her mental plea shot through him, and he knew he could hold nothing back. He'd give all that she needed and take all that she offered.

She reached for him, stretching her arm to where he waited between her open legs, his knees pressed against the underside of her thighs. Her fingers traced a light path along his fly. Through the rough material of his jeans, he could feel her heat. Nothing had ever been so seductive, so feminine as Madeleine's desire. She wanted him. Wanted his flesh in her body. Slowly, conscious that she watched every move, he slid his hands from her thighs to his own, moving sensuously across the rough fabric of his trousers to the fly. Her tongue slipped out the corner of her mouth, as if imagining the taste of him. With that simple move, his vision faded to red. He groaned and ripped at his jeans, fighting his own clothing until finally he was free and over her.

He thrust forward, entering her in one long, powerful stroke. Her body arched beneath him and her shocked cry shattered the room. He froze, the red haze clearing from his mind. He'd hurt her.

He started to pull out, wanting to save her from further pain. Her moaned protest and her strong legs wrapping around his waist stopped him. She clung to him, holding him inside her, as if she couldn't bear the loss of his flesh. She stared up at him, her eyes glazed with pleasure, not the pain he'd imagined.

"Stephen," she sighed his name as he settled fully inside her again. He held himself still, feeling the sweet pressure of her inner walls holding him. Never could he have imagined it would feel this good to be inside her. And he knew the truth—he was lost. He would never be free of her.

Mine. She gave a tiny gasp as he grew even harder inside her.

Locking her gaze with his own, he started to move. Steady pulsing thrusts, deep inside. Her body met his, stroke for stroke—begging him to go deeper, faster. His Maddie was a woman unafraid to seek her own needs. And he would give her what she sought, ease the unbearable ache that was forming, the need he saw in her eyes and heard in the silent cries that filled his head. He would give her what she needed, no matter the cost to himself.

He tilted her hips in his hands, positioning her so each thrust pressed against the most profound point of her desire. She groaned. Her arms wrapped around his neck, and she pulled him down to her. She met him with hungry, deep kisses that matched the fire between her legs.

Her taste overwhelmed him. He strained against her, his thrusts into her body becoming more desperate as her climax drew nearer. Her thoughts were vague, disjointed pleas he wanted to satisfy as her body tightened under his. He slipped his hand between their bodies, pressing, seeking and finding the touch that would bring her to completion.

Madeleine heard her own cry as the heat burst through her core and spread into her limbs. Each thrust of his hips milked the sensation further, bringing her to another peak quickly after the first. She groaned and pulled at him. The sound shocked her. Never before had she allowed herself that freedom or found the need to cry out.

He still moved above her, inside her, driving deep into her and holding himself to the hilt before slowly pulling out. Her own frenzy eased as she recovered from her climax. She relaxed, enjoying the long, deep slides of him inside her. She stared up at Stephen as he moved over her. With each thrust he bared his clenched teeth, as if he were fighting his own release, limiting his pleasure. The sharp tips of his eyeteeth—long and prominent—glistened in the dim light. Something held him back. He was fighting himself, fighting his desires.

A new longing burned in her chest—to bring Stephen to the same pleasure he'd created in her.

Instinct guided her. She cupped his head in her hands. Holding his gaze, she placed a light kiss on his tense lips, then guided him to the throbbing pulse in her neck. She shivered at the hot press of his mouth. His lips opened, then pulled away.

Maddie, no. She heard the sound inside her mind, a plea for release.

"Yes," she whispered in reply.

He groaned like a man tortured, and he ran his tongue across her skin, licking the line of her neck. She waited, needing this—needing it for him. She gasped as his teeth pierced her flesh and he entered her body again. The pain faded quickly and left only pleasure, his mouth pulling on her skin—the warm rush to fill him. Her thoughts wandered at the luxurious pleasure filling her. It was too delicious— his mouth on her neck, the steady thrusts between her legs.

With a final arch of his hips, Stephen lifted his head and cried out. A soft flutter of release scattered sparks through her body. The gentle climax left her warm and relaxed and smiling under the crush of Stephen's weight as he collapsed.

She smoothed her hands up his back, loving the feel of his body on hers. He still wore his shirt. It clung to his back, wet from the light sheen of sweat that covered his body. Stephen once more placed his mouth against her neck, this time lightly licking and soothing the wounds she knew were there. She forced breath into her lungs and let the sensation flow through her.

He raised his eyes to her, and she could see the questions. She had no answers. She wasn't ready for it to be over, for reality to return. She forced all thoughts but him from her mind and allowed her body to open to all the sensuous feelings he inspired. He stood, and seconds later she found herself lifted into his arms, his strength carrying her effortlessly.

"Tonight, you're mine," he whispered as he carried her to the stairs.

"Yes."

Madeleine nodded and rested her head against his shoulder. *For tonight.*

***

Madeleine stretched long in the bed, relaxing in the slither of satin sheets under her skin. An aching tenderness between her thighs stopped her movement.

Damn. Just when I think I've got a really good dream going, I wake up and find out it's real. Her eyes crept open.

She was in Stephen's bedroom. She vaguely remembered getting here, though it was more a haze of images than an actual memory. He'd carried her up the stairs. She remembered dropping her head against his shoulder and the fascination she'd had with the base of his neck.

He'd finished undressing her, her sated body enjoying

his slow touch. His lips had followed the path of bared skin, traced the line of her throat, kissed the soft skin of her breasts and her stomach and...

Memories ignited her body, arousing it, teasing it to life.

No! Stop!

Ignoring the ache between her legs, Madeleine rolled to her side and brought her knees protectively up to her chest. Each movement reminded her of him, the way he'd overwhelmed her senses and for a brief time became her whole world.

She stared at the empty pillow next to her. There was no indention where his head had lain. She was alone. He'd held her after they'd made love, touching her, whispering words in her ears and in her mind, words of passion and desire.

Never once mentioning love. Her heart cried at the bittersweet memory.

What did you expect? He'd declare his undying love? All the pulse points in her body wailed in assent. *No, dammit, this can't be happening. I cannot be falling in love with him.*

I can't.

Even as she mentally repeated the words, she knew they were a lie.

And knowing his touch, not just in dreams, would haunt her forever, a new memory to add to the bright light of the smile she saw in his eyes.

She tipped over on her back and looked up at the ceiling, letting the emotions wash over her. Fear and terror led the way.

She couldn't face him, couldn't see him. It was too new, too raw. He'd see it. Stephen, who could almost read her mind, would easily be able to look into her eyes and realize his little human was falling in love with him. She had to get out.

She threw off the sheet and climbed out of bed. Her body ached, but it was a satisfied, delicious feeling that only served to remind her of what she'd done. It would be so much easier if she could blame Stephen, but she couldn't. She could have stopped him. Hell, she encouraged him, teased him.

Damn it, I seduced him. She covered her eyes with her hands. It didn't help. She couldn't hide from the truth. He'd tried to back away and she hadn't let him.

He hadn't needed much encouragement, she admitted, but still, it had been her. What was she going to say to him now?

Her clothes had been tossed onto a chair. She pulled on her skirt. *This is one of the many reasons why I don't have casual sex. I never know what to say when it's over.*

She looked at the bed and stopped. Nothing about that had been casual. The warmth of the memory started in the center of her body and began to melt the resolve she'd been building.

Practical. Be practical. She took a deep breath. She would finish getting dressed, go home. And quietly panic.

She reached up to tidy her hair and looked into the mirror. Only there was no mirror. She scanned the walls. No mirror on the wall or the wood dresser.

"What kind of person doesn't have a mirror in his bedroom?" she muttered.

"One that doesn't cast a reflection."

Madeleine spun around at the sound of his voice. He filled the doorway, crowding the room with his presence. His shirt was open at the collar, a thin line of pale flesh visible in the light. She remembered tasting him there—and other places. A flush warmed her cheeks.

"How do you feel?"

"Fine."

"No dizziness?" He brushed his fingertips across her forehead, sweeping away the messy strands. She jerked away from his touch. Her body screamed in protest, wanting to be with him, near him, but she couldn't do it. She was too open to be near him. She took a step back and bumped into the dresser.

"I'm fine." She stared at the carpet, not wanting him to see the bare emotion in her eyes.

"Maddie, look at me."

His voice was rough, but she felt no mental compulsion to comply.

She shook her head. She wasn't up to a battle with him. "Please. I'd just like to go home."

He waited, and for a moment she thought he was going to say something else, but he just turned away.

"Come down when you're ready." His clipped reply made her wince.

When he was gone, she released the breath she'd been holding. Tears threatened, but she blinked them back. She didn't have the energy. She needed all her strength to keep the panic at bay.

Not only had she slept with a *vampire*—one she was probably falling in love with—it was very possible he was involved in her cousin's death. Oh God, what was she going to do now?

She opened the top drawer of his dresser, the practicality of looking for a comb or brush to untangle her hair easing her hurried mind. She shuffled through the bits of paper and notes that cluttered the drawer. Nothing useful. Then a flash caught her eye. A silver knife lay nestled in the edge of the drawer. The smooth blade was etched with swirls and circles. *Silver. It actually works*. Nick's words came back to her. Knowing it was too late to protect herself from Stephen—as he'd already entered her heart—she stared at the knife. Protection.

Without allowing herself to consider what she was doing, she pulled the knife from the drawer and slipped it up her sleeve, cupping the hilt in her palm.

Staring at the empty doorway, she took a deep breath and released it slowly. *Just hold it together for a little while longer.* Her legs shook as she walked down the stairs and waited at the bottom.

Stephen sat in the high-backed chair, one ankle crossed on the other knee. He stared down at a book resting on his calf. Without looking up, he spoke in a voice that reeked of boredom.

"Nicholas will take you home."

"I can get a cab."

"He feels the need to protect you."

She fingered the knife in her palm. "From who?"

"Tonight?" Stephen raised his eyes and impaled her with his glare. "Me."

A flash of pain, quickly crushed, flew into her mind. She tensed. It was foreign, as if she was receiving it from an outside source. Seconds later, the sharp pain was gone and a dull ache lingered.

Stephen dropped his gaze to the page in front of him, ignoring her. Madeleine walked down the short hallway where Nick waited. Stephen's voice reached her as they opened the door. "Good night, Maddie."

She stepped onto the porch and heard a quiet thump against the inside wall. It sounded suspiciously like a book being thrown across the room.

***

Stephen listened as his front door snapped shut. His hand shot out, flinging the book toward the far wall.

She'd walked out on him.

He stared at the empty space in front of him, his eyes blank. Emotions he'd eliminated years ago surged through his body. Human emotions. He snarled. He didn't want this.

Pain, frustration, and need battled inside him. He's spent two hundred years getting rid of these feelings—now they were back.

He propelled himself from the chair and followed Nicholas and Madeleine to the door.

Madeleine's arms were wrapped around her stomach, her shoulders hunched as if she was cold. He longed to be the one to warm her. He released the crushing grip he had on the door frame. She didn't want his warmth, his touch.

But that didn't mean he could leave her alone. It wasn't safe. Nicholas would be no protection. As they drove off, Stephen followed unseen.

Nicholas was only a fledgling, but he was smart. He scanned the streets as he drove and acted as a shield as he walked her inside. Stephen hovered in a vapor state nearby, following them upstairs, waiting to see if Madeleine invited the young man in. She didn't. She mumbled a barely audible good night and went inside.

"She's safe," Nicholas announced to the empty hallway. Stephen re-formed and faced the furious young man. "What the hell did you do to her? It's like she's crushed."

"It's not your concern." He tried to fill the words with venom but knew he failed. Leaving Nicholas in the hall, Stephen bolted from the building, too tempted to rip open Madeleine's door and beg her forgiveness. But how did he ask for forgiveness for what he was? It was a sin from which he couldn't hide.

The streets were slowing, losing their nightlife, as he stormed through the town. Gayle was waiting for him when he arrived at Death's Door. The other vampire opened his mouth, then snapped it shut. "Let's go downstairs." He led Stephen down a single dark staircase to the massive vault below the club. Stephen paced the length of the room while Gayle closed the door, sealing them from listening ears, and waited. "Is she dead?"

"No."

"Then what?"

Stephen glared at his friend. "She walked out on me."

"Whoa. You *are* out of practice."

Stephen ignored him. He shouldn't have come here. He wasn't in the mood for Gayle's teasing. He should have gone home and…and what? *Brooded, thought about Madeleine, paced the living room like a madman.* Pretty much what he was doing here. "Damn."

"Listen, why don't you—"

A buzzer interrupted Gayle's advice. They both looked at the vault door. "It must be important. No one bothers me when I'm down here." He walked to the wall and flipped a switch. A TV monitor came on, revealing what was on the other side of the door. Thomass and two Council Members.

"Just what I need tonight," Stephen muttered.

Gayle swung the door open and stepped outside to meet them. Stephen watched on the monitors. Gayle shook his head. Then again. Finally, he turned and came back inside.

"They want to search your house."

"For what?"

"They won't say. But we both know."

"My father's knives." He kept the strain out of his voice, knowing Gayle would recognize it.

Stephen wasn't worried they'd find the knives. He'd moved them, slipping them out of his room tonight while Madeleine slept. It had been a mindless activity to distract him from the lithe, sexy body lying on his bed. He'd had to do something or he'd have been on her again. He licked his lips. No hint of her flavor remained, but the memory was still sweet.

He shook his head to clear it. The knives weren't far away, just inaccessible to anyone but him. At worst, they'd find a lingering touch of silver, but that could be explained away.

No, the Council finding his knives wasn't Stephen's main concern. There was a bigger issue. He'd checked the case as he'd moved it—two more daggers were gone. Two more vampires were scheduled to die. Madeleine's abrupt departure tonight had briefly pushed the knives from his thoughts.

"Whatever happened to them?" Gayle's question drew him back.

"The daggers? They're safe. I assume," Stephen added when Gayle looked at him. Stephen ignored the question in his eyes and raised his chin to the door. "Go with them, would you?"

Gayle agreed and left Stephen alone. He could have gone himself, but his mind was beyond the Council tonight. Let them find what they would. He didn't notice time passing, his thoughts occupied with fighting off the memories of Madeleine and the silk of her skin, the taste of her.

Dammit, he'd known she'd be trouble when she first entered his life, but he'd never considered how distracting she'd be. When he should have been focusing on who was framing him for killing off the Council—and figuring out how they were doing it—he'd been thinking of Madeleine. Now, he used the murders to distract his mind from images of her. He had to look at the possibility that a vampire was working alone, killing Council members with silver daggers. But how? Stephen looked at his own past. What made him different? Why was he able to—

The whir of the vault opening grabbed his attention.

Gayle slipped in, concern and confusion replacing the usual lightness on his face.

Stephen waited for Gayle to speak. Finally, Gayle shook his head. "Nothing. They checked the whole house." The lines around Gayle's eyes crinkled for moment as he thought. "There was some concern in the bedroom."

"The safe in the closet," Stephen offered with as much amusement as he could create.

"No, they saw that. It was something else. Thomass

thought he sensed something in the top dresser drawer, but Charles and I searched and didn't find anything."

The dresser drawer? He'd never had his knives in the dresser. Too accessible. Not that their previous location had been that secure. Someone obviously knew how to get them.

"Someone's out to get you, my friend."

Stephen nodded. Someone who knew the truth. He flipped through his history again. Had anyone known about the knives? It was possible someone had seen them as he'd packed for the trip to America. If that were the case, why wait two hundred years to reveal it? A vampire keeping silver daggers, daggers specifically designed to kill their kind, would have instantly become the Council's target. Anyone who knew would have used the knowledge before now.

"Stay here tonight."

Stephen agreed to Gayle's advice. Dawn was close, and the temptation too great. If he left, he would find himself at Madeleine's.

Gayle came and went for another hour, leaving Stephen alone in the vault. He walked the length of the cavernous room, unable to settle. The second he stopped moving, he was hit by Madeleine's memory.

She'd left him. It wasn't physical. He knew she'd been satisfied, but when sanity returned, she'd run from him.

What did you expect? She'd declare her undying love? The idea was insane. A human in love with a vampire. No wonder she'd escaped.

Madeleine.

The image of her in his bed was too easy to conjure. He'd been teased by dreams and fantasies. They'd been nothing compared to the reality of touching her skin, feeling the heat of her body as he joined with her.

Dawn arrived as Gayle reentered the vault and sealed the door. For once, Stephen welcomed the oblivion of death. Pain wracked his body as the night pulled him back. He lay down on a bed, knowing he wouldn't fight it this morning. He'd let it take him. He closed his eyes and waited.

Madeleine turned to him and smiled. She spread the edges of her gown and bared herself to him. She was strong and powerful. He wanted her. She knew it, could see it in his hot eyes. She curled her fingers and beckoned him closer.

Stephen's eyes snapped open, and he stared at the dark in front of him.

Miles away and she was still with him.

Ten

Madeleine turned the key and looked over her shoulder. Nick was at his usual spot in the hallway, just down from her apartment. Tonight, she'd finally managed to nag him into leaving the overhang across the street and come into her building. In the past three days, since the night Stephen had sent her home with him, Nick had continued to escort her to and from work, and he'd stayed outside through the night. She saw him less during the days. He disappeared shortly after he took her to work and returned just before sunset. Each day, the exhaustion hung on him more heavily.

She cocked her head and stared at the young man propped up against the wall. She sighed. "Nick, you don't have to stand out here all night."

"I'm supposed to watch you."

"You don't have to stay out here. Would you like to come—"

"Don't say it!" The sharp slap of his words shocked her. "Don't invite me in," he commanded. His voice held the deep, impenetrable darkness that so often surrounded Stephen.

"Nick, I'm not afraid of you."

"You should be. I'm one of them, Madeleine. I might hate it but you can't ever forget it."

The quiet, dead tone made the tiny hairs along her arms stand up. She suppressed a shiver, not wanting him to see her fear. Silently, she nodded and entered her apartment, dragged down by the depressing reality of Nick's existence.

Great, she thought. *Sympathy for a vampire.* She closed her eyes for one moment and took a deep breath. A least it was something to distract her from thoughts of Stephen. She hadn't heard from him since that night. She wasn't surprised. After the way she'd behaved…she cringed at the memory. She wouldn't have called her, either.

She'd wigged out on him. Oh, she'd had a good reason. She'd just had mind-blowing sex with a vampire. Twice. It was enough to throw any woman off her game. But still...

Maybe he was waiting for her to apologize. Maybe that's why she hadn't heard from him.

"Or maybe he got what he wanted, and he's just waiting for a full moon so he can kill me," she muttered aloud.

That thought was way too grim to face. And she'd faced some grim thoughts in the past two weeks.

Unfortunately, making love to him hadn't lessened the fantasies. The dreams had been bad before—now they were overwhelming. Her fantasies, his fantasies, reality—it all blended together to keep her body and mind in a constant state of arousal.

She pressed her shoulders back and lifted her chin, strengthening her resolve. She would not be lured by mere physical pleasure—no matter how good it had been. It was just sex. Hot. Mind-blowing. But still just sex.

It was more.

At least for her. Damn it, for one night, she'd felt connected and sexy and—she winced at the word—loved.

She pushed away from the door and walked to the bedroom, pulling off her work clothes. Silver glittered across her bare arms and hung in strands around her neck as she took off her blouse. Over the past few days, she'd bought enough silver to start her own mint. She wore the necklaces and bracelets at all times.

She'd promised herself she wouldn't take them off for any reason—well, except for one. If Stephen came by. She shook her head. That wasn't likely.

She missed him—missed his surprise appearances in her living room, missed the long talks, exploring his mind. And his body. She shuddered as the thought opened the door to another fantasy—this one pure memory. The power and strength that had moved through her from his body, the sweet touch of his mouth on her skin.

He's a vampire!

It no longer made her heart pound. He was Stephen. And she wanted him.

One good thing had happened as a result of their lovemaking—the whispering in her head had faded. It had been completely gone the day after, but the noise was slowly returning. Maybe she should call Stephen and get another dose of the cure. She shook her head. The thought was too tempting. She'd have to live with the voices for a while longer.

With a sigh, she wandered into the kitchen and stared into her cupboard. The last can of soup stared back. Tomorrow was Saturday, and she was determined to use some of the daylight hours to go grocery shopping. The restriction of being home by sunset had left her little time for errands or shopping. She was down to the last can of soup. If she didn't shop soon, she'd be forced to delve into the dark recesses of her freezer—an idea almost as scary as vampires.

While the soup warmed on the stove, she moved to the living room and sat down in front of the couch. She wasn't doing office work tonight—tonight it was research, or what she was calling research. She'd thrown the stakes out the day after they'd made love. There was no way she could stab Stephen with a wooden stake. She couldn't do it. She had to find another way.

She opened her briefcase and pulled out a stack of comic books—*Vampire Warrior*. Nick's comics. Nick was part of that world. Maybe there was something in one of the stories that would help. Plus, she liked them. Her free time dedicated to research, she'd made a quick run to a comic store at lunch. The staff there hadn't found it unusual that she'd purchased two years' worth of *Vampire Warrior* comics. They'd simply recommended others as well. Madeleine decided to try them after she'd gone through Nick's. He had personal experience after all.

She'd started reading during lunch that day and had instantly been caught up in the story. Each issue ended with a cliffhanger, and she had worked her way through three comics before she'd had to go back to work. Now, she had to find out what happened. She finished one, and then another. As she read on, she noticed the shift.

In the first editions, Galor, the vampire hero, loved his power and strength—he reveled in being a vampire. Then the character started to change, the drawings and story turning from the exultation of power to the search for an escape. Anguish crept into the vampire's eyes and his soul grew tortured. Madeleine felt her heart in her throat as the woman who could have saved him died in his arms.

Tears streamed down Galor's face.

The phone next to her rang, tearing her from the story. She took a sharp breath and squinted at the clock, giving her eyes a few seconds to focus. It was late. She'd been reading for a while. Stephen rushed to his place in the front of her mind as she picked up the handset.

"Hello?" She waited for Stephen's deep, dark voice to answer.

"Madeleine?"

"Hi, Char." Madeleine relaxed against the sofa. She took a deep breath to calm her pounding heart and sniffed the air. "Wait. I'm burning my soup." Madeleine pushed herself to standing and stumbled into the kitchen. She clicked off the burner and pushed the pan of boiling soup onto the cool flat of the stove. "So, what's up?"

"Madeleine, I'm scared."

The noise behind Charlotte's voice came into focus. She wasn't home.

"What happened? Are you okay?"

"I'm fine. Just scared."

"Where are you?"

"The Jungle Club." Madeleine swore silently. "Jesse called and asked me out for a drink. I couldn't spend another night in my apartment."

"What happened?"

"Nothing, but Jesse went to the bathroom and didn't come back. That's not like him."

Madeleine rolled her eyes. Jesse, Charlotte's sometime boyfriend, was more likely than not to disappear. Still, the coincidence was too great.

"I think someone's following me. It just feels strange, you know."

Madeleine nodded even though Charlotte couldn't see her. She'd experienced that in the past week—that strange sensation that someone was watching her, and only her. Icy tremors filled Madeleine's chest.

"Okay, stay in public places, don't talk to anyone. Go sit by the bartender and don't worry about being rude. If anyone comes up to you, ignore them and walk away. I'll be there as soon as I can."

She clicked the phone off. She needed help. *Stephen.* She grimaced. It was logical to call him. He would know what to do, but she couldn't call him. Two things stopped her. One, she had completely freaked on him after making love. And two, she didn't know if he'd help. He'd made it more than clear that death and life had different values in his world. She couldn't risk Charlotte to his indifference to a human life.

Still, she needed help. She opened the line and hit the speed dial for Scott's number. She hadn't spoken to him since they'd searched Stephen's house, and she'd discovered vampires were real. After four rings, the machine picked up. *Great. What a night for him to have a date.*

"Scott, it's Maddie, I mean Madeleine. Listen, if you get this message soon, can you meet me at the Jungle Club? I think Charlotte's in some kind of trouble."

She hung up. It would have to do.

Madeleine threw down the phone and raced to her

bedroom. She needed protection, anything she could find. She didn't have any crosses and wasn't really sure they would work, but she had silver.

She draped another row of silver chains around her neck, adding to the strands already there, and looped more bracelets across both wrists. It was a gaudy mismatch of styles, but she ignored it. She wasn't going for fashion. She opened the drawer beside her bed and pulled out the knife she'd taken from Stephen's house. Sliding the dagger up her sleeve, she looked in the mirror. The stark glow of determination in her own eyes startled her.

Madeleine Bryant, Vampire Hunter.

She was still pulling on her coat as she opened the front door. Nick lounged at the end of the hall. He straightened when she walked out.

"Where are you going?" he called as she stormed by him, headed for the stairs. "Oh, this is a really bad idea."

She glanced over her shoulder. The vampire trailed close behind, worry etched in his young face. The stairwell was dark, as usual. She clutched the silver dagger in her hand and bolted downstairs. The comforting clatter of Nick's footsteps followed her.

"Madeleine, you can't," he shouted when they'd reached the outside of her building.

She turned on him and pointed the knife at his chest. "Who's going to stop me? You?" He backed away. "I didn't think so." She spun away and stalked off into the dark streets, her whole focus on getting to Charlotte before something happened.

The next street over was busy enough for her to find a cab. She used the ride over to calm herself and try to devise a plan. Nothing came to mind except grab Charlotte and get the hell out of there. It was simple but effective. She had enough silver that it should protect both of them—if Charlotte was still okay.

This is my fault, she reproached herself silently.

Charlotte was being threatened because of her. She took a series of slow, deep breaths, trying to concentrate on the hope that Charlotte—practical, stable Charlotte—was simply having a moment of hysteria.

The club was jumping when the cabbie dropped her off out front. Music pulsated through the walls, and people spilled out of doors and hung out of windows. *The neighbors must love this.* Of course, the pawnshop on the corner and the liquor store nearby probably didn't care. More business for them.

She inhaled through her teeth and moved toward the front door. She hoped Charlotte had listened to her and stayed at the bar. She didn't know how she would find her friend otherwise.

Ignoring the people around the door, she started up the steps.

In the distance, over the noise, she heard it—her name. "Madeleine!"

The crowd seemed to evaporate to her left for one moment, leaving a clear view of Charlotte. And another young woman. Panic poured from Charlotte's eyes as she fought against the stronger woman. The stranger didn't seem to notice her captive struggling. She just kept walking, moving farther away from Madeleine, pulling Charlotte behind her.

Madeleine plunged into the crowd, using Charlotte's screams as her guide. None of the other patrons seemed to even notice. They moved aside to let Madeleine pass, but no one offered to help. Charlotte and her captor turned down a narrow alley.

Madeleine ran to the entrance and stopped. It was a trap. She knew it but couldn't think of a different option. She couldn't leave Charlotte in there. It was her fault Charlotte was in this mess. Of course, she had never intended to get involved with a group of vampires, but that didn't mean much, standing on the edge of a dark alley. She tightened her fist around the silver dagger and held it down by her side.

The alley was filled with shadows, colorless shapes that sucked light from the world. Her fingers twitched on the hilt of the knife, cascading down the handle in an unsteady rhythm. She stepped forward and stared into the darkness, waiting for her eyes to adjust to the low light.

One of the shadows—deeper than the others, more real and solid—lay at the base of the wall not far from the entrance. The dim pile groaned.

"Charlotte?" She rushed to her friend's side and knelt down. "Char?"

A cool rush of air swooshed by her head, and invisible nails scraped across her back.

"Aahh!" Five lines of fire burned across Madeleine's skin. Grinding her teeth together, she spun around and placed her back against the wall. She stepped a few feet away from her friend's body, needing room for whatever was next. She held the silver knife in front of her chest and waited. The air began to churn again. Madeleine tensed. A heavy wind burst from her left side. Listening to instinct, she stabbed forward. An inhuman howl reverberated off the walls as her dagger connected with a solid body. Materializing from the air, he fell and landed at her feet with a thump and pained groan. The snarling creature turned his dark eyes to Madeleine. She could see a black trickle of blood oozing out the slash in his shirt where she'd cut him. The vampire bared his teeth and pushed himself up on one arm, leaning toward her.

She reached up and tugged on a light silver chain around her neck. As she pulled, the metal cut into her fingertips. With a quick jerk, the necklace came free. Madeleine flicked her wrist and tossed the silver chain at the vampire on the ground. His neck arched forward as the silver draped itself in a line across his face. He screamed. Even in the dim light Madeleine could see the

burning wound that formed instantly across his face and
the pain in his eyes.

The vampire rolled to his side and grabbed at the chain
in frantic motions. The silver burned his fingers. He flipped
over and the chain fell to the ground. Slowly, he crawled
away, his burnt fingers clutching his scarred face. Grim
satisfaction tightened Madeleine's eyes as she ignored the
retreating vampire and focused her attention on the next
attack.

Like a magician's show, a body appeared to her right
and another to her left.

She bent her knees and dropped into what she hoped
was a fighter's stance. She didn't know. She'd never had
to fight her way out of a dark alley before. She kept both
hands low—one holding the knife, the other a silver chain.

As a unit, the two people in front of her attacked.
Madeleine swiped wide with the knife toward the vampire
on her right and kicked out at the creature on her left.
Searing pain raked through her back as the scratches from
the first attack scraped against the brick wall. She had the
satisfaction of hearing one of her attackers grunt as she
swung the knife in a wide arc in front of her chest. The
second vampire punched his fist forward and connected
with the side of her head. Bright lights burst through her
skull. She fell to the ground. Survival instinct spurred her
on. She rolled to her back and held up the dagger like a
shield. Shadows appeared out of the dark, creeping toward
her.

She was going to die. In a dark, dirty alley.

One of the creatures stood near her legs. Light from a
distant street lamp glinted off a streak of metal in his hand.
He had a knife, too. Just an ordinary knife, but it wouldn't
take a silver dagger to kill her.

She could sense her other attackers gathering around
her fallen body, but she kept her eyes trained on the one in
front. He seemed to be leading the charge. Her fingers

tightened on the knife in her hand. She might die, but she was going to take some of them with her. He moved forward.

An animalistic growl filled the sky and bounced off the buildings. The stalking vampires froze. Darkness flashed through the alley, and with a cry, the vampire with the knife flew into the air and hit the brick wall with a sickening thud. He slid down the side and landed in a lump on the ground. He didn't get back up.

The atmosphere grew still with anticipation. A figure appeared, standing over the fallen vampire. *Stephen.*

He slowly turned to face the others, his long coat swirling with the movement. His lips pulled back into a snarl, his long canines bared in warning to his enemies. Red glowed in his eyes. Before he moved, the others began to inch away from Madeleine. Stephen leapt forward. Madeleine gasped as he flew across the distance and landed heavily on one of the vampires.

She jumped to her feet and raced to Charlotte's side, revitalized by Stephen's appearance. Stephen fought two attackers. One remained to stalk Madeleine. He flashed his fangs and growled as he walked forward.

She took one of the heavier chains off and began swinging it in a circle over her head. Each pass of the chain drew closer to the threatening vampire. He bobbed back and forth trying to stay out of range of the necklace and the knife she still wielded. He lunged forward. Madeleine swiped the necklace down and across his neck. The air sizzled with his cry, and a black scrape instantly appeared at the open neck of his shirt. Madeleine raised the knife. She wasn't sure she could actually kill one of them, but she hid her indecision behind a hate-filled glare. The vampire backed away. She took one threatening step. He turned and ran.

She spun around, her weapons held ready.

One vampire lay at Stephen's feet, unmoving. Stephen

held the final attacker in one hand—that hand was wrapped around the vampire's throat. Madeleine shivered as she stared at Stephen. He looked barely human. He stared at the writhing vampire as if he were nothing more than a bug set before him to torture. His fingers tightened on the man's throat. Another whimper followed. Madeleine could see Stephen's fingers slowly squeeze. He was going to crush the man's neck. She slid the knife into her back pocket.

"Stephen!"

"She's mine!" Stephen growled with clenched, fanged teeth.

"Stephen, stop!" Her shout was ignored. She stepped forward and pulled on Stephen's arm. He snapped his head in her direction. Crazed fury filled his eyes, and he stared at her as if he didn't recognize her.

"Stephen?" she asked in a soothing voice. "Sweetheart? Are you listening? Put him down." She kept up a steady stream of words—soothing, calming words, mixed with commands to release the other vampire.

The vampire had stopped struggling and hung limp at the end of Stephen's hand. Slowly, he looked up at his captive, then returned his gaze to Madeleine. A faint glimmer of light stared back at her through the blackness of his eyes. After a moment, the light grew bigger.

"Put him down, Stephen."

At her firm command, he lowered his arm and released him. The body crumpled to the ground. Madeleine knelt by the fallen vampire and pressed her fingers against his neck. "Will he have a pulse?" She'd felt Stephen's heart beating when they'd made love but couldn't remember the sound.

"Of a sort." The words were cold and muffled. Madeleine glanced up. His canine teeth were still extended, making his words blurred. "It will be much slower than a human's."

A slow throb pulsed beneath her fingertips.

"He's still alive," she said with a sigh of relief.

"Good. Now I can kill him."

Madeleine threw her body in front of the injured vampire. "No."

Fire flashed in Stephen's eyes. She tensed, but she didn't back down.

"Get out of the way, Maddie." She shook her head, and he said, "He touched what is mine. It's my right."

The bold, overwhelming possessiveness should have bothered her, but it didn't. The feminist side of her protested, of course, but she decided now was probably not the time to tell him she belonged to no one. He didn't look in the mood for that sort of discussion.

The red glow in his eyes returned as he tried to move around her.

"Let him go," she whispered. Her gaze locked with his. After an eternity of mere seconds, the hatred faded from his eyes, and he nodded. Not quite trusting his easy capitulation, she kept her body in front of the other vampire.

"I'm not going to hurt him, Madeleine." She arched her eyebrows in disbelief, and he muttered, "Not much. I just want to ask him a few questions."

Now that was something Madeleine could get behind. She'd been set up and she wanted to know why. She nodded and moved to the side, though she stayed near the fallen man.

The vampire's eyes were half shut but snapped open as Stephen stood over him. His gaze darted between Madeleine and Stephen, finally landing on the glittering display of silver hanging around Madeleine's neck. His eyes widened, and he started to press himself up. With a look of disgust, Stephen pushed him down and placed his boot on the man's chest.

"Not so fast, Antonio. We need to have a little chat."

"I-I don't have to tell you anything." He seemed to gather courage with each word. Madeleine trailed her finger along the chains. Antonio flinched and turned back to Stephen.

Stephen's approving nod sent a warm flush over her body. This was something new. They'd talked, they'd made love—now they were working together. It was intimacy of a different sort.

"Really, Antonio, I think you want to tell me everything. Or I'll just beat the hell out of you until you're so weak you can't crawl to cover. The sun should be up in a few hours. I understand it's a very painful way to die."

"You wouldn't dare. I work for the Council."

Stephen's smile, more frightening than facing five vampires in a dark alley, sent a chill through Madeleine's chest. "And you know how concerned I am about the Council's good opinion. Now, before I crumple your body like a poorly written letter, who sent you?"

Antonio pressed his lips together. Madeleine could see him fighting for his courage. He surreptitiously looked around.

"Your friends are gone," she warned. "You won't get any help there."

"You're just a human. What do you know?"

Madeleine had had a bad day and a tough week. She wasn't in the mood for attitude. Without clearly thinking, she ripped off another chain and slapped it across the back of Antonio's hand. He yelped and jerked his hand away.

"Didn't they warn you she's got a temper?" Stephen interjected with an insincere smile. "Now, who sent you after Madeleine?"

Antonio looked away.

"Antonio, I'm not going to ask you again. Who?"

"The Council. They want her dead."

"Who on the Council gave the order?"

"Thomass."

Stephen nodded and stepped away.

Madeleine watched the defeated vampire crawl backward on his hands. Not far, just out of Stephen's reach.

"That's it?" Madeleine asked. "Don't you want to know why?"

"Does it matter?"

He had a point. Someone wanted her dead. It probably didn't matter why. In Stephen's world, there very likely wasn't a reason.

Stephen reached out and pulled back the collar of Madeleine's shirt. "This is my mark, Antonio. She's mine." He didn't make a threat. He didn't need to.

His fingers brushed the faded bruise. She couldn't control the flutter in her belly at his soft touch. It was insane. She was in a dark alley having just fought five vampires with a silver knife and some jewelry, and she was still able to lust after Stephen. *Too weird.*

She vaguely heard Stephen order Antonio away.

"Come on."

Stephen's coat swirled around him as he stalked away, heading toward Charlotte. Madeleine stepped carefully over a vampire and followed after him.

"But what about the others?" Two of the five vampires were still unconscious.

He kept walking. "What about them?" he asked without turning around.

"We can't just leave them there."

He stopped. Madeleine slammed into his back. Only the strength of his hands catching her as he spun around stopped her from tumbling to the ground.

"What do you propose to do for them?" His voice was as cold as it had been during his conversation with Antonio. "They're vampires. They'll find their way home before the sun rises. If not, the world is just that much better off."

He steadied her on her feet then turned away. She watched him for a few seconds, thinking he was joking and would eventually turn around. He didn't.

Stephen stopped at the end of the alley and bent over. When he straightened, an unconscious Charlotte lay in his arms. He turned the corner and left the alley. Madeleine caught up with them at Stephen's car. He'd left the Jag at home tonight. The black sedan sat alone and untouched on the crowded street. He raised his chin toward the back door, and Madeleine reached to open it.

A face stared up at her. Madeleine jerked back.

"Nick?"

"Oh, yes, we'd best go around." Stephen walked around to the other side of the car. Madeleine raced to meet him there. She opened the door and he slipped Charlotte inside. Nick barely glanced at the unconscious woman placed next to him. He continued to glare at Stephen.

"Madeleine!"

Her head snapped up at the call. *Scott.* She looked around, trying to find him in the swarm of people that seemed to hover outside the club. Stephen stepped into her line of vision and opened the car door.

"We have to go."

"But that's Scott."

"Madeleine!"

Stephen's jaw tightened. "Yes, and it would be very inconvenient to have the police find two wounded vampires in the alley and an unconscious woman in my back seat. Get in."

She allowed herself to be helped into the car. They drove off as Scott burst from the crowd. She was going to have to call him tomorrow and explain. Somehow.

"Will you unlock me, please?" Nick asked.

Madeleine twisted around in her seat. The young man ignored her and glared at the back of Stephen's head. A thin metallic ribbon linking Nick's hand and the door glittered in the dim light. He was handcuffed inside the car. A tiny set of keys flew into the back seat. Nick caught them with his free hand.

She looked at Stephen, silently asking the question.

"He would have gotten in my way."

Madeleine waited, not quite believing Stephen's explanation. She stayed silent and watched him. Finally Stephen sighed and said, "He would have been killed. He has no protection, no power."

Madeleine didn't try to hide her smile. She couldn't resist teasing him just a little bit.

"It's so cute." She reached out and pinched his cheek. "You're protecting the baby vampire."

She could feel a snarl welling up in the back of Stephen's throat and laughed. The evening was full of revelations. She could feel herself falling more in love with him. And it didn't matter. She wasn't frightened. She wasn't upset. She was in love. And smiling.

The light glinted off the stark lines of his fangs. Madeleine chuckled. She'd seen Stephen angry, and although he might be upset tonight, he wasn't going to hurt her. He'd just protected her.

She sat back in her seat and stared forward, stunned by the simple reality. Stephen had protected her. He'd claimed he was going to kill her, but he'd missed the perfect opportunity of getting her out of his life.

And he'd locked Nick in the car.

She smiled. For the first time in weeks, she felt safe.

Then Stephen spoke. "Back in the alley—did you call me 'sweetheart'?"

Madeleine tensed and lied, "No."

"I think you did." He reached over and patted her knee. "It's so cute."

Nick chuckled from the back seat.

"I'd stay out of this," she warned.

His only response was more quiet laughter.

"I take it you know where she lives?"

Madeleine snapped to attention. "I'm sorry. What?"

"Your friend. I'm assuming you know where she lives. We can't keep her."

"Oh. Yes." She quickly gave directions.

When they arrived at Char's apartment building, Stephen carried her upstairs and propped her outside the door. He stared down at the unconscious woman as if a heavy decision pressed on him.

"What?" Madeleine asked.

"I don't know what she saw, what she might remember later. She could cause problems for us."

Madeleine pushed herself between Stephen and Charlotte. "Don't kill her."

Stephen grimaced. "I'm not going to kill her. She's had enough alcohol that most of what she saw will seem like a dream. I'm just going to encourage that."

He waved Madeleine out of the way. She didn't move. "How?"

Stephen glanced up and down the hallway. "Well, if you'd get out of the way, I'm going to bite her and plant a suggestion in her thoughts."

"You can't plant a suggestion without biting her?"

"No."

"You did with me. The first time we met."

"Can you guys discuss this later?" Nick interrupted. "We really should be moving."

Madeleine held her hand up into Nick's face to stop his comments. "What about the hickey?"

Stephen smiled. "She won't have a hickey."

This time when he slid around Madeleine, she let him go.

"Then why do I?" Both times Stephen had bitten her, she'd ended up wearing turtlenecks. During the summer. It was annoying. And embarrassing.

"Passion."

"What?" She placed her hand on his shoulder and

pulled him back before he could put his lips on Char's neck. "What passion?"

The muscles along his jaw tightened as if he was stopping himself from answering. After a moment he said, "I'm biting her with a purpose—it's cold, it's calculated, and it's the most efficient course of action."

"But you bit me with a purpose."

He nodded slowly. "Yes, until passion became involved."

It was too easy to remember the first touch of his mouth on her throat, the lure of his taste. She licked her lips at the memory.

"Exactly. Passion." Before she could stop him, he turned back and opened his mouth against Charlotte's throat. Madeleine crushed the protest, knowing it wasn't concern for Char that wanted him to stop. It was jealousy. She hated seeing Stephen's mouth on another woman's neck. She pressed her lips together and forced herself to watch.

It was over quickly. Stephen lifted his head and whispered quietly in Charlotte's ear. The tiny puncture wounds on her throat were closing already. Moments later he straightened. Charlotte opened her glassy eyes and stared up at Stephen with adoration. She smiled and tried to lean forward to kiss him. Madeleine was preparing to intervene, but Stephen leaned back out of Charlotte's reach. The move was quick and subtle, so subtle it might have been an accident, but Madeleine didn't think so. He had avoided Charlotte's kiss for a reason. For her.

"I'll get her inside," she announced, helping the dazzled Charlotte into her apartment. Her friend was easily led, and Madeleine guided her into the bedroom. Another spike of jealousy hit her as she saw the sensual smile on Charlotte's lips. Madeleine had to force herself not to drop Charlotte on the floor. Instead, she helped her into bed and pulled the covers over her.

Stephen and Nick were waiting in the hall when she returned.

"She'll be fine." Stephen placed his hand around her back and began walking down the hall. "She probably won't remember the fight. She got scared, and she called you. You came and rescued her, brought her home, and helped her to bed. She had a little too much to drink is all."

Madeleine nodded. None of them seemed inclined to speak as they walked back to the car.

"Are we going after this Thomass guy?" Madeleine asked once Stephen had pulled into the street.

"No, I'm going to talk to Thomass. You're going home."

"But—"

"What the hell did you think you were doing tonight anyway?"

"Defending myself."

"Against vampires? They almost killed you tonight." Now that the conversation was started, Stephen seemed to have a lot to say.

"I was doing okay."

Stephen snapped his head to the right and stared at her with disbelief. "Okay, so I wasn't doing that well, but I have a right to be involved. It's me they want to kill."

"And that will happen if you don't do what I say."

"And that means going home and staying inside."

"Yes."

"No."

Stephen's fingers tightened on the steering wheel, and she knew instinctively he was fighting his temper. He was just going to have to deal with it. She wasn't going back to hiding in her apartment.

"Fine." He sounded resigned to her presence. "Nicholas, I'm going to Death's Door. I'll drop you off at the house."

"Why does she get to go, and I have to go home?" Nick protested. "I'm not helpless, you know. I can defend myself."

She didn't think Stephen's body could get any tighter— his whole being radiated tension. She crossed her arms over her chest and waited with a smile until Stephen finished glaring at her.

"Fine. We'll all go. But if either of you gets in trouble, you're on your own."

"Okay," she agreed. She didn't believe him for moment. She looked into the back seat and smiled at Nick. He smiled back. The two of them were enjoying the adventure even if Stephen wasn't. She knew she should be scared, should take Stephen up on his offer to take her home. It was the safe thing to do. But she didn't feel like being safe, and if she wasn't going to be safe, she should at least be smart. Staying with Stephen was smart. He would be her safety.

She didn't know what the night would bring, but she'd face it with Stephen at her side.

Eleven

"By the way, thanks for coming tonight. I appreciate the rescue."

Stephen didn't seem to be in the mood for thanks.

"It was an obvious trap. Why did you go in?" he argued.

"She's my friend. I couldn't let her get hurt. It was my fault she was there in the first place."

"You could have asked for help."

"I did."

Stephen glared across the car at her, and Madeleine winced.

"*Real* help. What good would that human cop have been? You should have called *me*." He sounded offended, almost jealous that she'd called Scott.

"I had no way of getting a hold of you. How *did* you get there so fast?" She glanced over her shoulder at Nick. "What did you do? Call him by mental telepathy?"

Nick held up a tiny black cell phone. She looked over at Stephen. He reached down and unclipped a similar phone from his belt.

"Cell phones," she said in a dazed voice. "How technologically advanced. I guess I was expecting something a little more spooky."

"We save the spooky stuff for later."

She didn't smile. She had no idea how much more spooky stuff she could handle. Vampires had been enough. Finding herself in love with one had pushed her spook quotient to its limit.

The city around them changed. They traveled through the business district and beyond, into a world of seedy clubs and adult bookstores. Streetlights became fewer and fewer. Stephen calmly watched the streets like a driver who knew the area well and knew what to expect around each corner. Dark streets didn't bother him. Madeleine checked her door, confirming she was locked inside.

The streets were almost empty, yet they seemed alive, as if the inhabitants stood just out of sight, watching as they passed. Movement flickered at the corner of her eye. She turned, but whatever had been there was gone.

"Where are we going?" she asked as he drove farther into this foreign land, her voice tainted with uncertainty she wished she could hide. Stephen turned the car and pulled into a long, curved driveway.

A sign hung above the door of the huge black mansion. "Death's Door" adorned the wood in faded black ink. Darkness emanated from the building. Madeleine instinctively leaned away. Stephen drove around to a full parking lot and found a place in the corner. People—humans and vampires, she assumed—lingered in the parking lot in groups of two, three, and four.

Stephen parked and came around to her door. He offered his hand.

"Welcome to my world, Maddie."

Madeleine almost refused—her common sense finally awakening enough to protest—but she couldn't. She'd pushed him to bring her along, and there was something in Stephen's eyes that dared her to stay. She placed her hand in his and climbed out of the car. Still holding her hand, Stephen started toward the door. Nick stumbled along behind them.

Their approach attracted the interest of several groups of people. Until they saw Stephen leading the way. Madeleine watched in amazement as first one crowd, then the next backed out of his path.

It was easy to tell why. Power reverberated from him, warning even the most unaware that he was dangerous.

Madeleine tried to focus on the people around her, tried to keep her mind on her situation. She didn't have time to be distracted. She'd just fought five vampires, let Stephen bite her friend, and now was going into what

appeared to be a local vampire hangout. It was enough to
keep anyone's attention. But she couldn't pull her eyes off
Stephen. The black duster he wore flowed with invisible
forces, swirling around his body, caught up in blind winds
that surrounded him. A very modern vampire.

Maybe it was the adrenaline flowing through her body
or the power flowing through his, but she wanted him.
Wanted to taste the line of his neck and feel his body tighten
within hers. Unconsciously, she trailed her tongue along
the inside edge of her teeth. The slight abrasion sent a
little shiver over her skin. The memory of his touch was
so sharp and the dreams so vivid that new images snapped
into her mind. Variations on a theme. Stephen behind her,
his hands hot against her cool skin, warming her, matching
the heat inside her body. His lips sliding down the column
of her neck and—

Stephen jerked to a stop, spun around, and pulled
Madeleine against him.

"Wha—?" His mouth covered hers. No gentling, no
teasing—his lips met hers and his tongue entered her
waiting mouth. Oh yes, this was what she wanted. She
wrapped her arms around his neck and met him kiss for
kiss. Warm hands held her hips and pulled her hard against
the strength of his body. She could feel his erection
straining against the confines of his clothes. She shifted,
cupping and cuddling him in the warmth between her legs.
A tiny moan slipped from her throat. It was good and she
wanted more.

"My, my, my. Interesting."

As quickly as it started, it stopped. Stephen lifted his
head and set Madeleine away from him. Her knees wobbled
for a moment before finding the strength to stand straight.

Blinking away her shock, she looked up. Stephen
stared over her head, his teeth bared and the long line of
his fangs gleaming in the dim light of the parking lot.

"Down, boy," the same voice teased, and Madeleine

followed the sound to the source. A tall blond man with long, flowing hair stood a few feet away, his arms folded on his chest. His mouth was curled into a mocking smile and his glittering green eyes were full of laughter. "I'd heard you were storming up to my place. I thought I'd greet you before you broke something. I never realized it might be the city's decency laws. Necking? In my parking lot?" Stephen didn't respond, but Madeleine felt some of the tension ease from him. She didn't know this newcomer, but Stephen seemed to trust him.

"And you *must* be Madeleine. I've been dying to meet you."

The man sauntered forward—she'd never seen anyone truly saunter before, but there was no other word for it. He offered an elegant, slightly limp hand to Madeleine. She inched toward Stephen and stared at the open palm.

"Oh, don't worry, dear, I know better than to play with one of Stephen's toys." She opened her mouth to protest, but he stopped her. "My dear, you are so obviously marked you might as well wear a glowing sign that proclaims it. Not to mention that lovely bruise on your neck." He smiled up at Stephen. "A hickey? Stephen. I've seen week-old fledglings with more control."

"Gayle—" The warning in Stephen's voice was obvious—obvious, it seemed, except to the man it was directed at.

Gayle ignored Stephen and winked at Madeleine. "Don't worry, my dear, he won't hurt me. Not unless I beg him to."

She laughed, more at the frustrated look on Stephen's face than anything else.

"Gayle—" Stephen started again.

"He's just so terrifying when he's in a temper, isn't he?" the blond vampire asked Madeleine.

She nodded. She couldn't help liking the teasing man in front of her. He didn't fit her image of a vampire, except for the tall, good-looking part. His green eyes twinkled merrily even in the dim light of the parking lot.

"I'm Gayle, darling. Stephen's best, and sometimes only, friend in the whole world." Gayle looked between Stephen and Madeleine and cocked his head to the side. "And who is this?"

Madeleine looked back to see Nick struggling to steady himself. She knew exactly what he was going through— the battle between the instinct of "run and hide" and the pride of refusing to back down. She had Stephen to hold on to. Nick was alone.

"He's not your concern." Stephen's cold words countered the fire that blazed in his eyes.

Gayle laughed. Madeleine tried to catch the blond vampire's eyes and warn him that Stephen wasn't joking. She didn't know how she knew that. Maybe because she'd heard that tone before, but she knew that Gayle should back off.

"You bring him to my club, he becomes my concern." He trailed his gaze up and down Nick's body. "He doesn't wear your mark, but there's something different about him." Gayle pursed his lips and stared as if he was trying to figure out a puzzle. Light and flirtation left his eyes, leaving behind an intense intelligence and curiosity. Strange, protective instincts welled up inside Madeleine. It was silly, of course. Nick was a vampire—only a half-vampire to be sure—but still, he was probably more than capable of dealing with the situation. That didn't stop Madeleine from worrying. She didn't like the way Gayle stared at him.

"Come here," Gayle commanded.

"Leave him alone." The words were out before Madeleine realized she'd said them.

A flicker of irritation crossed Gayle's face before it was replaced by a teasing smile. It was so fast that she almost thought she'd imagined it, but she'd learned too much in the past few weeks to discount her intuition. Until she learned otherwise, she was going to accept all insights as true, and there was something about Gayle that she didn't quite trust, something beyond the façade he presented.

His lips curled into an amused, mocking smile. "Your pet's protecting the cub. Is he hers?"

"He's mine," Stephen corrected. "Whether he bears my mark or not. Leave him alone."

Gayle shrugged, and Madeleine was a little less sure she liked him. "Whatever you say. But there is something different about him. His heart isn't right. I'll figure it out."

"Don't bother."

"Oh, Stephen, my love, you know I can never resist a puzzle." He stared at Nick for a moment more before turning back to Stephen. "I take it you're coming in?"

"I need to see some people."

Madeleine shuddered at the quiet statement. For a moment she'd forgotten why they were here. During the strange necking session and Gayle's arrival, that anger seemed to have faded from Stephen. It now returned full force.

"Stephen, think about my insurance rates," Gayle whined as his shoulders sagged forward.

Madeleine couldn't help smiling. He was as changeable as the wind, and she wasn't sure she trusted him, but he was amusing. Stephen's grim face didn't change.

Gayle held up his hands in surrender. "Oh, fine, come on in." He turned and walked away. "But she might want to lose some of that jewelry."

Stephen ignored the comment. "Nicholas, go with Gayle. He'll keep you safe." The young man took a deep breath and followed Gayle inside. Stephen turned the opposite way, dragging Madeleine behind him with the grip he still had on her hand. He stopped when they were in a dark, secluded corner of the parking lot.

"I need to focus here, Madeleine."

He seemed to have a message beyond the words he was saying, but she didn't know what it was.

"Okay."

"I can't afford any more distractions."

What distractions? The tight set of Stephen's jaw stopped her from asking the question.

"Okay," she agreed again.

"I mean it, Madeleine. Stay out of my head."

"What?"

"No more fantasies. No more hot little dreams." Madeleine rocked back on her heels and stared up at him as he repeated, "Stay out of my head."

"Are you crazy?"

"Very close to it, I'd imagine." The long line of Stephen's fangs still shone in the light. He hadn't calmed down. She knew from experience that they only appeared when he was angry or aroused. He seemed to be both tonight. The thought came to her mind unbidden, but she didn't push it aside when it arrived—was the rest of him hard? The lingering ache of desire curled in her stomach. And the knowledge that she had the power to arouse him lit a flame of need. Without much effort she conjured up an image of the two of them together, naked, bodies touching, searching. She let the dream wander freely through her mind and ease into her body.

"Damn it, Madeleine," Stephen growled seconds before he captured her mouth with his and pulled her hard against his body. A brief flash of triumph flared in her head but then it was gone, replaced by pounding desire. She didn't care how they'd gotten here. She sank her fingers into his hair and sucked on his questing tongue, drawing him deeper into her mouth. His large hands held her hips against his erection. She groaned.

Arousal flowed through her, into him and back. Each wave building on the other. She lost all awareness but

Stephen. His desire spiraled through her body like a trail of hot smoke, sinking into the tiny crevices. She had to have him. *Now.* She stepped back and brought him to her. The cool door of a car supported her from behind as his weight pressed down on her. *Yes, now.* Her hands moved to the long line of buttons on his shirt.

Alarms went off.

Real alarms.

Whoop. Whoop. Whoop. "Alert. Please step away from the vehicle." The mechanical voice filled the parking lot. "Alert. Please step away from the vehicle."

Stephen pulled her away. The car alarm continued to whoop in the distance, but Madeleine barely heard it. Breath seemed almost impossible to find as she stared at him. He wasn't gasping like she was, but the taut line of his back, the stretched press of his shoulders, told her he faced the same desire.

Oh my God, we almost made love in a parking lot.

"Yes," Stephen answered her unspoken statement.

"You can read my mind," she accused, latching onto anger to replace the arousal.

"No, darling, you're transmitting. I'm just receiving."

"But you can talk to me in my head."

"Yes. I can transmit thoughts."

"But how—?"

"I have no idea, but for some reason, I'm getting your thoughts."

"All of them?"

"No. Just the sexual ones." The smile was obvious in his voice. "So if you could please keep your mind off sex for the next hour or so, I'd appreciate it."

Her eyes popped open. Wide. And she was sure she saw Stephen smile before he turned away. She glared at his back but raced to catch up. She didn't want to be alone in this place.

Noise and smoke swamped her senses as they stepped

inside. She stopped, too deafened to walk farther. Stephen came back and took her hand. She had no choice but to follow. Voices shouted in conversations mixed with the music pounding from the speakers, bringing the noise up to almost unbearable levels.

A waitress stepped in front of Stephen, pausing to smile up at him.

"Hi, Stephen. I've missed you. It's good to see you again." The woman's red, ready-to-pout lips seemed to make promises Madeleine had no intention of letting her keep.

Madeleine stepped to Stephen's side, making sure their clasped hands were visible. "You're hallucinating, honey. He's not really here." The waitress glared at Madeleine with eyes so blue they had to be contact-lens-enhanced. Madeleine refused to back down. She stared back at her until the waitress lowered her gaze and walked away.

"I take it Blue Eyes is a friend of yours," Madeleine asked casually.

"Not anymore."

A path cleared in front of them as they moved past the dance floor, through an open arch, and around a corner. The sound dropped away to a conversation level. Madeleine shook her head, clearing the throbbing away. Tables lit with votive candles in glass holders were scattered around the room. A couple talked quietly in the corner, their heads bent together, hands touching on top of the table's wooden surface.

"What is this place?" she finally asked.

"A club," Stephen said, surveying the room. "It's Gayle's."

She looked out at the crowd. "And most of them aren't human, are they?"

"It's a mix."

"It's a hunting ground."

"Yes."

After a moment, he moved on, leading her into a dimly lit corner. Gayle and Nick waited. Nick's arms were folded tightly across his chest while Gayle stood draped against the wall, a smug, seductive glow on his face. Nick's eyes looked wild with the urge to run.

"I didn't do anything," Gayle defended before Stephen even asked. "We were just talking. It's the rest of the room that's freaking out your little friend."

"I need to go speak with Thomass. Watch them." Gayle, Nick, and Madeleine all opened their mouths to protest, but Stephen walked away before any of them could get the words out.

"Oh, great." Gayle stepped up to the edge that looked out over the crowd. "He's going to tear my place up."

Madeleine watched Stephen move through the crowd. Bodies slid away as he neared. She didn't need to see the look on his face to know that the anger had returned.

Stephen stopped in front of a table full of people. Madeleine couldn't hear what was being said, but six people at the table stood and hurried away. Only one remained.

Madeleine didn't recognize him. Even seated she could tell he was tall—probably taller than Stephen. He wore his hair cropped short. It seemed to accentuate the softness of his face. He was handsome but not intriguing. Madeleine had learned that she had a thing for power. Stephen had a power that came from inside. This man was weak. But smiling.

He looked up at Stephen and greeted him. The greeting seemed to have no impact on Stephen's mood. His hand shot out, and he grabbed the taller man by the throat and began lifting him from the chair. People at the surrounding tables turned to watch—a blend of curiosity and fear marked their faces.

"I'd be less concerned about your bar and more concerned about your patrons," Madeleine said. Gayle looked at her. She nodded toward Stephen.

Gayle started down the steps but stopped himself. The mocking light in his eyes was gone. She could see his indecision. He didn't know who to protect.

"We'll be fine." Madeleine ran her fingers over the dagger in her back pocket and touched the chains at her neck. "You should help Stephen."

Gayle followed the trail of her hand across the necklaces she wore and nodded. "Okay. I'll go deal with that. Stay here and try to stay out of sight."

Madeleine nodded and took a step closer to Nick. She didn't know what was going on, but it didn't look good. Even by human standards, it didn't look good, and she'd seen firsthand the exponential difference between human and vampire trouble.

***

Stephen felt the satisfaction of his fingers digging into Thomass' throat. He couldn't kill the other vampire this way, but he knew how painful the experience was.

"Stephen—"

He choked off the beginning of Thomass' protest.

"I told you she belongs to me. Do you understand what that means? She's mine."

"I can explain."

"I'm really not in the mood to talk. Can you tell?" He heard the drop in noise level in the bar as conversations stopped and patrons began to listen. For once he didn't care. Gayle would be pissed. Let him be pissed. Thomass had gone after Madeleine.

"I had to. The Council—"

"The Council agreed that I would deal with her."

"They—they—"

Stephen knew he wasn't giving him enough air to speak. He didn't care. It felt good to crush something.

"Stephen, put him down. The entire room is watching."

He ignored Gayle's command. The rage that had boiled

up inside him in the alley had momentarily faltered in Madeleine's presence. Seeing Thomass and his smug smile, it all came back to him—the fury at realizing someone had come after Madeleine. He pulled on Thomass' neck.

"Damn."

Stephen looked up at Gayle's whispered curse. After a moment, he followed his friend's gaze. Right back to Madeleine.

And Matthias.

The older vampire lounged next to Madeleine, partially hiding her from Stephen's view. Thomass was forgotten. Stephen dropped him and tensed, preparing to jump the forty-foot distance to Madeleine. Gayle's hand stopped him.

"Too many people watching."

Stephen growled. Gayle was right. The fiction had to be maintained. He pushed through the crowd, his eyes focused on Madeleine. She wasn't looking at him. She was staring at Matthias. Her eyes were squinted into a tight glare as she listened to him.

Matthias placed his hand on Madeleine's shoulder. She paused for a moment, as if dazed, then shook it off. Stephen was almost to her. Seconds before he reached her side, Matthias reached for her again. Madeleine wrapped her arm around her back and then jerked it forward.

Silver glinted in her hand as she held a silver dagger up to Matthias' throat. The older vampire froze. If Stephen hadn't been so terrified, he might have laughed. He'd rarely seen Matthias bested. And never by a human.

But he couldn't find the humor tonight. Shock flooded the crowded room. The world was watching. Stephen, Gayle, and Thomass, who'd followed them, stepped onto the raised level and surrounded Madeleine and Matthias.

She didn't know what she'd done. She'd condemned them both.

"Maddie, put the knife down."

Her hand didn't waver. "It's him. He's the one who's been whispering in my head. All week long I've been hearing this voice, and it's his!"

She'd never mentioned voices in her head. "I'll deal with it. Put down the knife."

The warning in Stephen's voice penetrated her anger, and she drew the knife back. When it had moved an inch from Matthias' chest, the old vampire stepped away and launched himself at Stephen.

Madeleine watched as the dark vampire lunged for Stephen and she reacted instinctively. She stepped between them. Their bodies clashed. Matthias' roar ripped through the air as her dagger slashed across his thigh. Stephen placed his hands on Madeleine's shoulders and picked her up. As he swung out at the vampire in front of him, he spun around and set her behind him. The crush of bodies couldn't be stopped.

Amid the swirl of fists, fangs glistened and long fingernails raked across flesh. A heavy body slammed into her, knocking her into the wall. The air left her lungs and a sharp pain tore through her side. Madeleine crumpled to the floor and the knife fell from her fingers. Almost instantly she was lifted into someone's arms. She saw a flash of blond and realized it was Gayle who carried her. He stood her on the floor away from the tangle of bodies. Madeleine hunched over, trying to catch her breath.

She watched Gayle plunge back into the fight and step into a punch meant for Stephen. Gayle pushed another vampire away. "Stephen, get her out of here," Gayle ordered, shoving Stephen in her direction. Stephen paused and looked into the crowd. "I'll take care of Nick. It's you and her they'll be hunting. Go."

Stephen's strong, familiar hand wrapped around her wrist and started to pull her away. A flash of silver caught her attention. She bent down and snagged the blood-coated silver dagger.

Blood. Where did the blood come from?

She raced behind Stephen, struggling to keep up.

They burst out into the parking lot. The small crowds had formed into larger groups. All watching them. Word traveled quickly. The crowds started toward them.

Stephen stopped and turned around.

"Are you okay?" she asked as Stephen reached for her. Blood poured from four matching scratches down the length of his neck, red glowing as black in the dim light.

He nodded. "You?"

She returned his nod and held up the knife. "But someone's bleeding."

"Hold on," he commanded. He lifted her in his arms and the world began to spin. Lights glittered and streaked across the sky. She knew they were traveling but couldn't feel the movement. And then they stopped.

The club was gone. They were on a deserted street.

Stephen set her down and took off walking, pulling Madeleine behind him. Madeleine couldn't seem to catch her breath as she stumbled behind him. Fear and adrenaline drained the strength from her legs.

"What just happened?" Her words struggled with her body's need for oxygen.

"Half the Vampire Community saw you with a silver dagger."

"So?"

Stephen stopped and looked down at her. "Four vampires have been killed by silver daggers just like that one."

She stared at the knife in her hand. Blood dripped from its blade. Stephen propelled her forward. "But I didn't do it." It was the only protest her fuzzy thoughts could form.

"I know that and you know that."

"So we tell them that."

"They won't believe it."

"Why not?"

"Because you're with me. And until you came on the scene flashing a silver knife, I was their best suspect."

"Why do they think you did it?"

"The vampires who died were members of the ruling Council. We don't exactly get on."

"Why not?"

"Because they made me." She shook her head, not understanding, and he explained, "They converted me as revenge against my father."

"Your father?" She took a deep breath and fought the blurring edges of her mind. Something was wrong. Dizziness assaulted her, and she blinked her eyes to get rid of it.

"He was a vampire slayer."

Madeleine jerked to a stop. "What?"

"He used to hunt vampires and kill them—with knives just like that."

Even through her fogged senses she knew the truth—what better revenge against a vampire hunter than to convert his son?

"Oh my God."

"Yes."

He turned and stalked off down the alley.

Pain radiated from her side like a stitch from running too much. She was about to call to Stephen and tell him to stop for a moment when he stepped onto the street.

He looked left and right. The dark road was silent, but she knew she couldn't accept what her senses told her. It wasn't safe.

"I'm going to take you home. You get inside and stay inside until sunup, and then you get the hell out of the city. Don't tell anyone where you're going. Just go."

"I'm not going to be run out of my life, out of my home. It isn't much but it is mine."

Her legs wobbled like springs.

Stephen spun around. Madeleine stepped back at the

fire in his eyes. "These aren't some garden-variety thugs that are threatening you. They're vampires."

"I thought they couldn't get into my house at night. I should be safe."

"Madeleine, if they rip the front wall off the building, I don't think your home's protection is going to work."

She was sure he was trying to scare her, and it was working. Protests were slow in forming in her mind. All thoughts seemed slow in her mind. Pride tightened her jaw, and she shook her head.

"No, I'm not—"

The bright light in Stephen's eyes swirled in front of her face.

"Madeleine?" His voice was distant, not inside her head, but really far away. Like down a dark tunnel.

"I don't feel so good," she whispered.

And her world faded to black.

***

Madeleine sank gracefully to the ground. Stephen snagged her just before impact. Energy pumped through his own body.

"Maddie? Oh my God." He listened. Her heartbeat stuttered in his ears. He hadn't been paying attention. His mind had been filled with escape and rescue. Getting her away.

He laid her on the ground and ripped the edges of her jacket open. The sweet smell of blood reached him. Red flooded her T-shirt.

She'd been stabbed. He looked at the knife in her hand. Blood on the blade. The fight. Somehow she'd gotten in front of her own knife. Or someone had forced it into her.

He hadn't noticed—he'd been so focused on getting her clear, he hadn't been listening for the subtle changes in her heartbeat. He could hear it now, and smell her blood. Damn, why hadn't he noticed? God, he was too late.

Her heart slowed, but the wound still seeped.

Stephen watched her life force flow from her body, the reality of what he'd done slamming into him. He'd killed her. He'd finally killed her. He pushed her hair back, away from her face. She was dying, and it was his fault.

Damn it. He hadn't wanted this.

Mixed with the truth was the painful cry of possession. She belonged to him. And he was going to lose her.

Two hundred years alone. Two hundred years of crushing human emotions and learning to be content with what he'd become.

Then she'd entered his life. All the human feelings, irritating as they were, had returned.

And now he was going to lose her. The warm memory of making love to Madeleine settled on him—never to experience that again.

He couldn't do it. He couldn't face another eternity alone.

An instinct stronger than self-preservation screamed through his soul. He bent low over her and placed his mouth against her throat. The normally steady beat of her pulse was gone, turned erratic and struggling. He opened his mouth and pierced her skin with his teeth. The familiar rush of pleasure surged through him, but he stopped it. After a single taste he lifted his head.

Blood already flowed from the wounds on his neck.

He crushed the better angels in his head. *Solitude for two hundred years.*

He wasn't going to lose her. She was his.

He lifted her mouth to his throat and silently willed her to drink.

Her lips opened against his skin and a few drops fell freely onto her tongue. It was enough. Her body reacted— lost in its own death, it clung to its one chance for survival. Her lips closed around the wound, and she began to drink, pulling his life into her body.

Ecstasy roared through him. As if her soul were

floating free, he captured it and held it. Her spirit sank into him. They merged through flashes of light and sparks of color. Her heart pounded in his chest. His thudded into hers, increasing the beat, strengthening her.

"Stephen. No!"

Pain ripped through him as the cry tore him away from Madeleine. His head snapped up. Nicholas stood in the alley. Fury flashed in his eyes.

Stephen looked down at Madeleine, stretched out in his arms. Her eyes were shut, but her heart beat stronger than it had before.

Oh my God. What have I done?

He blinked, trying to clear his eyes and his memory. Caught in the threat of losing her, he'd done the unthinkable. He'd done to her what had been done to him.

Stephen pushed himself to his knees, still staring at the fallen body. *Oh my God.*

"Stephen?"

He couldn't face Nicholas. Not after what he'd done.

"Take care of her." Revulsion, a self-hatred beyond pain, pierced Stephen's heart. "Take care of her," he commanded again, stumbling to his feet and running from Madeleine.

From the vampire he'd just created.

Twelve

Sunlight stabbed her eyes through closed lids, dragging her from sleep. Madeleine groaned, draped her arm over her eyes, and tried to drift off. God, she was tired. Her entire body ached as if she'd been slammed against a brick wall a few dozen times.

"Madeleine, are you awake?"

"Ahh!" She reacted, throwing herself across the bed, away from the voice. She fell off the mattress and landed with a thump on the floor.

"Are you okay?"

She blinked and opened her eyes. Nick's concerned face filled the space in front of her.

"Ahh!" she repeated, jerking back. "What the hell are you doing here?" She glanced around to make sure she was in her own house. She was. But what the hell was *he* doing there? "I thought you couldn't enter someone's house without an invitation."

"That really only works with full vampires." He backed up and leaned against the window ledge. "I just didn't think you should get in the habit of inviting anyone in."

Her mind was still a little cloudy from the night before, as if she'd been on a weeklong drunk, but that seemed to make some sense. The aches in her body invited caution as she slowly pressed to standing. She rested her legs against the side of the bed, using it for support. Exhaustion dragged her down. God, she needed more sleep.

Get the hell out of the city. Stephen's warning flashed through her foggy thoughts. He'd told her to get out of town and then he'd...

The rest was a blur, blackness and strange colors swirling through her head.

She licked her lips. A strange taste lingered on her tongue—sweet and exotic.

T. L. Sinclare

"What time is it?"

"Four o'clock."

"In the afternoon?" She looked down at her bed as if it had cast some spell. "I slept until four in the afternoon?"

"Yes." Nick pushed away from the wall and walked toward her. "Madeleine, you have to—"

Her scream stopped whatever he was going to say.

Madeleine stared down at her T-shirt. What used to be a white T-shirt was red—or mostly red.

"What happened? Did someone get hurt?" She tried to remember. They'd been at Death's Door and there was a fight. The memory came to her in flashes connected by dark empty spaces—claws and nails reaching across the dimly lit space, white fangs, growls of frustration. And a sharp pain in her side.

Madeleine put her hand against her rib cage, the memory as piercing as a knife.

A tiny tear in the fabric of her shirt stopped her exploring fingers.

She'd been stabbed. It came back to her. She'd been bleeding, walking after Stephen, his command to leave town.

"What happened? I was bleeding. This is my blood, isn't it?" She pulled the shirt out of the way. "Where's the wound?" She looked up at Nick, not wanting the answer she knew he would give her. "Why isn't there a wound? What happened?"

"Madeleine, don't you get it? Don't you remember?" Nick paused. The anguish in his voice blew cold chills across her skin. He drew in a deep breath. "Stephen turned you into a vampire."

She forced herself to laugh. It had to be a joke. A bad joke. The reality was too much to comprehend. "Funny, I don't feel the need to drink blood."

"You will." Nick didn't smile. Agony wracked his face, an absolute need gripping his body. He looked tired again, as if he was being dragged down, pulled to the earth by a force stronger than gravity.

"Nick, what's going on?"

"He turned you into a vampire. In that alley last night. When you were lying there. Don't you remember?" She shook her head, but it wasn't just in answer to his question. It was also to deny the spark of memory. Something was there—a moment, a connection, something so wildly outrageous, so deeply intimate it couldn't be true.

"He gave you some of his blood. You drank from him."

She sank slowly onto the bed, her legs weakening, the memory coming to her more clearly now. The strange sensation of having Stephen inside her—not in a sexual sense, but in a way beyond physical, inside her mind and her heart, capturing all the tiny corners of emptiness and filling them with himself. And of her sharing herself, filling him.

He was still with her. She could feel him, despite the presence of the sun, despite their separation. It was insane. She shook her head again.

"If I'm a vampire, why am I out in daylight? Shouldn't I be sleeping in a coffin somewhere?" She sounded snide and bitchy, but she couldn't make herself stop.

"You're like I am." He shrugged. "A half-vampire."

"This is like being a little bit pregnant, isn't it?" She stood up and started to walk. Finally, she turned and faced Nick. "How did it happen? *Why* did it happen?"

He shook his head. "It doesn't matter why."

"You know, people have been telling me that a lot lately—that the reasons don't matter. Well, it does matter."

"Madeleine, it's done."

"Then it can be undone."

"It can't." Nick placed his hand on her arm and squeezed gently. "Madeleine, listen to me. You were there, bleeding in the alley. Dying. And Stephen helped you—"

She jerked free of his grip and his attempt at comfort.

Her mind circled with a mixture of reality, dreams, and terror. "Helped me?"

"He gave you some of his blood. It healed you."

"And it turned me into a vampire!"

"Yes."

Her arms instinctively wrapped themselves around her stomach. She didn't want to believe it. She couldn't believe it, but that didn't stop her from asking the question. "What happens now?"

"You'll start noticing some changes. Soon. You'll be stronger, more sensitive to light. The hunger won't come for a few weeks, but then it hits and it gets stronger."

She tried to turn away. She didn't want to hear this, but Nick said, "Madeleine, I'm not saying this to scare you, but you have to know. You can fight it for a while, but—" He gripped the corner post of her bed. His knuckles turned white as he held the sturdy wood. "He'll probably start urging you to make the final conversion."

"How's that done?" She vaguely remembered them talking about this before.

"There are two ways. If you die, you'll wake up a vampire. You didn't actually die last night. If you'd been a little farther gone, you might have. Instead, Stephen's blood healed you."

"So, if I get hit by a car and die—it's instant vampire."

Nick nodded. "It usually doesn't happen that way. Most take matters into their own hands and kill someone."

Then she remembered what he'd told her before. The first kill. She was supposed to have been his.

"You'll stay a half-vampire until you make your first kill." His voice dropped low. "Until you do, the hunger just gets worse. Stephen can help for a while. He's helped me, but eventually it's going to happen."

The band around her heart tightened for a moment. *Oh my God.* It was too much to take in. She leaned against the windowsill. *A vampire?* She was going to turn into a vampire?

The logical portion of her mind couldn't grasp the unbelievable—couldn't form it into a concept she could handle. Reality had disappeared.

She finally lifted her eyes. "Why haven't you done it?" she accused, wanting to release some of the anger, focus it in some direction. She pushed away from the window and stalked across the room. "If you know it's inevitable, why didn't you kill me that night at Stephen's?"

Nick's jaw tightened. With anger or restraint, she didn't know. Finally he smiled. It was a sad, self-mocking smile.

"I guess I haven't given up hope."

The smile fell from his lips and he turned away.

"Nick, wait."

"I need to go." He didn't stop.

"I'm sorry, Nick," she called after him, regretting her snide comments. He'd been kind to her. She was even willing to call him a friend. And she'd chased him away.

"Talk to Stephen," was all he said as he left.

The door closed behind him with a quiet click. She stared at the space he'd vacated.

She slowly began to pace the room. The movement seemed to help. The aches and pains she'd felt on awakening had faded quickly, leaving her feeling strong, energetic. She thought about what Nick had said. Was she actually changing already? Or was it just her normal body?

She didn't know how long she walked. The fact that she was covering the same ten feet of ground didn't matter—she didn't see the world around her. She wandered in a daze of confusion, fury, and moments of abject terror.

A ring broke the deep silence.

She flinched and stared at the phone, but she let it ring. The answering machine picked up and Scott's voice filled the room. "Madeleine? If you're there, pick up."

She dismissed his plea. There was enough running around her brain. She couldn't handle any more.

"I'm going to keep calling until I reach you, so you'd best pick up."

Scott was tenacious. That's what made him a good cop. She lifted the phone.

"Hi, Scott."

"What the hell was that last night?" he said by way of greeting. "You call me for help, and then you go running off when I get there?" He sounded wired.

"Scott..."

"And what were you doing with *him*? One week you think he's a vampire, and the next you go clubbing with him?"

"Scott, it wasn't like that." Madeleine rubbed her hand over her eyes. She couldn't deal with this right now. She had too much happening. And she couldn't bring him into it. One of her friends had already been hurt. "Thanks for coming last night. Char's fine." *I think.* "Sorry for calling." She started to hang up, but Scott's voice stopped her.

"We think we've found the murder weapon."

Madeleine's hand tightened around the phone.

"Danielle's? How?"

"I got a lucky break last night after you ran off. A tip. And it led me to the weapon."

"And?" she encouraged, her beleaguered mind content to focus on something concrete.

"Knife, of course, but we knew that. It looks like a fairly expensive knife. It looks like it's made of pure silver."

"A silver dagger?" Her words were hollow and sounded surprisingly calm.

"Yeah."

"Etched designs on the blade?"

Silence met her on the other end of the line. "How did you know that?"

She gave a quick, humorless laugh. "Lucky guess."

"Dammit, who's passing this information on to you?"

Madeleine shook her head, ignoring Scott's rant. She

had too much to think about. Danielle had been killed with one of Stephen's knives. Stephen? Madeleine rejected the idea as soon as it came to mind. Vampires couldn't touch silver. She'd seen that last night. But who was using Stephen's knives? He'd said someone had killed other vampires with the knives. That same person had killed Danielle.

"I need to go."

"Madeleine. Stay out of this."

"I can't."

"Then at least be careful."

"I know what I'm getting into, Scott."

"I'm sure that's what Danielle thought."

An invisible fist punched into Madeleine's stomach. *Oh, God. He's right. This is what Danielle had thought.* Damn, she'd had almost the exact same conversation with Danielle a few days before she disappeared.

"I have to go." Madeleine dropped the phone back on the cradle without hearing if Scott answered and stumbled to the mirror. Her pale skin glowed against the hideous brown wallpaper that lined the bathroom. *Danielle.* Danielle had been pale and exhausted. She'd been evasive, even surly, toward the end.

Fire roiled in the center of Madeleine's stomach. She should have been swearing, cursing Stephen's name, but no sound would come out. She couldn't think. Nothing settled in her mind. Betrayal coursed through her blood.

It was so obvious. She didn't know why she hadn't realized it before. She knew Danielle had been stabbed and that someone in Stephen's crowd was responsible. But this?

Danielle had been converted. And then someone killed her with a silver dagger.

***

The light faded, releasing Stephen from the bonds that held him. As always, his mind woke moments before his body was able to react.

Madeleine.

She was the first thought on his mind, just as she'd
been since he'd first met her. Tonight, however, it stronger
than ever.

Madeleine.

She felt near. Impossible.

Or it should have been impossible. The flood of
memory from the night before awakened his heart. Had
she survived? Had he converted her? Conversion was a
chancy proposition. In the two hundred years since his
own change, he could find no one who could explain why
it worked sometimes and why it didn't others. Had he left
her dying in that alley? Or worse, had he turned her into a
creature like himself?

Life returned to his body and he allowed himself the
pleasure of his quickening senses.

Madeleine.

Her scent reached him. She *was* here. Near him.

He opened his eyes and stared up. The lid to his coffin
was open and the space above him was filled with
Madeleine.

The silver dagger she'd used last night was gripped
tightly in her right hand, and she held it an inch from his
chest. Fire flashed in her eyes.

Well, she'd survived, and she was converted. The
changes had already started, her heartbeat subtly different.
More would follow. A stab of regret he couldn't control
pierced his soul. He'd done this to her. The overwhelming
self-disgust he'd felt when he'd realized what he'd done
faded to a grim resolve.

He wouldn't do it to her, couldn't do it to any creature,
and there was only one way out. For both of them.

"Good evening, Madeleine." He tried to sound casual,
even bored. He saw he was successful when her eyes
widened, and the knifepoint moved a fraction closer to his

chest.

She was almost mad enough to kill. Almost. It was too bad, really. A lot would be solved if she'd use the knife for its proscribed purpose. Fear and affection mixed with her rage, confusing her. No, Madeleine couldn't kill him in cold blood.

"I want answers."

He nodded, keeping his eyes trained on the dagger. "Move the knife, and we'll talk."

"We can talk here. Who killed Danielle? And don't tell me it doesn't matter. She was killed by one of these knives, so that means she was killed by a human—a human who can be punished."

She had a lot of faith in the knife she held. She'd seen its power last night. She just didn't know the truth.

"Move the knife, Madeleine."

"No."

He gave her no warning. Moving at a speed her human eyes couldn't detect, he reached out and snatched the blade from her hand.

Madeleine backed away as he slowly climbed out of the coffin, her eyes locked on the dagger in his hand.

"You can touch silver."

"Yes."

"A vampire who can touch silver." It only took a moment for the truth to creep into her eyes. "You killed Danielle."

"Yes."

Madeleine's rage hit him moments before she physically landed against him, pounding at him with her fists. Stephen caught her, stilling her hands.

She jerked out of his grasp as if she couldn't bear his touch. "Why?" Her eyes glittered with tears. Tears of rage and betrayal. Stephen shook his head. He'd done what he had to do. Madeleine would never understand.

"I have a right to know. She was my cousin."

"She ceased being your cousin when she was converted."

"And then you killed her?" she accused.

She wanted the whole story, but he knew the explanation wouldn't provide the comfort or closure she sought. "I had to."

"Why?"

"She was a danger to the Community."

"All vampires are a danger to the community."

"*My* Community. Something had gone wrong in her conversion." He found himself making the explanation he swore he wouldn't give. He hated telling her this, hated the image it was going to leave with her, but he needed it. Needed her to understand just a little. "She was uncontrollable. She couldn't stop feeding. She killed three people in one night, and she would have done more if she hadn't been stopped. We have to protect ourselves."

Madeleine leaned against the table as the information hit her like a physical blow. She wrapped her arms around her waist, completely closing herself to him. What did it matter? He couldn't offer her the comfort she needed. He was the source of her pain.

She raised her eyes to him. "You're so set on protecting the Community, why haven't you killed me?"

"Oh, Maddie, I have. Your body just doesn't know it yet."

"Did you convert her?"

"Are you asking if I move through the city turning young women into vampires?" he mocked. He needed her anger, needed her strength. "No. You were my first."

Tears pooled in her eyes. "Why did you do it?"

He had no answer for her. Hell, he barely had one for himself. The moment of decision—if that's what it could be called—was a blur. Just the desperate need, the pain and fear of centuries of loneliness, and the desire to bind her to him for eternity.

"You can go back."

Her head snapped up. "What?"

"You can become human again."

Hope flared in her weary eyes, and Stephen knew it had to be done. He had to free Madeleine.

"Nick said nothing could be done."

"He doesn't know. It's not something we generally talk about."

"What do I have to do?"

"You can kill me."

"What?" Blood drained from her face, and he could see the beginning of her hope die.

"If I die before you make your first kill, you'll go back to being human. I don't think you've killed anyone today." He paused. "But the night is young."

He extended the dagger toward her, hilt first. He could touch silver but if it entered his blood, it would burn and kill him like any other vampire. Madeleine stared down at the knife. He'd offered her the implement of his death once before, and she'd refused. She'd learned so much since then.

He knew her response before she did, knew she wouldn't do it, but he wanted her to have the choice he'd never been given. If he'd been offered a silver dagger, he'd have decimated the Council. But Maddie didn't hate deeply enough.

"You can't be serious."

"I don't joke."

"I won't do it."

"Not even for justice?" he taunted, trying to push her past her human ideals. "Not even to kill the man who killed your cousin?"

She wrapped her fingers around the hilt of the knife. He waited. He wasn't afraid of his death. In reality, it would be peace. Nothing compared to the pain of watching Madeleine grow to hate him for what he'd done to her.

She shook her head.

"Think about it, Maddie. You'll become a creature like me. Is that what you want? Slowly starving for blood. You'll crave it. You'll need it. Can you do that?" He hated pushing her like this, but he needed her to understand—really understand—her choice. "Has Nicholas told you what it's like? He doesn't even know the truth yet. You'll need it to the point of madness."

When she didn't respond, he circled around her, whispering the harsh truth into her ear. "You'll kill then. It won't matter who. It won't matter where. The need will overcome you, and all that you've ever thought of yourself will fade."

Madeleine heard the pain in his voice, the misery behind his words, and sympathy crept in. She knew from the stark reality of his tone that he'd been through the torture he was predicting for her.

"What did they do to you?"

He stared at the wall behind her head as if he was trying to decide what to tell her. His voice was dead when he finally spoke. "They converted me, and when I refused to feed, they locked me in a cage—"

"Until you were mad with hunger," she finished for him. There was something else. Something more. "Who did you—"

He looked into her eyes. And Madeleine felt her heart stop as he said, "My father."

"Oh my God." She stared at him with a mixture of horror and pity.

"That's what you have to look forward to." He pointed the blade toward his chest. "Do it."

She bit her front teeth together. "No."

The tears that threatened now escaped and poured down her cheeks.

"No." She shook her head and threw the dagger away. It tumbled onto the stone floor with a metallic clank.

Stephen nodded. He trailed his fingers along the edge of her jaw. The soft touch soothed her for a moment.

He walked to the door and looked at her. "Good-bye, Maddie."

And he was gone.

Madeleine stared at the vault door as it swung shut.

He's leaving? Now?

Dazed, she looked at the empty room. He'd left her alone. It was probably best. She needed a few minutes to take it all in. *Danielle. Vampires. Conversion.* Her gaze dropped to the silver dagger. *Kill Stephen.* She had to kill Stephen in order to become human again. She couldn't do it. And he couldn't ask it of her.

He'd killed Danielle.

Alone, she allowed the truth to sink in. Had she known before? Had she ignored the truth?

He'd lied to her. She'd asked him directly if he'd killed Danielle, and he'd said no.

Well, he wasn't walking away from her now. They were going to talk about this.

She stalked to the vault door, grabbed the handle, and cranked it left. It stuck. She turned it right. It stayed.

He'd locked her in.

***

Metal scraping against metal snapped Madeleine from her doze. Instinctively, she grabbed the silver dagger that lay by her knees and jumped to her feet. Stephen was back, and they were going to have this out. In eight hours of being locked in the dimly lit room, she'd considered changing her mind about killing Stephen.

The heavy metal door slowly swung open. The space in the door frame was empty. Madeleine clutched the knife and growled.

"Madeleine?" Nick's hesitant voice called from the hall, obviously staying out of her range until he'd identified himself. "Stephen told me to come let you out, and then help you get out of town."

"Where is he?" she bit out when he stepped into the doorway.

Nick shook his head. "Madeleine..."

"Where is he?"

"They've got him."

All thoughts of revenge and battles were gone. Sure, she might want to kill Stephen, but *she* wanted to be the one to do it. No one else was going to touch him. Eight hours spent in the tiny vault—thank goodness it was equipped with a sink and bathroom—had given her time to think. She was still mad, but hours of walking in a circle had burned away most of her rage.

"*Who* has him?"

"The Council. Someone's been killing vampires, and they think it's Stephen."

"No." She stared at the silver dagger in her hand. "Stephen might hate them, but he'd never do anything to hurt the Community."

"He confessed."

"What?" Madeleine felt her jaw sag open. "Why? Oh God. He's doing it to protect me." She grabbed her discarded jacket and headed toward the door.

"You?"

"If he dies before my first kill, I'll go back to being human."

She hurried past Nick, headed for the door, and was jerked to a sudden stop by his grip on her arm.

"Explain that." The flash of fury she saw in his eyes was counteracted by a glimmer of hope. She quickly explained what Stephen had told her.

"I could go back to being human?"

She stopped. She needed Nick's assistance. She couldn't have him working against her. "Stephen didn't convert you, did he?"

"No. They just dumped me on Stephen's back porch

one day and he took me in."

The calculated image Stephen portrayed blended and smoothed with the reality. He hadn't killed her. He hadn't eliminated Nick, even though he could. He was a noble man—with fangs.

"Where is he?"

"Madeleine, you don't want to do this. If what you've told me is true, you're free."

This was her way out. She just had to let Stephen die. The silent cry of her heart drowned out the logic. She shook her head. "I can't let anything happen to him."

"You're in love with him." Nick sighed, and before she could respond, he said, "Okay, we've got work to do because Gayle warned *me* to hide out for the next few days. They're going to stake Stephen and leave him for the sun, and then they're going to go looking for his friends."

"That's us." Madeleine raced up the stairs with Nick following close behind. "Grab those curtains." She indicated the heavy coverings in Stephen's living-room windows. Blackout curtains. A home decorating requirement for any vampire. She made a half-joking mental note to get some for herself. The thought allowed a whole host of others to enter her mind, encouraging the panic that had threatened all night. She forced it aside. She didn't have time.

Stephen. She had to focus on Stephen. She couldn't let him sacrifice himself.

"Madeleine, we can't fight an entire group of vampires."

She used the dagger to slice through the material to pull the drapes down.

"We don't have to. They're leaving him for the sun."

"So, you're saying we just have to sneak up on a group of vampires, wait them out, and then beat the sunrise."

Put that bluntly, it sounded harder than she'd originally

thought.

"That's my plan."

***

The sun was almost up when Nick pointed to a small hill just outside of town. *Private property.* They were trespassing on vampire land.

Madeleine inched the car forward, hoping without hope that the crackle of the tires along the gravel road would go unnoticed. It wasn't much noise, and with the headlights turned off it might have been missed by a human, but never by a vampire. Every sound was probably being monitored. Her only hope was that they'd decided to seek cover with the onset of daylight.

They were in another of Stephen's cars—a convertible. They'd opened the garage door and she'd been stunned for the third time that evening. Stephen had *five* cars inside the garage. She'd wanted to take the Jag, but the convertible had the largest trunk.

Madeleine squinted through the darkness up the hill. In the coming day's pale light, she could make out a shadow on the slope.

"There he is."

"Let's go." Nick opened his door and started to climb out.

"Wait." Madeleine stopped him with her hand. "Isn't it strange that they'd just leave him here with no one watching?"

"Very good, Madeleine." She tensed at the eerily familiar voice. The voice that was constantly muttering in her head.

"Matthias."

The vampire stepped out of the darkness and strolled toward the car. "I've been waiting for you."

"Me?"

"I've been in your head for days. I knew you couldn't resist trying to save him. I volunteered to stay behind and make sure Stephen's little human friend didn't show up. They'll be pleased to know I meted out your punishment as well." He shook his head. "You shouldn't piss off vampires, Madeleine. We're a testy lot as it is."

"I didn't do anything, and neither did Stephen. Someone else is killing your people."

He stared at her for a long moment. "You actually believe that? Ah, well, even if he didn't do it, it will be my pleasure to see him die. Right after you."

Blood pounded in her skull. "Why?"

Despite Nick's convulsive grip on her arm, Madeleine opened the door and jumped out, confronting the danger when her instincts told her to run. She jammed her fists on her hips and faced the angry vampire.

Maddie, no! Stephen's voice echoed in her head. She looked up the hill. The dark shape twisted, struggling against its bonds.

"Leave her alone!" Nick shouted.

Matthias held up his hand. "Sleep." Nick blinked and slumped backward against the seat, his eyes closing in a deep sleep.

"Now, where were we?"

"Why are you doing this? What have I ever done to you?"

"Oh, not you. Him." He tilted his head toward the slope, his voice filled with hatred. He stepped forward. She braced herself against the car and waited.

"Why?"

"The sins of the father." Madeleine shook her head. "He hasn't told you the story? I would have thought him proud of it. His father was a vampire slayer. Took us quite awhile to find him. Twenty of our Community were murdered before we caught him."

His father. She remembered the pain and self-disgust in Stephen's voice. They'd starved Stephen and used his father to torment him. Her fingers tightened on the hilt of the dagger she still carried.

"You guys converted Stephen and killed his father. That's your revenge."

"That was the Community's revenge. Mine is personal." Matthias stepped closer. Madeleine wanted to back away, but she was pressed against the car. "One of the vampires he killed was my mate." A look of ancient pain accompanied his cold words and tore at Madeleine's heart. "So now, I'll have the satisfaction of killing you and sending Stephen to hell with that knowledge."

Madeleine. Matthias' voice was back in her head. She tried to think of Stephen, use him as a buffer, but the call was too strong. *Look at me, Madeleine.*

Fighting him with all her strength, she felt her head lift, and her gaze met his. It was nothing like the connection she shared with Stephen. She was trapped but felt none of the safety, none of the passion. Matthias put his hands on her shoulders and pulled her forward. Like a rag doll, she flopped against him, her strength gone, her will crushed beneath his.

"Stephen," he whispered in her ear. "Watch, Stephen. It's time for your love to die."

No!

Stephen's scream echoed through her head.

She couldn't respond, couldn't move. She could only watch the pale light glitter off the long spikes of Matthias' fangs as they moved closer.

A whimper escaped as he pressed his open mouth against the base of her neck. She mentally tensed, waiting for the sharp stab of pain she knew would follow.

But it didn't come. Matthias' grip tightened on her arms for a moment, and then she was free. She sagged against the car and forced calming breaths through her lungs.

He stepped away and glared down at her.

"He's converted you," he accused. "Why the hell

would he do that?" He spun around and stared up the hillside. "Why would he do it?" he whispered almost to himself. "Damn."

"Does this mean you aren't going to kill me?"

"You're a vampire." He flung his arm to the side and snarled. "I can't kill another vampire." He tilted his head and stared at her, confusion still lining his face. "He converted you."

"Yes." She could see it happening—the revenge he'd plotted for two hundred years failing before his eyes. Stephen was dying. She was out of reach. "It's been two hundred years. That's kind of a long time to hold a grudge."

Matthias looked at Stephen then back to Madeleine. "Tell me that at the end of *your* life." He glared up the hill. "The sun will be up in moments. You'll never make it."

"I'm going to try."

Matthias nodded. The glittering light of revenge gone from his eyes, taking with it all fire, all life.

"Good night, Madeleine." And he faded away.

She stared in the silence, somehow saddened. Everything had been stripped away.

"Nick?" A soft snore came back to her. "Nick?" She punched his arm. His body rocked, but there was no response.

The first glimmer of the day's warmth brushed across her cheeks. She had to move. She popped the trunk and grabbed the curtains, pulling them behind her as she raced up the hill. The first shaft of direct light moved across the lawn with alarming speed, like ripples on the water.

She forced air into her tight lungs as she made it to the hill's midpoint. Stephen's arms were tight, cocked inward as he strained against the silver chains that held him. She felt the tension in her own arms—the burning wrists and the heat that enveloped his skin. His pain tore through her. She didn't understand. He could touch silver. Why did it hurt so badly? It made no sense, but the reflected pain slowed her movements.

His eyelids fluttered. They opened for an instant and snapped shut.

"No, Maddie…" His voice was soft and fading. "Let it go."

Her protest was instinctive.

"No," she growled through clenched teeth.

She tossed the heavy curtain over his body and knelt down to work free the bands that held his hands and feet. Stephen could touch silver, but for some reason he hadn't had the strength to break these chains. As the first band opened in her hand, she saw why. Tiny stab wounds circled his wrists from spikes on the inside of the band. Blood pooled in his palms.

Fury and sympathy threatened to overwhelm her. She crushed the emotions and concentrated on releasing the cuffs. A strange calm settled over her as she worked, her mind free from the panic that lurked at the edge of her consciousness. Finally, the last band opened. He was free, but they were still on the side of the hill.

She slipped his hand underneath the blackout curtain as a line of sunlight inched across the green grass toward them. She didn't know how it all worked—if any part of his body was touched by sun, would he die? Or was she too late? She couldn't deal with the future. She had to get Stephen to safety.

Madeleine slipped her hands under his arms, scooping the curtains under him to encircle his body, and dragged him down the hill. The sun was fully up by the time she'd managed to haul his body over the lip of the trunk and snap the lid closed.

Her chest rose and fell in tortured breaths as she rested. How the hell she'd managed to get a two-hundred-pound body down a hill and into a trunk she didn't know, but at least he was inside. *Out of the light, I have to get him completely out of the light.*

She drove to Stephen's house, circled around back, eased the car into the garage, and closed the door.

She considered leaving Stephen's body in the trunk but gagged at the idea. If she left him there, it would seem like he was just a body.

Appalled shivers moved over her skin in tiny waves. *Best not to think about it.*

Making sure he was fully covered, she pulled him through the house and down the stairs. Exhaustion hit her as she stepped inside the vault. She couldn't move him anymore. She dropped his shoulders and stood up.

The curtain still covered his body. She left it there. She couldn't bring herself to look at him.

With a sigh, she shut off the light and closed the door. Her legs wobbled as she climbed the stairs. She needed sleep but knew it was impossible.

They would come for Stephen once they realized he'd escaped.

She didn't know what the night would bring, but she had until sunset to make Stephen's house a fortress against the undead.

Thirteen

The sun was almost fully set, taking with it all trace of light and color. Whatever happened, it would be soon. The vampires would be waking and they'd be looking for Stephen. Madeleine paced the elegant carpet in the living room and hoped she was ready.

She took a deep breath and wrapped her arms around her stomach. Her day had started at sunrise, and it wasn't over. She'd borrowed Stephen's car and purchased supplies, using a credit card that now bulged near its limit. Then she'd spent the day fortifying the house.

She'd combined everything she'd learned from Stephen and Nick, library books, and the Internet—a mixture of reality, legend and Hollywood. If it was supposed to ward off vampires, she'd used it. Stephen's house looked like something out of Sleeping Beauty.

Rose stems, twisted around one another, formed thorny covers for the windows and doors. Madeleine had ruined two pairs of gloves braiding the stems and stapling them to the house. It was impossible to pass through any of the house's openings without running into a rose stem. Cloves of garlic and pouches of wolfsbane littered the windowsills and were interspersed through the rose thorns. Silver knives and forks were taped and glued to the insides of the windows, designed to scratch anyone who made it through the thorns. Garlic paste covered the doorknobs. If there was any truth to the legends, they were at least marginally safe. As long as they stayed inside.

All that was left was to check on Stephen and find out if she'd been in time.

Exhaustion lurked at the edges of her mind, threatening to overwhelm her. Her body ached from physical exertion. She'd monitored her body all day, watching for the changes Nick had predicted. She hadn't noticed any differences. Was it too soon? Or had she been freed? If Stephen had died from the sunlight, if she'd been too late, she was fully human again. And alone. She shivered.

The sun had set. It was time. If Stephen was alive, he'd be waking soon. The hand crank on the vault spun easily in her hand, and the door swung open. Stephen was somewhere in the darkness.

The adrenaline spike that had sustained her through the day was fading. Even the caffeine from her four cups of coffee was beginning to wane. All that remained was courage. And she didn't know how much she had left.

Gulping in a deep breath, she flicked on the light and listened to the silence.

"Stephen?" She kept her voice soft. No answer.

She stepped into the vault. The weak light barely illuminated the room. The curtains still covered him. He hadn't moved.

"Stephen?" She stopped directly over him and placed her hand on the cover. Taking a deep breath, she clutched it tight and waited. *One. Two. Three.* She jerked the curtain back.

Stephen lay still, silent, and pale.

She extended her hand toward him, trying to ignore the shaking in her limbs.

His eyes snapped open. Insanity stared up at her. The blue of his eyes was gone. Blood red stared back at her.

He snarled, mouth open, teeth bared, canines extended. Madeleine screamed and jumped back. Stephen sat up. His clawed hand shot out and latched onto her throat. The grip of his fingers slowly tightened.

She fought him with all of her remaining strength. Giving up was not an option. Too much had happened to end this here. She tore at his hands, prying her fingers underneath his grasp. She struggled against the unrelenting pull as he dragged her downward toward the piercing whiteness of his teeth. With a full swing, she kicked out and planted her tennis shoe against his breastbone. The force knocked him back. And she was free.

She spun away and bolted for the steps. Her legs shook and wouldn't listen to her panicked commands to run. She peddled up the stairs on hands and feet, her breath coming in tortured gasps.

Claws raked across her back.

"Aah!" She kicked out behind her. She didn't look back to see where she'd hit him, but she was once again free.

A sob of relief broke from her lips when she reached the door and slammed it shut behind her. She leaned her back against the wood while her shaking hands turned the bolt in place.

A heavy thud hit the other side of the door. She jumped back and stared at it, waiting for Stephen to break through. An erratic thumping beat against the wall.

My God, what happened to him? She waited, listening as the pounding subsided. A howl reverberated through the door and pierced her soul. Madeleine closed her eyes and pressed her fingers to the wood.

She sensed him on the other side. They stood in silence.

"I'm sorry, Stephen," she whispered and backed away from the door.

Moments later, she heard heavy footfalls on the steps as he went back down the stairs.

She stabbed her fingers through her hair and paced across the living room, the ache in her throat a continued reminder of Stephen's fall from sanity. This was the one scenario she hadn't imagined. She'd figured he would either be alive or dead, but never insane. *I can't handle an insane human, let alone a crazed vampire.*

There was only one source of help for this—another vampire. Nick would be no help. Not against a crazed Stephen. She needed a vampire.

Damn. First they're everywhere, now I can't find one when I need them.

Nick was still asleep in the garage. She hadn't moved him after they'd returned home. She'd checked on him several times, but the exhaustion she'd seen him battle seemed to have won.

She walked the length of the living room. She hadn't had time to replace the curtains, but the vines and silver blocked peeping eyes—human eyes at least. She needed help, but how was she supposed to find any of the others? Look in the phone book under "vampires?" She smiled then stopped. Stephen probably had speed dial. Madeleine picked up the cordless phone and hit the first speed dial number. It rang twice.

"This can't be Stephen, so who the hell is it?"

She recognized the voice—Gayle—though none of the flirtation and teasing remained.

"Madeleine? Is that you?"

Gayle had declared himself Stephen's only friend. Madeleine clenched her hands into indecisive fists. She would be trusting him with Stephen's life. She had to trust someone. She couldn't handle Stephen alone.

"Yes."

"What's going on? Why are you at Stephen's house?"

How did he—? Then she realized he probably had caller ID. She wasn't going to be able to hide. But she also wasn't going to give him any warning. "I need your help. I need you over here."

"Why?"

She thought about Stephen and his attitude. He didn't ask—he commanded. "Just get over here. Now." She hung up the phone before Gayle could respond. *That will get him here.*

Seconds later the phone rang and the caller ID flashed *Gayle-Cell.*

"Hello?"

"I'm here."

Madeleine walked to the window and looked out.

Gayle stood on the front steps and waved. He didn't look happy. Madeleine hung up the phone. She'd dealt with unhappy vampires before. She could do it again. She clutched her silver dagger, ready to use it to protect herself. And Stephen.

She opened the front door and peered through the vines and silver but made no move to step outside. Gayle folded his arms on this chest and smirked at her.

"I love what you've done to the place."

"I like it."

"Hmm, yes. I bet the neighbors are going to be thrilled."

"They'll live."

Gayle cocked his head to the side. "Yes, but will you?" Gone was all semblance of the light, flirtatious man from the club. His eyes glittered with power and anger. And intelligence. He was going to be a dangerous enemy. Madeleine swallowed and reminded herself why she was doing this. *Stephen.*

"I see you've decided to take over his home."

Gayle clearly thought Stephen was dead. "He would have wanted me to have it."

"What do you want, Madeleine? We're going to have quite a busy night. The execution of a vampire makes everyone a bit edgy, and that's good for business." He sounded snide and sarcastic, but she thought—hoped— she heard a faint trace of regret and anger in his voice.

"Come in."

"I can't."

"I just invited you," she snapped. She was too tired for this. She didn't have time for any more stupid vampire rules.

"Yes, but you've also booby-trapped the door. I'm impressed." He scanned the web of vines. "Not many people know about the rose thorns. And I smell garlic but I don't see it."

"It's on the doorknobs."

"Of course." He looked through the rose thorns and leveled his gaze at Madeleine. "What are you protecting?"

"You'll have to come in and see." She held the silver dagger in one hand, making sure Gayle saw it. She didn't want any misunderstanding about her trust. Taking one of the work gloves she'd used to braid the rose stems, she grabbed the middle section of vines and pulled it to the side, leaving a small opening, barely large enough for a man Gayle's size to slip through. He bent down and slid into the opening.

When he'd made it through the maze, she dropped the vines and pointed the knife blade at Gayle's chest.

The smug look on his face as he leaned against the wall irritated her. He didn't think she'd do it. Didn't think she would actually hurt him. Two weeks ago, she might have agreed with him, but after the day she'd had...

She turned the knife and slapped the flat of the blade across the back of his hand. Instantly, a red streak appeared across the skin. Gayle snatched his arm back and curled his free hand into a claw.

"What the hell are you doing?" he snarled, his fangs bared.

"Just checking."

"Excuse me?"

"Someone is killing vampires with silver daggers. I just wanted to make sure it wasn't you."

Gayle raised an eyebrow, but Madeleine ignored the silent question and thrust her chin forward. Stephen obviously had a reason for not telling Gayle about his immunity to silver. She wasn't going to share the secret.

"Can we get to the point of my visit here? As I said, it will be a busy night at Death's Door."

Madeleine heard the subtle threat in his words and felt a shiver slide down her back. A decision faced her. One that could cost Stephen his life.

"Madeleine? What's going on?"

She took a deep breath. "Stephen's downstairs."

"What? He was left for the sun. No one could save him ..." His voice drifted away, but then the light appeared in his eyes. "Except a human."

Madeleine bowed her head in acknowledgment. "Matthias was watching. How did you get past him?" Gayle was obviously as suspicious of her as she was of him.

"Matthias and I came to an agreement."

Questions flittered over his face, but he stayed silent. "Where is he?"

She raised her chin to the door leading down to the basement. "In the vault. He's not right."

"They're going to be pissed when they discover he's gone." Gayle said it almost to himself. "What's wrong with him?"

"I went downstairs at sunset, and he attacked me. I barely got away." She showed Gayle the bruises on her neck. They didn't hurt as much as she would have expected.

Gayle nodded. "He's starving. He hasn't fed properly since you came into his life." Madeleine's hand automatically lifted to the base of her neck. The tiny marks left by Stephen's teeth were gone when she'd awoken yesterday morning. After he'd converted her. Stephen hadn't fed except with her. She couldn't stop the tiny flash of pleasure—purely possessive, feminine pleasure. "Exactly." Gayle shook his hair back away from his face. "Fine. I'll handle him."

She started toward the door, intent on going with him. She wasn't going to leave him alone with Stephen. Not when someone was killing vampires. So Gayle couldn't touch silver—that didn't mean there wasn't another way.

"I'll come with you."

"No. Stephen will hear your rapid little heartbeat, and we'll spend the next ten minutes prying his fangs out of your flesh. I'll go alone."

The strong, commanding voice was a direct contrast to the flighty persona she'd seen at Death's Door. She didn't know which personality was real or if either of them could be trusted. She waited until he'd started down the stairs and then she followed. She wasn't going to let him hurt Stephen. Not after everything she'd been through.

She inched down the steps and crept to the edge of the vault door. Gayle knelt with his knee pressed on Stephen's chest, holding a weakly struggling Stephen to the floor. Gayle slid his hand into his pocket and pulled out a tiny black case. With a quiet snick, a blade appeared. She was too far away to stop him.

"No!" she shouted seconds before the blade slashed across Gayle's wrist. He turned and glared at her over his shoulder. Stephen struggled harder, reaching past Gayle.

"Damn it, Madeleine, get out. I'm not going to hurt him." Blood dripped down Gayle's arm. He slowly lowered it to Stephen's mouth. Stephen avoided it, his focus on Madeleine. The red glow of insane hunger still burned in his eyes.

"Get out," Gayle reiterated.

This time she nodded and backed away. Stephen had looked at her with all kinds of desire, but never like this. He didn't even recognize her.

Stephen's harsh voice filled her head. *You'll kill then. It won't matter who, it won't matter where. The need will overcome you, and all that you've ever thought of yourself will fade.*

He hadn't been able to see through the hunger. She stumbled up the stairs and entered the living room. What did she do now? There was nothing to do but wait. She didn't like it. It gave her too much time to think.

That poor creature. She wouldn't think of him as Stephen—Stephen would never hurt her. Even as she thought the words, she knew they were true, and the last little bit of fear eased inside her.

She loved him. A vampire.

A creature like her.

She allowed her mind to consider the impossible. If it came down to it, could she do it? Could she actually bite someone? She tried to imagine herself with fangs. And a long black cloak that swirled in the wind. A chuckle that bordered on hysteria rattled out of her throat.

The rapid tap of a fist on wood snapped her from her thoughts. Cautiously, she peered down the hallway to the front door. A shadow moved outside the thin, etched-glass windows that framed the door.

Vampire!

She stared at the door, waiting for it to open. The knock sounded again.

A polite vampire? One who couldn't enter Stephen's house? But no, she had enough garlic, silver, and rose vines wrapped across the door that whoever was knocking was probably getting bloody knuckles doing it. She walked down the hall, waiting to see how persistent the human was.

She shook her head at the thought. She'd already divided the world into humans and vampires.

She peeked out the edge of the window. A large male body filled the frame, his hands shoved into his pockets as he scanned the street.

Madeleine moved without thinking and jerked the door open.

"Scott, what are you doing here?"

She had to look at him through the crisscross of rose stems and silverware.

He turned. He looked pale and tired. Madeleine felt an empathetic pang. Her own mind was hazy from exhaustion and stress.

"I was looking for you. What the hell is all this?"

"It's a little hard to explain."

"I think I deserve some answers, Madeleine."

She nodded. He was right. He did deserve the answers, but she couldn't be the one to give them to him.

"Scott, I need you to understand and just hold off. I'll tell you all I can when I can."

He looked like he would object, but he just shook his head and put his hands on his hips. "At least tell me you're okay. I've been trying to reach you since yesterday. Charlotte's frantic. Just what the hell is going on?

"Listen, Scott—"

"Madeleine, I don't think you know what kind of people you're dealing with." He hunched down and lowered his voice. "I didn't believe you before, but I do now. I think Stephen had something to do with Danielle's death. In fact, I think he killed her himself."

The long mind- and body-numbing day hadn't dulled her senses enough to avoid the spike of pain that hit her. She shook her head.

"I'm worried about you, Madeleine."

"I'll be fine." A tight throb began behind her eyes. "You should drop Danielle's death." The words crept from her lips, forced there by logic but restrained by the ache in her heart. Justice wouldn't be satisfied. She had to get Scott away from it. If he pursued Danielle's death, he would be putting himself in danger.

She knew that from experience.

"I'm a cop. I don't just *drop* homicides."

"You were right. It was a mugging. It's time to move on."

"Is he threatening you?"

Madeleine shook her head but couldn't resist a glance over her shoulder. Stephen wouldn't be pleased about Scott's presence. She couldn't forget the fire in Stephen's eyes when he realized she'd called Scott for help, almost as if he'd been jealous. *Not likely.* He'd made it clear he was above human emotions—including jealousy, guilt.

And love.

It didn't matter. Despite the fact that he didn't—couldn't—return her love, she'd thrown her lot in with him.

"Madeleine, I'm worried about you. Will you at least talk to me?" He stepped back, opening a space for her on the porch.

She had to get Scott to leave. If Stephen came upstairs and found him …

In his present state, she didn't know what would happen. She nodded and grabbed the work glove she needed to get into and out of the house. She lifted the panel of rose vines and stepped onto the porch. The wave of heat hit her as she left the cool air-conditioning of Stephen's home.

"Madeleine, I think you should come with me. I don't think you're safe here."

"I'll be fine." She cocked her head and stared at Scott. Something wasn't right.

The humidity drenched her skin, and sweat trickled down the back of her neck. Droplets of water lined Scott's forehead.

It was no wonder. He was wearing a sweater.

A turtleneck.

Her tired mind slowly caught on. She inched back toward the door. She'd recently worn turtlenecks on hot days. To hide a vampire bite.

Scott's hand shot out and grabbed her elbow.

"You need to come with me." His hand covered her mouth, and the world turned black.

Fourteen

Stephen sat on the floor, still hidden in the darkest shadows of the room. His body hummed with the need for blood, barely sated from the small amount Gayle had given him.

"Did I hurt her?"

Memories came in sharp spikes, slashes through waves of rage and red. Debilitating fear in Madeleine's eyes, his hand on her throat. He looked around. No body lay on the floor. He hadn't killed her. At least not downstairs. She'd only escaped him because of his weakened state—the strain of the silver and the burns of the rising sun had drained him.

"Bruised but alive." Gayle waited for a moment, then pushed himself away from the wall and planted his feet in front of Stephen. "What the hell were you thinking?"

Stephen raised his eyes at the sharp snap of Gayle's words. He wasn't really surprised by the dramatic change from the man who inhabited Death's Door. He'd always known Gayle had hidden sides.

"I don't know what came over me." He said it sarcastically, but it was the truth.

"Insanity? Stupidity?"

Stephen wanted to fight back, but damn, Gayle was right.

"All of the above," Stephen finally agreed. "She was lying there, and I thought she was dying, and I—" He stopped. The rambling explanation wasn't going to justify what he'd done.

"What?" Gayle interrupted. "What are you talking about?"

"Madeleine. Converting Madeleine."

"You converted her?" He answered his own question. "Of course. That's what's different about her. Well, good for you."

"Good for me?" Stephen pushed himself to his feet. "Don't you see what I've done?"

"You've created a mate for yourself. Madeleine will make a fine vampire."

"She'll never survive. She's not tough enough."

Gayle raised one mocking eyebrow. "Excuse me? You're talking about the woman who just saved your ass by dragging you to safety and threatening me with a silver dagger. Strength and courage are two things she's not lacking."

Stephen folded his arms across his chest. Gayle was right. Madeleine had strength and courage, but she didn't have the survival instinct. She was too concerned with others, and he didn't want to see that change.

"You overly noble son of a bitch." Gayle's voice was filled with wonder. "You tried to suicide. That's what this was about, wasn't it? You tried to kill yourself by confessing to the Council."

"I…"

Gayle held his hand up. He didn't want explanations, and Stephen wasn't sure he had one to give. "Don't try to explain it to me. I understand your twisted thought processes. You'd sacrifice yourself? For a human?"

"For Madeleine."

"She'll make a great vampire, you know. Just like you. And it would give you something to think about besides hating the Council. Everyone would win."

The truth tightened its grip around Stephen's throat.

"I can't do that to her. The choice was taken away from me." He leaned against the wall, his body weak. The blood Gayle had given him was enough to keep him upright, but just barely. He hadn't fed properly in days. Now, he needed it desperately. "I can't do it to her, Gayle."

"You gave her the choice last night. She could have let you die. What would be more painless to her than that?"

The same thought had crossed his mind as well and

plagued him in the few minutes since he'd returned to himself. Madeleine had saved him. Even knowing what she would become, she'd risked her own life, faced down Matthias, and rescued him.

He'd given her the choice. And she'd chosen to rescue him. The tight band that had settled around his heart began to loosen. She'd chosen him.

"She'll make a great vampire," Gayle repeated.

"Yes, once we get her to complete the conversion, convince the Community she's not a slayer, and she forgives me for killing her cousin."

Gayle hitched his hips backward and jumped onto the table that held Stephen's coffin. "You've got time. Lots of time." He pursed his lips together and looked up, thinking. "It's fate, you know. Destiny." The laughter returned to his eyes. Stephen couldn't help responding in kind.

"Think about it," Gayle added with a teasing chuckle. "You're obviously meant to be together. You were connected to her long before the conversion—you were getting her dreams, hearing her thoughts. Destiny."

Stephen was sure there was a logical explanation for the same thing, but he didn't mind Gayle's romantic view of it. It might help convince Madeleine to stay with him.

"I have to say, she's taking it all rather well for a human."

Stephen's lip curled up into a smile. "She threatened me with a silver dagger when she found out."

"Ha! Me, too." He jumped off the table and patted Stephen's shoulder. "I like her, Stephen."

"Me, too."

"But we'd better get upstairs. She's probably worn a hole in the floor and—"

"Getting crankier by the moment." He wasn't looking forward to facing Madeleine. There was still so much to talk about.

Gayle stopped him at the bottom of the steps. "No

more noble attempts at suicide?"

"No, she's made her choice." And he'd made his. He was going to keep her.

Stephen led the way upstairs. God, he was tired. He hadn't been this tired since he'd been human. He needed to feed, and he needed a little less stress.

And a little more Madeleine. His body reacted instantly to the image. He rubbed his fingertips across his forehead, willing away the seductive thought. It obviously didn't matter how tired or weak he was—Madeleine was enough to inspire him.

They stepped into the hallway. Stephen listened, scanning the house for the distinctive sounds of Madeleine's heart. Only the muted pounding of Nicholas' reached him.

"Nicholas!" he called. The fledgling appeared at the kitchen door. "Where's Madeleine?"

"I haven't seen her. Not since morning."

The warm scent of sultry heat filled his head. Stephen turned. The front door was open.

"She's gone." She'd left him. A hollow feeling entered his stomach. Had she panicked? He'd attacked her. Had he scared her so much that she'd run?

It didn't make sense. Madeleine had faced five vampires with a knife and some silver jewelry. She didn't panic easily. But why had she left?

"Well, we have a problem," Gayle announced.

"Yes," Stephen agreed. "The whole Community is going to be after her."

Gayle grimaced. "Okay, then we have two problems."

Stephen raised his eyebrows in question.

"Have you seen what she's done to your house?" Gayle asked.

Stephen looked at the door. Rose vines interspersed with white lines of silver dinnerware were woven across the opening, creating an impenetrable web.

"No one can get in…" Gayle's voice trailed away.

"And we can't get out," Stephen finished.

Madeleine had been busy. Resourceful. But then she always was.

And she was out there alone. What was she thinking? Stephen rubbed his fingers along the line of his neck.

"Can't you just vaporize and slide out?" Nicholas asked.

"We'd be sliced to ribbons," Stephen replied. "The thorns and silver still scratch in a vapor state. You'll have to let us out."

Damn, he needed to find her. The Council and every vampire in the Community would be looking for her. But there was one vampire in particular.

Stephen looked at Gayle.

"Matthias has been whispering to Madeleine in her head. He had her last night, but he let her go. He might decide to use her as bait to get to me directly. He could have lured her out." Stephen turned away from Gayle. "Nicholas, find some way of getting through that mess on the door. Tear it down if you have to." He leapt down the stairs to his vault.

He'd never approached the knives when another vampire was in the house, and he'd never considered leaving the house with one, but tonight was different. They could stake him later, but tonight, he was using every weapon he had. He knelt down and opened the floor panel. Special shielding masked the silver's vibration. For Stephen, it didn't matter. Where silver burned the others, it felt no different than wood in his hand. The change had begun a year ago—or that's when he'd noticed it. After spending months experimenting, he'd approached Joshua. Joshua had agreed to research it quietly. This kind of immunity would not be welcome among the Community— especially not with Stephen's history. Two weeks after Stephen had told his mentor, Joshua was dead. Death by silver dagger.

Stephen had done his own investigating in the months that followed, but he'd been blocked at every turn. There was no way to find out without revealing too much, without exposing another to Joshua's fate.

Stephen opened the black case. Five silver slashes lay in lines across the dark velvet. He was going to do it. He was going to hunt another vampire with the daggers his father had given him. The memory returned like a knife through his skin. His father's pain, the desperate hunger. He had no memory of it—just the pain and fury of the hunger, and the slow return to sanity, his father's broken body on the floor of the cell. They'd had their revenge.

He pushed the memory aside as he picked up the first knife. Tonight, he would have his.

Someone else knew about the knives and was able to use them. Was it a vampire working with a human? He looked at the daggers. Or was there another vampire out there who could touch silver? Over the past year, he'd analyzed the differences—how was he different from the others created about the same time? Or was it simply age? No one knew Matthias' real age, but could he have moved beyond the restrictions normal vampires faced?

There were too many possibilities. Stephen had to face them logically. He would direct his energies toward his enemies first—Matthias and the Council—and then start looking at his friends.

Alone in the vault, Stephen flipped the knife over in his hand. The weight of the metal, the shape of the hilt was familiar. The hours he'd trained with his father learning to fight with and throw the knives came back to him. Two hundred years had passed, but his body hadn't forgotten. He slipped two knives into his back pocket and a third up his sleeve.

That would be enough.

He came upstairs, feeling the heavy weight of silver

in his palm. He stopped only inches away from Gayle. "How strong is your constitution?" Stephen asked.

"Strong."

Stephen raised his hand and revealed the silver dagger lying across his fingers.

Gayle blanched. "Not that strong." He held up one hand and took a step back. "And before you try it, Madeleine already slapped me with a knife blade to see if I can tolerate the touch. I can't." He shook his head. "How can you?"

"I have no idea, but it's obvious that if I can do it, so can someone else."

"So, they're all looking for a vampire and human working together, and it's just a vampire." Gayle folded his arms over his chest and continued to stare at the blade. Finally, he sighed. "I don't think we have time tonight, but we are definitely going to have to talk about this."

Stephen nodded. He'd instinctively liked Gayle when they'd met twelve years ago. It was only in the past few hours that he could determine why. Gayle was loyal, he didn't ask stupid questions, and he had great timing.

"Go to the Council," Stephen said. "Find out what they know. If they have Madeleine, don't let them hurt her. If they don't have her, keep them from doing something stupid."

"Like what?"

"Like tearing the city apart looking for her. Or me. I need a little time. If Matthias doesn't have her, it's a good bet the Council will soon."

"And if the Council doesn't have her?"

"Then it's a good bet someone with a silver dagger does." Stephen didn't want to consider it. He needed to be methodical. Go with the obvious enemies, and eliminate them first before he started looking at so-called friends.

Gayle's forehead crinkled with concern. "Maybe I should go to Matthias. You two have a way of getting distracted."

"If Matthias has her, he's using her as bait for me. He'll at least let me inside. The Council won't give me the chance to speak."

Nicholas called out that he'd cleared Madeleine's defenses. When they were outside, Stephen led the way down the steps. "Nicholas, go to Madeleine's apartment. If she's okay, that's where she'll go. I've got my phone. Let's stay in touch." The other two nodded and went their ways.

Moments later new blood sang through Stephen's veins. He'd hated to take the time, but he needed his strength. The young woman he'd found walking the night streets wouldn't remember the experience in the morning, and Stephen could at least function now. It hadn't been enough but he'd been cautious, not wanting to kill her. Days of starving himself followed by the silver spikes in his wrists and the heat of the previous day's sunrise had taken too much from his body. It would take time for him to recover. But at least he was strong enough to find Madeleine.

Stephen stopped in front of the house Matthias used as his lair. It was nondescript, plain, and set back from the street. Stephen had never been here before, but he knew about it—*know thy enemy*. Matthias was in for a surprise tonight. Stephen knocked on the front door and waited. Nervous energy fluttered in his stomach—fear for Madeleine and concern about facing Matthias. Matthias was old and strong.

It wasn't hard to imagine what it must have felt like for Madeleine standing on *his* doorstep. Of course, she hadn't known what was on the other side. Stephen shook his head. It wouldn't have stopped her. Madeleine was fiercely loyal to those she loved.

An intense longing hit him. She'd rescued him, but he wouldn't allow himself to believe he was one of the people

Madeleine loved. He needed to find her, then he'd worry
about where he fit in her life.

The door swung open without assistance. He stared
down the empty hallway, waiting for the necessary
invitation. After long seconds, it came from a disembodied
voice that echoed through the house. Stephen stepped
inside, immediately listening for the familiar beat of
Madeleine's heart. Silence. If Matthias had her, she was
hidden away. Matthias had a vault somewhere. She was
probably there.

If he had her.

Stephen stalked down the hall and turned the corner
at the first opening. The muted sounds of movement led
him down another short hallway into a large living room,
not visible from the road. The house looked plain from
the outside, but opulence ruled on the inside.

Matthias sat casually at a grand piano, the fingers of
one hand strumming the keys.

A pale light flashed at Stephen from Matthias' eyes—
eyes that for two hundred years had glowed with hate now
seemed to have lost their fire. He stood and walked toward
Stephen.

"So, she was able to rescue you. Pity."

"Where is she?"

"You've lost your little fledgling? And you come to
me? I'm honored."

Stephen didn't have the patience or strength to mess
around. He let the silver dagger hidden up his sleeve drop
down into his hand. A quick flick of his wrist flipped the
point toward Matthias' heart.

"Where is she?"

Matthias stared down at the knife. Anger and shock
hit Stephen as Matthias raised his eyes.

"This is the second time in three days I've had a silver
dagger pointed at my chest. I don't like it." His fangs
glittered in the light. "So, you've found a way to touch

silver and now you're finally taking your revenge. Nice to know I'm in the top five of your enemies. Madeleine almost had me convinced it wasn't you. Worse yet, she believes it herself. You're being a bit obvious on who you kill. The Council knows your history. You should have killed a few friends instead of just your enemies."

"I don't want to hurt you. I just want Madeleine." He looked into the vampire's eyes and waited.

"I don't have her."

"Damn." Stephen lowered the knife and backed away. He didn't know why he believed Matthias, but he did. Maybe it was because Matthias had had the opportunity to kill Madeleine last night and let her go. "I was afraid you were going to say that."

"You didn't kill them, did you?" Matthias' question startled Stephen.

"No."

"Someone did."

"Yes." Stephen held up the knife. "With these daggers."

Matthias' lips pulled back in disgust. "Could you put that away? I find it particularly unnerving to see a vampire holding silver." Stephen complied, sliding the knife back up his sleeve. "Vampires dying. We all thought it was a vampire working with a human—what else could it be?" he said thoughtfully.

"A vampire who can touch silver."

Matthias began a slow wander across his living room. "How's it done?"

"I have no idea, and to be honest, I have other things on my mind tonight."

Matthias held up his finger. "No. It's important. Madeleine wouldn't leave you, not willingly. So, whoever has her…" Stephen waited. He'd tried reasoning this out on his own, not trusting any of the others. But Matthias seemed willing to help. "Why you? It's not age. I can't stand the presence of the stuff." He stared at Stephen. "What's different about you?"

"My conversion." It was the only thing he could think of—his conversion hadn't been typical. It had been neither fast nor painless. But if conversion was the key, than at least one other person would have his same abilities. Stephen shook his head. It was impossible. The memories hit him hard and fast.

Matthias nodded. "You wouldn't feed. I remember now. You became an experiment of sorts for the Council. They were quite amazed at how long you lasted. And you just kept getting stronger. All the strengths of a vampire but none of the weaknesses."

Two hundred years hadn't dulled the pain. Anger still roiled in his stomach at the thought. "It lasted until the final conversion, and then we became normal, at least by vampire standards."

"So after two hundred years you lose those weaknesses? Sounds far-fetched." Matthias looked skeptical.

Stephen agreed, but what else could it be?

An electronic buzz interrupted Matthias. Stephen unclipped the cell phone that perpetually hung at his hip. He glanced at the number. *Thomass.* He flipped the end of the phone down.

"Yes?"

"Stephen? Oh my God, it's true. You escaped. What happened? How?"

"Thomass, I'm kind of busy right now."

"Stephen, the Council's got that woman. Madeleine."

His stomach tightened. "What? Where's Gayle?"

"Gayle?"

"Are you at the Council Chambers?"

"Uh, no. They have her hidden."

"Where?"

"Stephen, let her go. You escaped once. They won't

let it happen again. Get out of town." Thomass paused.
"Joshua would have told you the same thing."

Stephen ignored his last statement. Thomass was right.
Joshua believed in survival at any cost. And Joshua had
taught him well. He'd helped Stephen become the creature
he was. But Joshua was dead.

Thomass rambled on, pleading and coercing at
different intervals. Stephen let his voice echo in the
background.

If conversion *was* the key, that left only one person.

"Where is she, Thomass?" Stephen asked, cutting into
Thomass' rant.

There was silence on the other end of the phone, a
reluctance. "That warehouse," he finally said. "Where they
found the other girl. I think they're hoping to pass it off as
a serial killer. Stephen, don't—"

Stephen flipped the phone shut, cutting off any further
protests.

"Who was that?"

Matthias would have heard most of the conversation.
"Thomass."

"The Council has her?" Stephen nodded. "But she's
not at the Council Chambers. Odd."

"Yes." *Very odd.* Stephen turned and started toward
the door.

"I'll go to the Chambers, see what I can find out."

Stephen straightened. *Matthias? Offering to help?*
"Why?"

Matthias' smile was not comforting. "I think
Madeleine's going to be her own revenge. I've spent a lot
of time in her head over the past week. When she completes
her conversion, you'll be responsible for her, and she's
going to make your life a living hell."

"I certainly hope so."

They stopped at the front door.

"You weren't in that cage alone. Who was with you?"

Stephen looked at his phone for a moment before answering.

"Thomass."

***

Madeleine glared at the man's back. She kept her movements small, rubbing the rough edge of duct tape against the chair's metal spine. She'd seen it in movies, but she'd never realized how truly uncomfortable it was to be tied with her arms behind her.

Where is this super vampire strength I'm supposed to get? she inwardly groused. *I could use it now.*

The man pressed the button on his phone and turned around. His head blocked the light and for a moment he was silhouetted, his short hair appearing dark in the shadow. The shape of his head, the dark whisper—it was familiar. The man from the alleyway. It seemed like a lifetime ago, but it was him. He stepped forward, baring his face to the light. His feral, slightly insane smile made her pull harder on the bonds that held her. She had to get away.

"Your boyfriend will be here any moment." She pressed her lips together and continued to glare at him. She hadn't said anything since she'd woken up tied to the chair. She wasn't going to give him the satisfaction. He was obviously working up to something big, and he wanted an audience. She refused to give him one.

"Still hoping he'll save you? Me, too." He looked so serious, so sincere. If it hadn't been for the touch of madness lurking in his eyes, she might have believed him. "I was surprised he didn't kill you first off. It really would have made so much more sense." His lips curled up into a sneer. "But Stephen never did have the necessary instincts." He shrugged. "But in the end, it all worked out. Stephen was distracted, busy with you. He didn't have time to think about vampires and silver daggers."

"You killed them." The accusation left her mouth

without conscious thought.

A flicker of irritation crossed his face.

"So, he's told you about them, has he? How very open of him. Yes, I did. It was simple. Who would have ever expected a vampire to carry a silver dagger? It seems those months locked in a cage with Stephen had some value after all." He wandered in a path in front of her. Madeleine kept her eyes focused on him but continued to work at the tape holding her to the chair. "I wonder if Stephen's figured it out. Most conversions are completed within hours, days of the transfer." Pure hate crinkled the edges of his eyes and an unholy glow of red sparkled inside. "But not Stephen. He was so damn noble. He lasted months— months—without blood. I stayed with him of course."

"Why?" It was so obvious he hated Stephen.

"I could see it, even then. The others would come by, tempt him, offer him humans, and he'd turn away. It frustrated them, but you could see their admiration, too. They were so impressed by the vampire slayer's son. I wasn't going to let him get all the glory."

"Glory!?" Stephen's infuriated voice echoed through the empty warehouse.

Her captor spun around and stepped behind her, dropping his open hands on her shoulders.

Stephen walked into the light, his fingers clenched into fists at his side. "Glory? Thomass, you twisted son of a bitch. That wasn't glory, that was torture."

"You still can't see it, can you? You hate the Council, hate what they did to you, hate what they made you, and in return, they admire you. You never hear it, but I've had to listen to it for two hundred years. They actually wanted to offer you a seat on the Council to make up for everything." His fingers dug into Madeleine's shoulders. "Such a good little vampire. It was so satisfying to see them slowly turn against you. A few hints here and there and suddenly everyone remembers your father's knives.

Even your favorite admirers were starting to turn."

Madeleine ignored the furious words spewing from Thomass' mouth and stared at Stephen. He stared back.

Are you all right?

Madeleine heard the words in her head and shrugged. She didn't try to transmit to him the real answer: Hell, no, I'm not all right. She didn't know if she could actually send the message, and he didn't need the distraction right now.

"What is this all about, Thomass?" Stephen's voice was calm, belying the tension she sensed in him.

Thomass laughed. "I don't like you, Stephen."

"I don't like you, either, but I've never gone after you with a silver dagger."

"You should have." As the words left his mouth, Madeleine felt the press of metal against her throat. She could only see the edge. It was a silver dagger like the one she'd used. "As soon as you could touch silver, you should have started killing anyone who would get in your way. That's what a real vampire would do."

Stephen shook his head. Madeleine couldn't read what he was thinking, but she could tell he had something in mind. "What do you want?" he asked.

"I want you to die."

"Then you'll be the only vampire who can touch silver."

"Yes, funny how that works."

"But if you kill me, who will you blame the future murders on?"

"I think I'm done for awhile. The Council is quite impressed with me. They see me as the loyal, wronged companion of a murderer. I've played my part very well. I was able to appear loyal to you but still wanted what was best for the Community. Besides, you're just going to disappear. We'll be able to blame you for years to come. Now, do you want to die before or after your fledgling?"

"Let her go, Thomass." Stephen stepped forward, a glint of silver flashing in his right palm.

"Stay back. If I drive this dagger into her heart, she'll die. Just like any human. And she won't come back. The silver will kill the vampire as well."

Stephen stopped. "She has nothing to do with this."

"No, she doesn't. She was just a lucky break." He ran his fingers through her short hair. Madeleine started to pull away—his touch made her skin crawl—but the hot edge of the knife stopped her. Instead she glared at Stephen, hoping he had something in mind to get them out of this. She kept steady pressure on the tape holding her hands, surreptitiously rubbing it along the chair frame. "I never would have picked her for your type," Thomass said. "I always thought you'd prefer perky and cheerful to mouthy and crabby."

Madeleine stopped moving. "Danielle," she whispered.

"Yes. She was a great little helper. Got the knives for me. At least at first. Then I had to find my own way inside." He tilted his head to the side. "You need better security, Stephen. It wasn't that difficult to get in and take them. But you found the one I planted in the dresser drawer."

"*You* brought the Council to my house."

Thomass smug smile made Madeleine's teeth ache but she ignored it, letting the two men talk. While Thomass was focused on Stephen, she began again on the tape that held her.

"Yes. It was time to add a little more suspicion to you but it didn't work." He sounded irritated by that.

"Sorry."

The knife bit into her skin at Stephen's sarcastic apology. Madeleine tensed. She needed more time, she needed to keep him talking.

"You converted Danielle?" she asked.

Thomass laughed softly. "Yes. It was her reward for helping me. Unfortunately, she remained just a little too human afterward. Started asking questions, feeling guilty about vampires dying. I needed to get rid of her."

Madeleine felt Stephen's shock from across the room. "You said her conversion was flawed, that she had to be destroyed. You asked me to handle it to protect Dylan."

"I lied. Joshua came to me, asking veiled questions about vampires and silver. I knew he knew something. But he never told me where he got his information, and then after he was dead, he was no use. I figured it had to be you. Joshua wouldn't protect just anyone. I needed to find out for certain." He laughed, so confident in his victory. "You were so easy to set up, Stephen. A few concerns for the Community, and the girl ends up with a silver dagger in her chest. You might say you hate them, but you are certainly willing to help when they're in need."

"Why not just come after me? Why the setup?"

"It was more fun this way. I got to see you squirm."

"Let Madeleine go. It's me you want."

"I still need her. I need her until you're dead."

Stephen held himself still for a moment. He couldn't let Thomass see the impact of his words. His own death he expected, but he had to free Madeleine. She didn't deserve this. He needed something to distract Thomass, something to move him away from Madeleine.

Stephen opened his arms wide. Thomass' gaze flickered to the dagger in Stephen's hand. He uncurled his fingers and the knife clattered to the floor. "Here I am."

Thomass pulled his dagger away from Madeleine's neck an inch or so. "I don't trust you."

"I never wanted this life, you know that."

Thomass stepped forward. Stephen backed up, leading Thomass away from Madeleine. Thomass was right. She wouldn't survive a silver dagger. Thomass peeled his lips back and bared his extended eyeteeth. Stephen remained calm and continued to back away.

"Fight me," Thomass commanded.

Stephen shook his head and took another step back. He could see what Thomass wanted. He wanted to best Stephen in a fight. A simple execution wouldn't be enough.

"So controlled. So noble," Thomass sneered. "I know what you're doing. You're trying to show her how *human* you are. You don't want her to see what an animal you really are. Madeleine, did he tell you about his father? How he ripped open his own father's neck and fed?"

Stephen steeled his will. He knew the taunts were designed to anger him. It worked, but he didn't attack. Still weak from the silver in his veins and the brush with sunlight, Stephen didn't know if he had the strength to beat Thomass. He wanted to give Madeleine time to escape if he failed. She had to be free first. Though retreat was counter to his character, Stephen ignored Thomass' words and continued to back away, silently pleading for Madeleine to free herself.

Thomass seemed to sense Stephen's attention was elsewhere, and he laughed. That was when Stephen realized Thomass was truly insane.

"You didn't do it, you know," Thomass sneered.

"What?" Stephen stayed focused on Madeleine. He needed to keep Thomass distracted.

"You didn't kill your father." Tension pulled Stephen's body tight, grabbing his attention. Thomass chuckled. "I did. They weren't going to let you go until you'd fed, and I wanted out. You cowered in the corner, mad for it but still refusing to feed. I wasn't quite that noble. I killed him and then poured his blood on you. You woke up never realizing I'd done it." Stephen lost all awareness except the hatred. He reached behind him, whipped out the second dagger and lunged at Thomass. Years of regret and guilt converted instantly to fury. Thomas jumped back, laughing as he sliced his hand across Stephen's arm. A thin trail of fire burned, but Stephen barely noticed it.

His only thought was to kill. He could have thrown

the knife—he'd practiced for hours with his father—but he wanted to feel the knife enter Thomass' flesh. Stephen stalked forward, his fangs bared. He swung in wide arcs, forcing Thomass back. Rage gave Stephen strength, and Thomass had stopped laughing. He blocked each of Stephen's blows, but Stephen could see the other vampire was weakening. Thomass stumbled backward. Stephen moved in, desperate to kill the creature in front of him.

"Stephen." Madeleine's quiet cry snapped him back into himself. He turned to her and fell into her eyes. In that brief moment, he saw the forgiveness and comfort for years of anger and guilt. He looked at her and saw the humanity he thought he'd lost. And he saw the love. Calm cleared his mind and he realized he couldn't do it—he wouldn't kill in front of her—not with those frightened eyes watching him.

From his right, Thomass pounced, aiming his knife at Stephen's heart. Stephen stepped back, slicing his own blade down across Thomass' forearm. Thomass growled and dropped low, snarling like a wolf as he turned. He hunted Stephen and Stephen backed away. He would stop Thomass but not kill him, not unless he had to. He let Thomass stalk him. Stephen's defensive stance seemed to infuriate Thomass even further. Thomass swung wide arcs with his arm, nicking Stephen's skin with each pass. The thin cuts burned, but Stephen ignored the sensation.

An exultant cry echoed from across the room and Stephen felt one level of fear disappear. Madeleine stood up and ripped the last of the tape from her arms. She was free.

Stephen kept Thomass in sight but watched Madeleine, willing her to escape. He should have known better.

She ran from the chair and leapt toward them, landing hard against Thomass' back. Her arms wrapped around his neck, her knees grabbing his hips. Thomass rocked forward under the impact. She pulled on Thomass' neck, her muscles bunching as she tried to tip the vampire backward. He tore her arms away from his throat and, with a shrug, tossed her off his back.

Her body flew through the air and crashed hard to the ground with a sickening thud. Her heart stuttered as she landed. Anger swamped Stephen, his sight turning red as he stared at Madeleine's crumpled form.

Thomass had touched Madeleine. Stephen attacked. The anger he'd felt before was nothing compared to the fury he experienced now.

Thomass backed away, defending and dodging each strike of Stephen's knife. Stephen pushed forward, becoming the hunter once again.

A scuffle in the distance vied for Stephen's attention. For a moment, he thought Madeleine had woken up, but then he realized the sound was coming from much farther away. *Gayle or Matthias.*

Thomass cocked his head to the side. He heard it, too, and was distracted by the sound. Stephen took the opportunity. He slashed the knife across Thomass' chest, gouging deep into the skin. A scream erupted from deep inside the other vampire. Stephen could feel nothing but satisfaction. The silver would spiral through Thomass' blood stream, poisoning him, weakening him. Stephen knew the sensation. He'd felt it last night when the Council had wrapped spike-lined cuffs around his wrists and ankles. The silver might not kill him, but it was painful and draining. Thomass' arm fell to his side as blood oozed across his chest.

"That's going to leave a nasty scar," Stephen said, moving toward his opponent.

"Yes." Thomass glared at him, then flipped backward and landed beside Madeleine's fallen body. "So will this." He drove his hand downward and forced the knife into Madeleine's heart.

With the silence of death, her heart stopped.

Fifteen

Stephen stared at the silver dagger imbedded in Madeleine's heart and felt his own skip one of its rare beats. Too stunned to move, he watched Thomass fade into a mist and slide toward the exit. Stephen let him go. He would find him later.

Madeleine was gone. His feet were leaden as he stumbled forward.

"Oh my God, Maddie."

He dropped to his knees, aching to touch her but not knowing how. She was gone. His fingers traced the back of her hand. Her skin was warm but rapidly cooling. The stark silver of the knife glowed against the blood that stained her shirt. He couldn't stand it. He jerked the knife free and tossed it on the ground beside her body.

He had no hope of her return as Thomass had predicted. The silver in the knife had killed the vampire just as the blade had killed the human.

Tears burned in his eyes. He hadn't cried since he'd been converted.

His heart beat with a hollow thud, and the emptiness of his soul flooded in with each pulse.

"Stephen?" Gayle's voice broke the quiet. "I'm sorry."

He nodded but didn't turn around. He wasn't ready to see the sympathy. How pathetic, he mocked himself. A vampire mourning the loss of a human. He pressed his lips together and forced himself to stand.

What had he told Madeleine? He was a good vampire. He would do what needed to be done. Stephen crushed all emotion.

"We, uh, need to get rid of the body. This is what Thomass wanted, bad press. Two women killed in the same manner. Particularly these two. Cousins. The police will—" He went blank for a moment. He clenched his fists and continued. "Uh, the police will latch on to it. We need to get rid of it."

"I'll do it," Gayle offered.

Stephen shook his head. He would do it. It was the right thing for the Community. He would do what needed to be done.

"No," another voice said. Stephen lifted his head and saw Matthias. He hadn't realized Matthias was there, and he expected to see some light of triumph in his eyes, but there was nothing. "You're in no state to do it. You'll muck it up."

Stephen felt his lips curl back into an unconscious snarl but didn't act upon it. Matthias was right.

"Let Gayle take care of it."

Stephen nodded and started to walk away. He looked down one last time at Madeleine's silent body. She was gone. His legs were weighted with reluctance and an exhaustion that went beyond the physical. He didn't want to leave her, but he had to. Had to move on.

"Go with him." He heard Matthias' command, and seconds later Nicholas appeared at his side.

Stephen's first reaction was to send him away. He didn't want anyone with him—he didn't need their sympathy. Nicholas was silent, offering nothing but his quiet presence, and for once, Stephen was glad for the company. After two hundred years alone, Madeleine had entered his life and now it seemed empty without her. It didn't make sense. He'd only known her for two weeks, but there would be a hole in his life.

She was gone.

And the memory would linger. Forever.

***

Gayle watched Stephen and Nick walk away. He waited until they were out of hearing distance before turning to Matthias.

"Any brilliant ideas about where I should stash the body?" Gayle folded his arms on his chest and cocked one hip out to the side. "Most of my guests walk away from the encounter. I don't usually do this."

"I'll take care of it. You go with Stephen."

Warning bells went off in Gayle's head. "Matthias...what are you up to?"

"Nothing." The answer was too innocent to be believed, but before Gayle could respond, Matthias commanded, "Go. I'll handle the disposal."

Gayle started toward the door. He wanted to check on Stephen, but that didn't mean he was going to trust Matthias.

It would be interesting to see if Nick could keep up with the ancient vampire.

***

Madeleine felt the sun lift from her chest and the night close on the earth. She was awake—she burst from the darkness and bolted upright. Her body felt strange, foreign, powerful. She stared into the dark room. She knew it was dark even though she could see each line clearly.

"Good evening, Madeleine." Matthias' mocking voice greeted her. She shivered. The voice inside her head. In person.

"Where the hell am I?"

"My home."

"What am I doing..." She licked her lips, and her tongue brushed across the sharp spikes of her teeth. "Oh my God. I have fangs!"

Matthias smiled, showing his own extended canines. "Welcome to our world, Madeleine."

"Where's Stephen?" She needed him. A sudden longing, a desperate ache filled her chest. She would be safe with him. She suddenly felt very vulnerable next to this powerful creature.

"Looking to be rescued?"

His answer didn't tell her much. Hell, it didn't tell her anything. An instinctive growl welled up in her throat but stopped when her lips moved over the long spikes of her canines.

"What happened?" she asked.

"You were turned into a vampire."

"I remember that part. What happened last night?" She pulled her red-stained blouse away from her body. It was blood. Her blood. This was the second time in three days she'd woken up with her own blood on her shirt. She could remember the dagger fight between Stephen and Thomass but little beyond that. "I assume it was last night."

"Yes. There was a fight. You were killed."

Madeleine nodded. Nick had told her about this. To become a full vampire she either had to kill someone or die herself.

"Is Stephen okay?"

"I've never cared for him much personally, but—" He held up one hand to stop her next protest. "As far as I—" A deep pounding in the distance stopped his words. "Ahh, I expect that's him now." Seconds later there was a crash of wood and Stephen's shout.

"Matthias!"

"Downstairs," Matthias replied in a quiet voice that seemed to echo through the house. The door burst open, and Stephen stormed in.

Madeleine stared in amazement. She'd thought she'd seen Stephen upset on every level, but this was one step beyond everything she'd seen before. Not even during the fight with Thomass had rage flowed through Stephen's body as it did now. He was focused and furious. And he didn't look beyond Matthias, didn't even see her.

"Gayle just told me you took Madeleine's body. What the hell are you doing?"

Matthias smirked. "My good deed for the century." He tilted his head toward Madeleine.

Now Stephen saw her.

"Maddie? Oh my God, Maddie." He started to move

forward and stopped. "How? The silver should have killed her."

"The dagger wasn't left in her chest long enough."

"It should have killed any vampire," Stephen still protested.

"Any vampire but you." Matthias curled his fingers and inspected the line of long fingernails, as if the conversation were only of mild interest to him. "You're immune to silver. If you'd been thinking correctly last night instead of mourning, you would have realized there was a good possibility that you transferred that to Madeleine when she was converted. There was at least some possibility. It appears I was right. I like being right. She's going to torment you for decades."

Madeleine waited, watching. She was a vampire, and she was Stephen's responsibility. She knew enough to know he would have to take care of her until she was strong enough to be on her own. On her own. She pressed her lips together. She didn't want to be on her own. She wanted to be with Stephen. But he'd never really planned on this. He'd even been willing to die to free her.

Matthias faded from her awareness as Stephen stared at her. Desire like she'd never felt before flooded her system. She felt her teeth extend long. And she was hungry. Hungry for more than food. She wanted Stephen. And something else.

A fire matching her own flared in the blue depths of his gaze.

"I'll leave you two alone."

Madeleine barely noticed the door closing behind Matthias. She could only see Stephen. Her mind raced to counteract the dictates of her body. Throwing herself on him and dragging him to the floor kept coming to mind as her best option.

She tried to stop herself. *You're a vampire! You have other issues besides the fact that Stephen would look really good without his clothes right now.*

"Stephen, I don't know what's wrong with me—"

"Your senses are heightened. You feel everything more strongly."

She moaned as another wave of lust hit her. Her body tingled, tensing and releasing, preparing for Stephen's touch. The picture of their bodies entwined together was so clear in her mind.

Maddie, his voice whispered in her head, *you're transmitting again.*

She nodded and licked her lips.

Stephen groaned, and she heard it through her whole body, the sweet vibrations fluttering through her nerve endings.

"Maddie."

The plea, the need she heard in his voice was too much to resist. She flew at him and landed in his welcoming arms. Stephen continued to whisper as he covered her mouth with his. The first stroke of his tongue into her mouth sent orgasmic shudders down her spine. She could only cling to him, allowing the overwhelming sensations to move through her.

Stephen. She released the cry inside her mind, too enraptured to consider pulling her lips from his.

It's all right, love. It's new. The intensity will lessen.

He didn't add "a bit," but she knew it was there. Her new senses were strong, and with them came strong pleasures. Her mind turned hazy as Stephen slid his hands down her back, cupping her bottom and pressing her against his erection. Her legs spread to allow him contact with that sweet spot between her thighs. He made one slight thrust of his hips. Madeleine squeaked and threw herself backward.

Stephen released her. She bent over, clutching her stomach, though it wasn't precisely her stomach that was throbbing.

"Oh my," she whispered when her chest had relaxed enough for her to speak. "I almost…with just that."

Stephen smiled, pure seduction in his eyes. He walked slowly toward her. She wanted to back away, not from fear of Stephen, but fear of too much pleasure. She turned away. Sensations, feelings, emotions, in an intensity she'd never had to deal with. She wanted him. She could smell him, remember the taste of him on her tongue.

"Yes. With just a touch." His voice dropped to a husky whisper. "Imagine what it will feel like when I'm inside you." He stepped up behind her. Close but not quite touching her. She could feel his presence all around her, filling her. "Deep inside you."

She groaned and dropped her head back, the image forming easily in her mind and sparking wild fires of need in the center of her being. Stephen wrapped his arms around her, holding her, skimming his hands across her body. The tension that had started with the look in his eyes continued to build.

He gripped the edges of her stained blouse and tugged, efficiently popping off the buttons. She barely noticed, so smooth was his touch. He spread his legs and pulled her back against his chest, fitting her body to his. The hard line of his erection pressed into her backside. She arched her back, pressing up into his large hands as they cupped her breasts.

"Stephen!" He answered her cry by spinning her around and tearing at first her clothes and then his. In seconds they were naked. She couldn't think, couldn't speak, could only feel, the need vibrating through her. Stephen eased her down to the bed and followed her. There was no prelude, no long, teasing kisses. He covered her mouth, plunging his tongue inside as he drove his hardness into her depths. Her body shuddered to a fast, hard release, and her cry resonated through the room.

Stephen slowed his thrusts, and they moved together.

The physical intensity beyond anything she could have imagined as a human, each nerve ending seemed to sparkle and glow, every sensation magnified. But beyond that, beyond the powerful tremors through her body, was the light in Stephen's eyes. He stared down at her as he moved, as he loved her body—and he loved her mind.

They were connected by body and blood, part of each other. His voice in her head whispered while his body moved within hers. She relaxed and let his soft, sweet words flow through her.

The mind-melting combination of his words and his flesh pushed her to the edge. They moved together, faster now, still it wasn't enough.

"Stephen!" she cried, needing him, needing something.

Yes, love.

He placed his mouth against the base of her neck. The slice of his incisors and the slow suction of his mouth sent her spiraling out of control. Pleasure crashed through her, the newly excited sensations shimmering across every inch of her skin. She felt Stephen tense in her arms and thrilled to his harsh groan. His strength faded, and he sank down on top of her.

Madeleine wrapped her arms and legs around him and held on, holding him inside her body. After a moment, she felt him relax and bury his nose into her neck.

They lay there, listening to the silence of the room.

Her body was sated and a lingering tiredness filled her limbs, but she felt no desire for sleep. As the passion eased, worry filled the open space in her mind. The Council, the other vampires—they were still after Stephen. And what if now that she was a vampire, Stephen didn't want her? Oh, she knew he *wanted* her, but what if he only wanted sex? It was great sex but she wanted more. She needed more.

He had to know she was in love with him. No woman would go through what she'd been through without true love inspiring it. But Stephen had never mentioned love, had never shown any emotion besides passion.

A vulnerability she'd never felt when she was human came over her. If Stephen didn't want her, she would be alone. Forever.

"Madeleine, we must—"

A fist pounding on the door broke off Stephen's words.

"Are you decent? We're coming in." As the door was opening, Stephen threw a sheet toward Madeleine and grabbed his own trousers. They were barely covered when Gayle and Nicholas walked in. The cheeky grin Gayle sported made Madeleine smile. Nicholas looked worried, but she'd grown used to that look on his face.

Two more bodies filed in behind them, filling the cramped vault. Madeleine knew Matthias but not the other man. He was short and pudgy, completely atypical of what Madeleine expected a vampire to look like. She thought for a moment that he was human. But then she realized she heard only one true heartbeat—Nick's. The slow steady pulse of his heart pulled her attention, inspiring a craving deep within her. She licked her lips and stared at the long line of Nick's throat. She pressed herself up on her knees, eager to be closer to—

"Later, my sweet." Stephen's whisper into her ear pulled her back.

Gayle winked. Nick looked around the room, oblivious to the potential threat. Madeleine shoved aside this new urge and turned to the pudgy little man.

He had to be from the Council. Well, he wasn't taking Stephen. She'd been through enough to keep him alive— they weren't taking him now.

"You just back off there, mister." She held the sheet across her chest and scooted into position so she was in front of Stephen. "He didn't do anything wrong, and you're not taking him."

"Yes, so I understand." The smooth agreement startled

Madeleine for a moment. He looked beyond Madeleine to
Stephen. "Matthias and Gayle have given me a *detailed*
accounting of what occurred last night. I'll pass along the
facts to the Council. I'm sure they'll eventually want to
hear from you. I'll give you a few days to get your stories
straight," he said, flashing a mocking smile at Gayle and
Matthias.

Gayle glared at Matthias. Matthias ignored the younger
vampire.

"Thank you, Charles," Stephen replied.

"She's got quite a lot of spirit, I understand." He lifted
his chin toward Madeleine.

"Yes, she does."

"She's also not deaf," Madeleine said, tension making
her cranky. Stephen wrapped his arm around her and pulled
her against his side. The warmth of his chest soothed some
of the stress from her shoulders.

"No. Welcome, young one. Stephen's a good teacher.
He'll teach you how to be a proper vampire." He nodded
to the others in the room and walked out.

"So, what exactly did you tell him?" Stephen asked
when Charles was gone.

"That Thomass was working with a human to kill
vampires."

"Scott was helping him, wasn't he?" Madeleine
interjected. "What happened to him?"

Gayle shrugged. "He seems to have disappeared."

Guilt spiked Madeleine's chest.

"We'll look for him, Maddie," Stephen said, answering
her unspoken concern. "While we're looking for
Thomass." Stephen looked up. "You didn't say anything
about the silver?"

Matthias shook his head. "We decided if they knew
Thomass could touch silver, they might continue to
investigate."

And that might lead back to Stephen. Madeleine

rubbed her fingers over the back of Stephen's hand, wanting him to know she was there with him.

"Well, we're off to the club. I have lots of gossip tonight." Gayle rubbed his palms together gleefully. "And some rumors to spread." He flipped his long hair over his shoulder and gave a dramatic sigh. "We can't have too much truth out there. What fun would that be?"

"And it's too dangerous," Matthias added.

Gayle rolled his eyes. "Yeah, yeah, yeah. Mister Practical. Oh, we should warn Stephen." He reverted back to the serious, commanding man who'd stood in Stephen's house and demanded answers. "It looks like Dylan's dead. He disappeared right after you and he had that 'discussion' at my club."

"Our guess is, he was going to be the next to be found," Matthias said. "We cleared it with the Council. You couldn't have done it."

"I made up some great alibis for both of you, but Matthias wouldn't back me up," Gayle said.

Matthias glared at Gayle. "Your lies are too elaborate."

"But more fun."

They turned and left, sniping at each other as they walked out. Nick followed but stayed just out of reach of both the vampires.

"Gayle seemed so normal for that short period of time," Madeleine mused.

"I think Gayle has depths we'll never understand."

The door swung shut and they were alone again.

Silence dominated the room—silence filled with unasked questions.

Stephen took Madeleine's shoulders in his hands and turned her to face him. He looked so serious, so intense, she wasn't sure she wanted to hear what he had to say.

"I'm sorry about Danielle. I truly thought I was doing what was best for the Community." It was easy to hear the regret in his voice. He couldn't hide it. Not from her.

Madeleine nodded. Somehow, through it all, she'd come to understand, at least a little. Stephen's sense of responsibility was strong, and he'd done what he thought was right. But there was one question she had to ask.

"Why didn't you tell me about Danielle at the beginning? I couldn't have done anything."

"Sheer, undiluted terror."

Madeleine's eyes widened. "You were afraid I'd attack you?"

"I was afraid you'd hate me."

"Never."

"I was afraid you'd leave me."

Her heart fell and all strength of resistance disappeared from her body. She shook her head. "Never," she repeated.

"Be careful." The caution and vulnerability that hummed through his body made her move closer, wanting to touch him, wanting to give him the comfort he needed. "Never is a very long time for you now."

"I know."

"Once I have you, I'm not letting you go."

"I love you." It was as simple as she could put it.

She waited, open before him, needing his response.

"I love you. Forever, Madeleine."

She nodded and returned his pledge.

"Forever."

About the Author

T. L. Sinclare began writing romances (during Trigonometry class) at the age of sixteen. During her senior year in high school, the class dressed up as what they would be in twenty years—she dressed as a romance writer. She began to write seriously in 1992 when she joined Romance Writer's of America (RWA). Her manuscript *A Christmas Elf* was a finalist in the national Romance Writer's of America Golden Heart™ Contest in 1998.

Ms. Sinclare is currently the Morning Weather Anchor at KTUU-Channel 2 in Anchorage, Alaska. She also works for the station as their remote productions coordinator. Prior to joining KTUU, she worked as Assistant Media Relations for Alyeska Pipeline Service Company, where she was in charge of advertising coordination, local and state media interaction, and internal communications programs.

Ms. Sinclare has lived in Alaska for thirty years. Her family moved to Alaska in 1972 when her father was transferred to Elmendorf AFB with the U.S. Air Force. She received her Bachelor of Arts in English and Broadcasting from Gonzaga University in 1986.

Printed in the United States
47424LVS00002B/101